ream

Dreaming *of* Tuscany

T. A.
WILLIAMS

San Diego, California

Canelo US
An imprint of Printers Row Publishing Group
9717 Pacific Heights Blvd, San Diego, CA 92121
www.canelobooksus.com

Printers Row Publishing Group is a division of Readerlink Distribution Services, LLC. Canelo US is a registered trademark of Readerlink Distribution Services, LLC.

This edition originally published in the United Kingdom in 2020 by Canelo.

Published in partnership with Canelo.

Correspondence regarding the content of this book should be sent to Canelo US, Editorial Department, at the above address. Author inquiries should be sent to Canelo, Unit 9, 5th Floor, Cargo Works, 1–2 Hatfields, London SE1 9PG, United Kingdom, www.canelo.co.

Publisher: Peter Norton • Associate Publisher: Ana Parker
Art Director: Charles McStravick
Senior Developmental Editor: April Graham
Production Team: Beno Chan, Julie Greene, Rusty von Dyl

Library of Congress Control Number: 2021950591

ISBN: 978-1-6672-0133-7

Printed in the United States of America

26 25 24 23 22   1 2 3 4 5

To Mariangela and Christina, as always. With love.

Chapter 1

'Beatrice, can you hear me?'

Bee heard the voice as if through a curtain. A warm hand touched her wrist and the voice reached her again. It was a man's voice and it sounded friendly.

'Beatrice, can you hear me? I'm Doctor Bianchi. You're here at the hospital in Siena.' His English was fluent. He sounded like an Italian who had spent time in America.

As his words registered, Bee struggled to work out how she could have ended up here, but she couldn't make sense of it. Hospital?

'Yes, I can hear you.' Her voice sounded as if it belonged to somebody else.

She shook her head in an attempt to get her brain working again and winced with pain. Very cautiously she tried wiggling her fingers and toes. Reassured, she stretched her arms and then her legs. As she did so, a sharp pain shot up her left thigh and into her back.

'Ouch.'

'I'm afraid you've taken a bit of a beating, but you'll be fine. Your thigh's badly bruised, but there's nothing broken.'

Bee raised her free arm and ran her fingers across her face, unsurprised to find it swathed in bandages. Only then did she open her eyes. She blinked a couple of times before the realisation struck her that everything was black. A wave of panic began to sweep up and engulf her and she fought as hard as she had ever fought in her life to suppress it.

'I can't see.' Her voice was still very weak, but the terror in it was audible.

'It's all right, Beatrice. The pads over your eyes will be coming off very soon and your eyesight should be unimpaired.'

The sensation of relief she felt was palpable. She breathed out with a long sigh and felt her body relax again. She let her fingers run on up to her head and, for a moment, she couldn't understand what had happened there. It took several seconds before her befuddled brain worked out that her hair, her lovely long hair, had gone. But how could it have just disappeared?

'My hair? What happened to my hair?'

All she could feel on her head was a mixture of stubble and surgical dressings.

The doctor's fingers gave her wrist another encouraging squeeze.

'Don't worry, it'll grow back. You took a blow to the head in the accident and suffered a number of cuts and grazes. I'm afraid most of your hair was singed in the blast and we had to shave the rest off so as to get access to the scalp to stitch you up. But apart from the main wound, none of your other cuts were too serious. Your hair'll soon grow back and hide everything and you'll feel fine again before too long.'

What blast? A bomb? Had she been in a terrorist attack? Bee shook her head in frustration. If only she could remember...

'Beatrice, is there anybody you'd like us to contact? Friends? Family? We've located your mother and I spoke to her personally to reassure her. I was surprised to find that she's Italian.' He switched to Italian. 'Does this mean you speak Italian too? Could we be having this conversation in Italian?'

Bee found she was able to answer in Italian without apparent difficulty and she took that as a good sign that her brain hadn't been seriously damaged. 'It's a lot easier for me in English, thank you, if you don't mind. I do speak Italian, but I'm not sure how good I'd be at medical terminology.' She switched back to English again. 'It was really kind of you to contact mum. Thank you very much Doctor...?'

'Bianchi... Dario Bianchi. I work in the trauma department here at the hospital in Siena.'

Bee lay back and, as she relaxed, the mist in her head gradually began to clear and she started to remember.

'Siena, you said? I've been working in Siena.' She tried her hardest to concentrate, and memories came flooding back with a rush. 'I've been working for a film company.'

'That's right. That's dead right.' The doctor sounded pleased, and maybe a bit relieved. 'You were on the set of a new film that's being made here. Can you remember what happened to you?'

Bee lay back and concentrated, finding she could remember the name of the film, the hotel where she and most of the crew had been staying, but nothing about

3

what had happened to her. She tried her hardest, but as far as the accident was concerned, there was just darkness.

'Let me see. The film we're making is called *The Dark Prince*. It's an epic, set in the Middle Ages, and I've been employed as the historical consultant. I've been here for almost two months now and the film's just about finished.' She gave a little snort of frustration. 'I can remember all that, but my mind's a complete blank about the accident. I've no idea how I ended up here.'

'Never mind, Beatrice. It'll probably come back in time. Apparently, the accident happened on set. They said a lighting gantry collapsed on you and the lights exploded, showering you with flying glass.'

In spite of Bee's best efforts, she still couldn't recall anything at all of the actual event. 'Was anybody else hurt?'

'I'm afraid so. Mimi Robertson herself. She was luckier than you, though. She didn't get the blow to the head and her cuts were less serious.'

'Wow.'

This was a name Bee instantly recognised. Mimi Robertson was the most famous British actress of her generation and one of the most famous names in Hollywood. She was starring in *The Dark Prince* and Beth had been introduced to her weeks ago when filming had started, but they had barely exchanged more than a few words since then. The stunningly beautiful star kept herself very much to herself, and the other crew members had warned Bee not to be surprised if Mimi – 'Miss Robertson' as she preferred to be called – completely ignored her. She was apparently renowned for her glacial manner and her prickly personality, and Bee had wisely kept out of her way.

She was, however, box office gold.

Once again Bee relaxed, relieved her memory appeared to be returning, although the thought of her lovely mane of long hair having been lost threatened to bring tears to her eyes. Her thigh was really sore and she wondered whether all these injuries would have an impact upon the rest of her life. Doing her best to quash a rising sense of panic, she spared a thought for Mimi Robertson, wondering how she was coping with her injuries. After all, to film stars like her, appearance was paramount.

Then another name came to mind: Jamie. For a moment, she wondered whether she should ask the doctor to contact him and tell him she was all right. No sooner did the thought occur to her than she dismissed it as irrelevant. That was all over now. They had broken up some months ago and she had no difficulty remembering the last troubled weeks leading up to their separation. In fact, if she could have permanently lost those memories as a result of the accident, it would have been a blessing.

She lay there, pleased to feel that her brain was definitely functioning better now, even if the events of that day on the film set were still a blank. She had a thought. 'Doctor Bianchi, if you've got time, maybe you could ask someone to let the people at Pan World know I'm awake.'

'That's already been done. In fact, I believe there's somebody from the company coming to see you later on. She's been coming in here all week.'

'All week…? How long have I been here?'

'Five days. You've been in an induced coma. There was some swelling in your brain that had us worried, but I'm pleased to say that's all gone down again now.'

'Five days? So, today's what…?' Bee struggled to make sense of what she was hearing. '…Friday, Saturday?'

'Saturday – that's right. You were brought in on Monday morning.'

'And the swelling to the brain…?' She tried her hardest to keep her voice level. 'That sounds serious.'

'It could have been, Beatrice, but don't worry. As far as we can tell, you've sustained no permanent damage.'

'As far as you can tell…?' Suddenly the loss of her hair paled in comparison. Fighting once more to calm her fears, she did her best to turn the conversation away from her own problems.

'And Miss Robertson? Is she still in the hospital?'

'No, she was released almost immediately. Anyway, like I say, you'll be visited by one of your colleagues quite soon. She'll be able to tell you more, but we're just waiting for the pads to come off your eyes and for my head of department to have the chance to see you. Now you just lie there and relax. Everything'll be fine.'

'Thank you, Doctor Bianchi.'

'You're very welcome. I'm off now, but you're not on your own. The nurse has just arrived and she'll stay with you until the pads over your eyes are removed.'

Bee heard a brief exchange in hushed tones and then his footsteps recede, and for a moment she felt terribly alone in the darkness. There was a light touch as a hand caught hold of hers. It was warm and soft; it reminded her of her mother. Bee reached for the fingers, squeezing them just as she had done as a little girl. The sensation was very comforting.

'Hello, my name's Rosa. I'll stay with you. Don't worry now.'

The voice was as warm as the hand. She was speaking Italian, but slowly and clearly, unsure whether Bee would understand. This simple gesture of human kindness suddenly broke the dam and Bee felt the tears begin to flow. She found herself sobbing like a little baby, as a sensation of relief flowed through her, tempered by very real fear for the future.

She felt the nurse's other hand gently stroke the unbandaged side of her face until the tears began to subside. It took a while, but Bee finally found the strength to speak again, marshalling the words in her head before launching into Italian.

'Thank you so much, Rosa, you're very kind. I suppose it's just the reaction. I'm sorry I've soaked your bandages with my tears.' She was pleased to hear her voice sounding pretty strong and her Italian flowing well. Her mother had always spoken Italian to her, even though Bee had been born and brought up near London, and after two months in Tuscany, it wasn't too much of a challenge.

'Don't worry, Beatrice. Let it out. You've been through an awful lot, but you're safe here now and you're going to be all right.' After a pause, the nurse changed the subject and Bee was grateful to her. At first...

'So, have you got any friends or family coming to see you?'

Bee shook her head. 'I don't think so. My parents are in England. My mum's got a problem with her ears and can't fly, and it's too far for my dad to drive.'

'No man in your life? A fiancé or a husband, maybe?'

'Nothing like that. I had a boyfriend, but that's all over now. It all fell apart a few months ago.'

'I'm sorry. Did you have a fight?'

'No, not really. I suppose we were arguing more about little things towards the end, but I think we both realised it wasn't going anywhere. At least, that was the way I felt.' She took a deep breath and tried to hide the heartbreak she had felt as four years with James had dissolved into dust. 'Splitting up was the sensible thing to do, but it's been a tough year all in all.'

'Never mind, you're a very pretty girl. You'll soon find somebody else.'

Bee shook her head slowly. The last thing she needed was another man any time soon. She ran her free hand up to her face again and explored the bandages.

'Rosa, are these bandages just to protect my eyes, or has something happened to my face?'

'I'm afraid you got a bit cut up in the blast. It's the left side of your face and your left ear that got the worst of it. As well as the top of your head.'

'Is it serious?' Bee's mind was racing.

'I heard them say your hearing and eyesight should be all right, but there's a bit of damage to the skin of your cheek. It'll probably take a while to recover.'

'But it *will* recover?'

'You'd better talk to the doctor about that, Beatrice. I really don't know.'

'Will I be scarred for life, Rosa?'

'I can't say, Beatrice, but they can do the most amazing things these days. You'll see – our surgeons are second to none.'

'Oh, God…'

'Don't you worry, dear. It'll be all right.'

–

8

They took the pads off her eyes about an hour later. The lights in the private room had been dimmed and the blinds drawn, and at first all Bee could see were three vague shapes. As her eyes adjusted and her focus sharpened, she felt an overwhelming wave of relief wash over her. She made out two men and a woman standing around the bed. The man nearer to her was the first to talk.

'Miss Kingdom… Beatrice, I'm Dr Esposito and this is my colleague, Dr Bianchi.' He was speaking Italian and he started slowly, but seeing her comprehension, he gradually speeded up. He didn't introduce the nurse, but from the friendly smile on her face, Bee deduced it had to be Rosa and did her best to smile back at her, although how much of it would be visible beneath the dressings was unclear.

'Hello. Thank you for taking such good care of me.'

'You're very welcome. It's not often we have patients from Hollywood here.' He repeated Dr Bianchi's words, but Bee decided not to break the news to him that she had never been to the US, let alone Hollywood. 'We're all delighted you've pulled through. We were a bit worried about you for a while, but you're making good progress now.' The specialist stepped a bit closer and leant towards her face. 'Now, can you see me quite clearly? How many fingers am I holding up?'

'Fingers? Three. And, yes, my eyesight's really fine, thank you. And I can hear you loud and clear as well, although there's a lot of ringing in my ears.'

'Don't worry about the tinnitus. It's only to be expected after the sort of damage you've incurred. It'll gradually calm down, but it may take a few more days.'

Bee nodded, reassured. 'But what about my face?'

9

The two doctors exchanged glances and it was Dr Bianchi who replied. In the background, Bee saw Dr Esposito motion towards the nurse who went over to the window and opened the blinds. Light flooded into the room and Bee blinked, delighted to find she could see everything with complete clarity.

'It's only the left side of your head and face we have to worry about. Your ear and neck were protected to a certain extent by your hair, but your scalp and your left cheek have suffered some burns and lots of little shrapnel wounds – mainly caused by broken glass, I'm afraid.'

'Will I be scarred for life?' Bee was pleased to hear her voice sounding level and measured – very different from the turmoil inside her head.

'We don't really know at this stage, Beatrice. We'll have to keep the dressings on for a while until the skin starts to heal, and then it'll be a few more weeks before we can say definitely. But I'm confident that by the end of the summer you'll be looking much more like your old self.'

'But not *exactly* like before?'

She saw the doctors exchange glances again. It was Dr Bianchi who replied once more.

'We'll do our very best, Beatrice, but it'll be a slow process, and there's no way of knowing at this stage what the final outcome will be.' He smiled encouragingly. 'But there's a lot we can do to help you and, remember, it's only cosmetic. None of your internal organs have been damaged, your brain's returned to normal, and you can see and hear as well as before. So, just try to relax and rest assured that we'll do our very best for you. You've been very lucky.'

Chapter 2

'You've been very lucky. It doesn't look bad at all.'

Bee harrumphed quietly to herself. Why did everybody keep telling her she'd been lucky? Surely being banged on the head and ending up with a face full of broken glass was anything but lucky. However, hiding her frustration, she summoned a wry smile.

'Gayle, you're a lovely lady but a terrible liar. Tell me honestly – what do I look like? They only took the dressings off a few minutes before you arrived, and the nurse has gone to get me a mirror. Is it awful?'

'No, honestly, Bee, it doesn't look too bad. Sure, there's a bit of blistering and it all looks pretty red and raw, but I'm sure it'll heal up fine.'

Bee scrutinised her closely.

'I'm sure I saw your nose grow longer as you said that.' She looked round in frustration. 'If only I could see it. Where's Rosa with that mirror?' She caught Gayle's eye. 'You haven't got a mirror in your bag, have you?'

'Sorry, no.'

This time Bee felt sure she spotted the nose elongate. Fortunately, at that moment, Rosa came back in with a hand mirror.

'Here you are, Beatrice. Now don't you worry. It's still a bit inflamed at the moment, but the doctors say it's all healing well.'

She went back out again, leaving Bee and Gayle alone.

Bee took a deep breath and looked into the mirror. What she saw confirmed her assessment of Gayle as a barefaced liar.

It looked awful.

Her left ear was bright red and raw, as was the skin around it all the way down to where the collar of her shirt had been. Her cheek, however, was far worse; it also looked red and raw, but it was laced with white and yellow and the few patches of unbroken skin were a deep blue, almost purple colour – presumably severely bruised. The rest of her face was a spectral white and her eyes bloodshot. The damage extended right across her cheek, almost reaching her nose and mouth, but not quite. She swallowed hard and took a final look before setting the mirror down again.

'A sight for sore eyes, eh?' She did her best to sound upbeat, while, inside, she could feel her whole world collapsing in on itself. She struggled hard, but couldn't stop tears springing from her eyes. Somehow this was just another bitter blow to be added to the run of bad luck this year had brought her. She reached for the edge of the sheet and wiped it gingerly across her face as Gayle leapt in with further encouragement.

'I told you it didn't look so bad.'

Bee waited until the tears stopped before emerging from the shelter of the sheet.

'Sorry about that, Gayle. Anyway, it's all right; you don't need to keep up the charade. I've seen it now. My face looks like a cross between the surface of the moon and a trifle.' She did her best to sound resolute, but it was far from easy. 'Anyway, thanks so much for coming.' She glanced around, but they were quite alone in the room. 'So, how's Mimi Robertson handling it?'

Gayle replied in similarly guarded tones. 'You can probably imagine. She's been screaming blue murder. Her agent's threatening a billion-dollar lawsuit, claiming criminal negligence, demanding exorbitant damages. Rick says the board are crapping themselves.'

Gayle was Liaison Officer, acting as intermediary between the production team of the film based here in Italy and the mother company back in Hollywood, and Bee had got to know her well over the past weeks in Siena. She was ten years older than Bee and had worked for the company for twenty years now and very little went on in Pan World without her knowledge. If she said the top brass were crapping themselves, they most probably were.

'So, where is she? Has she gone home?'

'Not yet. She's hunkered down in a suite on the top floor of the Grand Hotel Continental here in Siena and she refuses to come out of the door. There's a paparazzi encampment on the square outside.'

'That sounds grim.' Bee tried to raise herself into a more upright position, but the combination of a stab of pain up her thigh and a sudden throbbing ache in her head stopped her in her tracks. 'Ouch.'

'Just take it easy, Beatrice. You need time. I've been in every day, but they wouldn't let me see you until now. You've been all wired up to loads of machines in Intensive Care. To be honest, they were very worried about you at first. They said you were hit really hard on the head and there was talk of possible brain damage. Thank goodness you're all right now.'

'In a manner of speaking. There's the small matter of my face...' Bee took a deep breath and did her best to rally her spirits. She was an intelligent woman, after all. What mattered was what she was like on the inside, not her outward appearance. She repeated this a few times to herself, but without any appreciable success. What was life going to be like in the future if she ended up seriously scarred? Would she be able to cope? Thrusting that thought to one side – at least for now – she tried to sound positive. 'But you're right, it could have been a lot worse.'

'Has anybody else been in to see you yet?'

Bee shook her head as she dabbed her eyes once more. 'No. you're the first. I still can't get my head round the fact that it's now Saturday. I've lost a week of my life.'

'But you've survived – and they say you'll make a full recovery.'

'I don't know about full, but the doctor said he hopes to have me looking a lot better by the end of the summer.'

Gayle leant forward. 'Listen, Bee, about that: we at Pan World are very conscious that the accident happened on our watch and we're going to look after you. I know your contract was due to finish in a few weeks' time, but I've been told to assure you that we'll keep paying your salary until you're fully fit again.' She hesitated for a moment before adding, 'And expenses. So, why don't you take it easy for however long you need to get you looking and feeling good again? It was pretty serious, you know. You deserve a bit of time off.'

'That's very kind, Gayle.'

Bee had a sneaky suspicion this generosity by the company was a pre-emptive attempt to ward off a claim for damages, but she didn't comment. Accidents happened. The amount the company had been paying her for her services was at least twice what she had been earning as a university lecturer, and another month or two at that rate would make a real difference to her finances. What was more important was how she would look at the end of it.

'I must admit the idea of a few weeks off does appeal. Please thank your superiors. That's very generous.'

–

The doctors gave her something to help her sleep that night and, in consequence, next morning Bee woke up feeling rested and a bit more positive. She turned on the television and went instinctively to the news in English. After a fairly long piece on the latest developments at Westminster, just as Bee was beginning to tire of it, she saw a familiar face.

'World-famous British film star, Mimi Robertson, is reported to be recovering well after the accident in Tuscany on the set of the new film, *The Dark Prince*, which resulted in her being injured and hospitalised. A spokesperson for Pan World Movies told our correspondent that Miss Roberson is now out of hospital, making good progress and hoping to be back in action before long.'

This was accompanied by a montage of shots of Mimi, mostly taken from last year's Oscar ceremony. Then, to Bee's surprise, she heard her own name mentioned.

'Also injured in the freak accident was British-born Doctor Beatrice Kingdom, thirty-one, a Medieval

History specialist and historical adviser to the film company. She remains in Siena hospital.'

Even more surprising was a close-up of Bee taken, by the look of it, fairly recently on the film set. In spite of the circumstances, she felt a little flash of pleasure to see herself on television and not looking too bad. In fact, with her clipboard, she did rather look the part of the visiting academic.

'Doctors say Doctor Kingdom suffered a fractured skull and serious bruising, but her injuries are not thought to be life-threatening, although she is reported to be badly scarred.'

Bee let out a long, heartfelt sigh. Somehow, hearing her injuries described on the television made it all so very, very real. She let the remote slip from her hand as she felt another wave of emotion threatening to engulf her. The shaky confidence she had been starting to build disintegrated as if had never existed, as those few words rammed home to her the extent of what had happened, and the consequences for her future. She was badly scarred and these scars, no doubt, would be with her for the rest of her life. Her eyes filled with tears and she found herself sobbing inconsolably, the repressed emotions pouring out as she descended into the abyss of despair she had been fighting so hard to avoid.

An hour later, by the time Rosa appeared with her meal, Bee had managed to pull herself together again, but it hadn't been easy. At least the nurse brought something that helped to cheer her. On the tray was a familiar, if battered, object. As Rosa picked it up and passed it over, she apologised to Bee.

'We had to cut you out of your clothes so, unless you want what's left of them, we plan to burn them. They're a bit of a mess, so I didn't bring them. But your bag here and your phone are in pretty good condition. The outside of the bag's a bit burned, but the contents, including your phone, are fine, though. Here...'

Bee took the bag gratefully, registering the information she had just received. Burning her clothes would be no great loss. Since arriving in Tuscany, she had spent most of her working days in shorts and a T-shirt and their total value, including her underwear, was probably not much more than the cost of a decent meal in a good restaurant over here. She glanced inside the bag and saw her phone, purse, and other bits and pieces just like she had left them, and she heaved a sigh of relief.

'Thank you so much, Rosa. I was terrified I'd lost my phone with all my contacts. Go ahead and burn the clothes by all means.'

After eating her unexpectedly good dinner, she felt strong enough to phone home and speak to her parents. They had a long conversation, in which she did her best to convince her mum and dad that she was well on her way to recovery, and by the time she hung up, she felt pretty sure they were reassured – even if she herself was still far from certain how things would turn out. She was just setting the phone down again when it started ringing. She didn't recognise the number.

'Hello. Beatrice Kingdom.' As she was in Italy, she added a greeting in Italian. '*Pronto, chi parla?*'

'Beatrice, hi, great to hear your voice.'

She would have recognised the voice anywhere, and she was impressed. It belonged to no less a figure than internationally acclaimed, Oscar-winning film director, Amos Franklin, the director of *The Dark Prince*. They had spoken quite a bit over the past few weeks of filming, but mainly just about technical historical details, and they had certainly never got to the point of exchanging phone numbers. He sounded genuinely pleased to hear her voice and she felt herself blushing even though she was alone in the room. She felt genuinely happy for the first time since waking from her coma.

'Hello, Mr Franklin. Thank you so much for calling.'

'My pleasure. It's the least I could do. So, how're you feeling?'

Bee was mightily impressed to be called by the great man himself. She shared with him the optimistic report the doctor had given her, finishing with the words, 'So, hopefully, they'll let me out in a week or so'

'I do hope so.' He sounded sincere. 'You take it easy. I heard you almost died, after all.'

'Did I?'

Gayle had said pretty much the same thing, too. Bee knew the doctors had been worried about her, but almost dying…?

'So Gayle told me. She said you've been in a coma.'

'That's right, but I'm feeling much better now. But tell me, how's Miss Robertson? And was anybody else hurt in the accident?'

'No, just the two of you. Mimi's doing well, I believe.' His voice was studiously neutral.

Bee remembered what Gayle had said about Mimi's legal team baying for blood. No doubt relations between her and the director were strained as a result. Sensibly, she didn't comment.

'That's good. Have you been able to finish filming? Is Miss Robertson heading back to LA?'

'We'd almost finished anyway and we've been able to shoot round her for the last few scenes, so we've got all the footage we need. As for Mimi, I'm not sure what her plans are. She refuses to let me or anybody else see her, and the doctors say it'll be a month or two before the scarring to her face disappears completely, so my guess is she's thinking of lying low for a while – you know, out of the way of the paparazzi.'

'Lying low?' Bee's voice tailed off. Mimi Robertson's face was so well-known all around the world, it would surely be next to impossible for her to disappear for long before being discovered.

'Anyway, Beatrice, I'm delighted to hear you sounding bright and I just wanted to thank you for making sure the film is historically accurate. That means a lot to me.' Bee felt a thrill of professional pride. 'Your knowledge of the Middle Ages is impressive and I've really valued your input. I look forward to working with you again in the future. Just look after yourself now and get well soon. So long.'

Then he added a short sentence that came as a real surprise to Bee.

'Oh, and Joey told me to tell you he sends his love.'

–

Gayle dropped in the following afternoon with a massive bunch of roses and a cardboard box. From it she extracted a wig and handed it to Bee.

'It's real hair. Luis found it in Wardrobe. We wondered if it might be useful to you when you're allowed out

19

of here – you know, until your hair grows back. Why don't you try it on, if you're allowed to do that without disturbing all your cuts and bruises?'

Bee took the wig from her and studied it. The hair was a rich auburn colour, straight cut, and it looked as if it would just about reach to her shoulders. Very carefully, so as not to disturb the dressings, she perched it on her head and smoothed the sides.

'Wow, it really is like looking at a completely different person.' Gayle sounded impressed.

Bee reached for the mirror that Rosa had left on her bedside table. Hesitantly, she checked her reflection. Gayle was right. The wig changed her quite considerably and it looked remarkably convincing. And if she turned her head to the left, she looked almost normal again. Of course, if she turned the other way, she looked like a zombie. She dropped the mirror and glanced up at Gayle, forcing a smile.

'I look like Scully from *The X-Files*.'

'Well, you certainly don't look like you, that's for sure. It's a hell of a change.'

'Thank you, and do say thanks to Luis, too. I'm sure it'll come in very handy.' She reached up and removed the wig once more. 'Listen, Gayle, can I ask you something?' Bee knew she needed to know. 'I got a call yesterday from Amos and at the end he mentioned that Joey sent his love. Is that just Hollywood-speak or do you think there's more to it than that? I like him all right, but not in that way.'

Gayle smiled. 'Don't worry your head about it. Joey loves everybody. He loves you, he loves me… he loves Amos. Of course, you're a very pretty girl, Bee, and he likes very pretty girls.' Her smile broadened. 'And there are lots of very pretty girls who like him. Trust me, the queue is very, very long. You don't need to worry, it's just his way.'

Bee smiled back at her. The last thing she needed now was some kind of involvement with a man, however rich and handsome he might be. Joseph Aquila, known to the world as Joey Eagle, was one of the best-known faces in Hollywood. He was tall, he was ruggedly good-looking, and he had the body of a Greek god. And he knew it. In the course of filming, Bee and the rest of the crew had seen quite a lot of his divine body, and she had to admire the obvious effort he must have put in to getting himself into such amazing shape. His pairing with the beautiful Mimi Robertson in *The Dark Prince* had attracted the attention of the world's media, and the film was no doubt eagerly awaited by millions of devoted fans.

Bee had met him a few times on set and he had been smiley, friendly and complimentary and, to her surprise, more than a bit flirty. She had always liked him as an actor and felt flattered to be on the receiving end of the attentions of such a demigod, but his reputation as a womaniser would have been enough to put her off the idea of getting involved with him, irrespective of her present lack of interest in the male of the species. A real hunk he most definitely was, but as far as Bee was concerned, she was very happy to leave him to the 'very pretty girls' who liked him. For a moment, Amos's comment had worried her that she might be in Joey's sights, but she now felt relieved. After everything that had happened over the past few months, she didn't want to find herself in any man's sights at the moment. Mind you, she told herself more soberly, with her face chopped to bits, he was hardly likely to come knocking on her door now anyway.

'Well, if you see him, tell him I send him my love too.'

'Will do.' Now Bee saw a more serious expression appear on Gayle's face. 'Look, Bee, I have something to ask you.'

'Of course.'

'What plans do you have for when you're discharged from hospital?'

'Nothing definite. If as you've told me the company will keep paying me for a while, I was thinking about having a holiday, although I'm wondering whether I should really be looking for a new job.'

'What happened to the old job? Teaching history at university?'

Bee took a deep breath. 'I've still got it officially, but I've been on compassionate leave since Easter. I left in a bit of a hurry.'

Gayle didn't look in the least bit phased. Presumably in her world, people leaving jobs overnight was so common as to be unremarkable. 'Trouble?' Seeing Bee nod, she probed a bit. 'Something happened at work?'

'Afraid so.' Bee hadn't told anybody here what had really happened, but she felt she could talk to Gayle. 'I had a problem with my Head of Department.'

'What sort of problem?'

'A groping sort of problem.'

To her surprise, she saw Gayle smile, albeit grimly. 'Wow, I thought that was the prerogative of my profession.'

Bee shook her head. 'Don't you believe it. There are predatory perverts in the gloomy halls of academia as well, I'm afraid.'

'So, what's the deal? What's happened to him?'

'It's all very British. He's being allowed to work out this term and resign his position next month at the end of the academic year with his reputation intact. Basically, he's jumping before they push him, and I've been shifted out of the way – on paid leave – while it all happens.'

'So he gets away with it?' The smile had disappeared from Gayle's face now. 'Surely in the present climate, with the whole "Me Too" movement, they should have done more than that?'

Bee just nodded. 'That's why I'm thinking about making a complete change. It's a good university, and lecturing positions are like hen's teeth in my field, but somehow I know I'm not going to feel comfortable back there again. They should've backed me up far more than they did. Besides, I think I'm ready for a change of direction anyway. I've loved these weeks working for Pan World. It's been like a breath of fresh air. It would be great to find something like this again.'

'And everybody says you did great. The problem is there are only so many historical movies being made. I tell you, Bee, if we could offer you a full-time job we would, but we just don't have any plans to get involved with historicals again any time soon. Of course, if *The Dark Prince* is a box office success, we'll almost certainly be going for a sequel, but that's some way up the road.'

Bee nodded. 'I quite understand, but maybe it wouldn't hurt me to look around.'

'Sure. But anyway, your job, new or old, wouldn't start back until the autumn, right?'

Bee nodded.

'So, for the next month or two, you're kind of free?'

Bee began to wonder where this might be leading. She soon found out.

'Tell me, Bee, how might the idea of a few weeks in a luxury villa here in Tuscany sound? All expenses paid and, of course, you'd still get your salary from us.'

'It sounds wonderful, but…?'

As she spoke, Bee began to put two and two together, remembering what Amos Franklin had said about Mimi Robertson and her intention of hiding herself away. Gayle confirmed her suspicions.

'Mimi wants to disappear and we were wondering if you'd like to disappear with her.'

'What, me and Mimi Robertson?' It sounded unreal. Beatrice Kingdom, the nobody, and a global megastar? And an irascible, spoilt one as well, if the tales told about her were true.

'That's right. All we'd ask of you is that you keep an eye on her.'

'Keep an eye…?'

'You know what they're like, these film stars. They don't carry money, they don't lift a finger, they're completely helpless without somebody to look after them.' No doubt spotting the expression on Bee's face, Gayle hurried on. 'Don't worry, the place we've found comes complete with staff who'll do all the housekeeping, cooking, laundry and so on. We just wondered if you might be prepared to keep her company, stop her going stir crazy. Besides, you speak Italian and she's gonna need an interpreter.'

'And where's this villa?' In spite of the very scary thought of being asked to pair up with a global megastar, Bee could hear the animation in her own voice.

'Here, not too far from Siena. Apparently it's out in the wilds, well out of the way of the paparazzi.'

'Do places like that exist here in Tuscany? Surely this whole area's swarming with tourists.'

'That's what I thought, too. But our guys have found just the place. Or so they tell me.'

Bee wondered idly who these 'guys' might be. Gayle appeared to have a 'guy' for just about everything. Not for nothing was she referred to by the film crew as 'The Fixer'.

'So, are you interested, Bee?'

'Of course…' Her voice tailed off as she considered the ramifications of this offer. 'It's just… Mimi Robertson… I don't know…'

Gayle nodded. 'I hear you, Bee. I know her better than you and I know she has a reputation for being difficult. That's the way so many of these big stars get to be. They're spoilt rotten. But, underneath, she's a good girl, believe me. I've known her since she was a young bit-part actress and we've always gotten on well. You'll see. Once she's away from all the glitz and glamour, she'll be fine. Trust me.'

'If you say so, Gayle…' The more Bee thought about it, the weirder it felt.

'More to the point, are you sure the idea of a month or even two in the wilds of the country doesn't sound too scary or too boring?'

'To be honest, Gayle, I'm not sure how I might handle being dumped in the middle of the country. I've lived in a big city most of my life.' Even so, as she thought it over, Bee felt her spirits lift for just about the first time since the accident. 'Mind you, for years now I've been dreaming of spending time in Tuscany. I came over to Florence on holiday with my parents years ago when I was just a little a girl and I've been in love with the area ever since. The idea of spending a month or two here *is* pretty wonderful, even if I have to do it from underneath a red wig.'

'And trust me, I know you can hack it with Mimi, even if she can be pretty demanding.'

'Well, all right then, if you say so. Why not? It sounds amazing and it'll give me the time I need to get over all this, and hopefully find myself a new job.'

'Great, if you're sure I'll tell Mimi and see what she says. How long do you think it'll be before they discharge you?'

'I don't really know. I imagine they'll keep me here as long as I have dressings that need to be changed. I'll ask the doctors.'

'So, maybe, another week or so?'

Bee nodded slowly. 'I suppose so.'

'Mimi should be able to survive here in Siena until then. How long she'll be able to stay undetected when you both move out to the countryside is another matter. Her face is all over the local as well as the national papers, as is yours by the way.' Bee must have looked surprised. 'Reflected glory, Bee.' She grinned. 'Enjoy your moment in the limelight. I just hope my guys are right when they say the place they've found is really remote. If the paparazzi get word of where Mimi's gone, there'll be hell to pay.'

Bee turned the idea over in her head. As a confirmed city dweller, a prolonged sojourn in the wilds of the countryside sounded a bit scary, but, certainly, this would keep Mimi a good long way away from prying eyes and give them both a well-earned break. She had often dreamt of a long holiday in Tuscany, but had been thinking rather more of art galleries, museums and gorgeous architecture. Being stuck out in the middle of nowhere wasn't quite the same but, still, Tuscany was Tuscany.

'I suppose it really has to be in the back of beyond, hasn't it, Gayle? No shops, no cafés, no cinemas, no theatre. I'm pretty sure I can cope, but the question is whether Mimi can.'

No doubt seeing her hesitation, Gayle changed to a more encouraging tone. 'It won't be too bad. Don't you worry. My guys say the place is very beautiful and very comfortable. There's TV and broadband, but you'll both need to find something to do to pass the time.'

'That's the least of my worries. I suppose it depends how demanding Mimi's going to be. If I get some free time to myself, I can get down to some serious job-hunting and catch up on my reading. You never know; Mimi might even decide to write her memoirs. Although she's a bit young for memoir writing, really.' She caught Gayle's eye. 'How old is she, actually?'

Gayle winked. 'She's thirty-nine. Just like she was last year, and the year before...'

'Wow, I thought she was my age.'

'And that is?'

'Thirty-one.'

Gayle's smile broadened. 'Mimi's looking at *forty*-one in the rear-view mirror, let alone thirty-one. Anyway, you and she'll get along fine, I'm sure. Just give it a bit of time. And you'd be doing us a big favour. We won't forget it.'

Chapter 3

'When your guy said the place was out in the wilds, Gayle, he wasn't joking!'

Gayle had instructed the driver of the big black Mercedes to stop the car at the top of the hill to give Bee and Mimi a panoramic view of where they would be spending the next few weeks or even months. Gayle's unspecified 'guys' who had managed to find this place had promised it would be suitably remote. From what Bee could see, they had been spot on. Virtually everywhere she looked, there were just woods, fields, trees and vines.

She glanced sideways at Mimi and another little shiver of apprehension ran through her. What was it going to be like, living with a highly strung actress out here in the middle of nowhere? She still hadn't got over the fact of finding herself sitting alongside the megastar on the way here today. Goodness only knew how scary it would be when she found herself all alone with her. She struggled to get her head around the fact that she was in the presence of somebody whose face was known to millions and millions of people around the world. The knowledge that a large portion of those millions of people would love to swap places with her alongside Mimi should have helped bolster her confidence, but it didn't.

She climbed gingerly out of the car into the stifling heat of the late June sunshine, stretching her sore leg as she did so. The bruising had reached the multicoloured stage by now and, although the doctors had told her she was doing fine, her thigh muscles and the whole area still ached. She leant against the side of the car and breathed deeply. After almost three weeks in hospital, it was good to be out in the open once more. The sun was shining brightly from a cloudless sky and after the air-conditioned interior of the car it was really hot out here, but she didn't mind. It was a delightful day and the view was equally delightful.

'What a fabulous place.' She glanced across at Mimi Robertson, who had decided to come out from behind the anonymity of the tinted glass of the luxury car, and risked speaking to her directly for the first time. 'What do you think, Miss Robertson?'

'It's pretty. I'll give you that.'

Gayle had warned Bee not to expect effusive comments from Mimi. That wasn't her style. At least the fact that she had answered in a civil tone and hadn't immediately found fault with the place was a positive start and Bee relaxed slightly. Beside her, she got the feeling Gayle shared her relief.

'You know you were worried about the neighbours recognising you, Mimi? Not many of them around here.' Gayle looked across at her hopefully.

Mimi made no comment. As Gayle represented Pan World, and as Mimi was still angry with them for letting the accident befall her, relations between her and Gayle were strained. The half-hour journey from Siena to here had been conducted in stony silence and Bee felt almost sorry for Gayle, although she knew her to have the thick skin of a rhinoceros.

From where the driver had stopped the sleek black car, the ground sloped steeply down through dense woodland that lined the hilltop until the trees gave way to a tapestry of vineyards further down, the regular, mathematically arranged rows giving the whole valley the impression of a knitted patchwork quilt. The countryside was a symphony of different shades of green, from the deep lustrous colour of the hollies and conifers to the more delicate shades of the deciduous trees and the bright green of the new growth on the vines. The verges were filled with striking patches of orange poppies, clumps of wild roses and a host of other wild flowers. The vineyards and fields were criss-crossed by the famous *strade bianche*, the 'white roads' of Tuscany, surfaced with white gravel. It was a stunning view.

Further down the valley, as it opened out more, a pyramid-shaped little hill rose up incongruously from the vines and on it, surrounded by a spectacular selection of cypresses and umbrella pines, Bee could just make out the unmistakable outline of an old Tuscan villa. It was a big building, light ochre in colour, with a pink tiled roof just poking up above even the highest trees. The house blended perfectly in with its surroundings and looked as if it had always been there.

Bee looked across at Gayle. 'Is that the place?'

'That's right. That's the Villa of Montegrifone. It was built about five hundred years ago, apparently.'

'What a place! I wonder if there really was a griffon here. Miss Robertson, the name translates as Mount of the Griffon.' She shot a quick glance across at the actress,

31

but saw only a stony expression on the bits of her face not covered by a huge pair of sunglasses. Looking hastily away, she carried on. 'In fact, the whole area's amazing. And it's so quiet.'

Just to prove her wrong, a woodpecker chose this precise moment to rattle off a series of hammer blows against a tree just down from where they were standing. But, when it stopped, Bee could hear nothing but the breeze rustling through the leaves.

As it wasn't far from here to their destination, Bee reached for her bag.

'I think I'd better put my wig on now. I don't want to scare the locals when they see me for the first time.'

She did her best to keep her voice expressionless, but it wasn't easy. She had now reached the point where she could look at herself in the mirror without welling up, but it had taken time. The doctors had told her the scars on her head were beginning to heal well by now and they had removed the last of the dressings a few days earlier. Her head looked a lot better than it did, but the combination of stubbly hair and scabs wasn't exactly alluring. As for her face, they had all told her back at the hospital that this was also healing as expected, but it still looked more like a recently ploughed field than the smooth skin of her other cheek. She had started to get used to her lopsided appearance, but she was under no illusions that people unused to it would get quite a shock. At least the wig would cover her head, but there was no way of hiding her damaged face, short of adopting a burka.

'They know there's been an accident and of course they won't mind, Bee.' Gayle was sounding encouraging.

'Besides, you're improving every day. I hardly even notice it now.'

Bee gave her a sceptical look, retrieved the wig from inside the car and carefully pulled it on, trying not to let it sit too tightly against her scalp. She checked her appearance in the wing mirror and was relieved to see the red hair looking pretty convincing, even if it made her head very hot. She looked up and managed to summon a smile for Gayle.

'Right. Agent Scully reporting for duty.'

Before Gayle could respond, they were both surprised to hear Mimi Robertson.

'And you're sure the people in the villa aren't going to rush off to the tabloids to reveal the fact that I'm staying here?'

Bee and Gayle exchanged glances. These were just about the first unprompted words she had uttered all day. Gayle was quick to answer.

'No, Mimi, it's all taken care of. Our lawyers have drawn up a non-disclosure agreement and all the people who live here have signed it. They won't utter a word to anyone.'

'Including Beatrice? Has she signed?'

'Including me.' Bee did her best to keep any hint of annoyance out of her voice. Of course she wasn't going to reveal anything, with or without a gagging order, but it would have been nice to be addressed directly.

'And the driver?' Mimi waved vaguely back in the direction of the car.

'He's a trusty. He comes well recommended. He'll keep his mouth shut, I promise.'

The expression on Mimi's face showed just what she thought of Pan World's promises. Out here in the bright sunlight, Bee could see that her face, while scarred, was nowhere near as seriously injured as her own. And yet, from what Gayle had told her, Mimi and her lawyers were still breathing fire and fury. She sighed inwardly and hoped both she and Mimi would get back to normal as soon as possible.

As they drove down the narrow winding road, the valley gradually opened out on either side of them. Just as they reached a clump of trees near the bottom of the slope, the driver suddenly jammed on the brakes, hard enough for Bee's wig to slip forward over her eyes and for a stab of pain to shoot up from her thigh as her injured leg was jarred. She pushed the wig back up just in time to see why he had stopped so abruptly: two little stripy creatures, the size of small dogs, were just disappearing into the undergrowth on the other side.

'What're those?' She leant forward and spoke to the driver in Italian.

'Wild boar, Signorina. Those were babies, but their mother must be around somewhere. I don't think we'll hang about, just in case.' He accelerated away once more.

'I had no idea they were so sweet.'

'Yes, they're sweet to look at when they're little, but they do an awful lot of damage to the vines.' He shot her an oblique glance. 'And I know I wouldn't want to meet one without a rifle in my hands.'

After translating what he had said to the others, Bee reflected on it. She didn't much like the idea of living in a place infested with dangerous wild boar, but she kept her reservations to herself for now. She already knew that living in the country was going to be a challenge. And, from the severe expression on the actress's face, living with Mimi was going to prove to be every bit as testing.

They carried on down the valley until the road curled round to the right and they got a better view of the villa ahead of them, perched on the conical hill, protected by trees. It was as imposing and as gorgeous as it had looked at first sight. The Mercedes slowed down as they came to a sign marked 'VILLA MONTEGRIFONE' and turned off to the left. Sturdy metal gates blocked their way and the driver pulled up alongside a keypad set in the gatepost and pressed the buzzer. Seconds later, the gates began to swing smoothly open. They drove through onto a white gravelled *strada bianca* that led up the hill with a couple of sweeping curves. The drive was lined on both sides with the iconic Tuscan cypress trees and, in spite of her concerns, Bee felt a mounting sense of excitement as they approached their destination. The views over the vines opened up on both sides as they reached the top and drove into the shelter of the trees. The shade, after the heat of the sun, was very welcome. Bee opened her window fully and breathed in. A cuckoo somewhere nearby welcomed them with its distinctive call. She found she was smiling as she leant forward again and tapped Gayle on the shoulder.

'What a place!'

From the front seat, Gayle smiled back at her. 'Isn't it? And it's only taken us half an hour to get here from Siena, but it feels so very remote. It really is cute, and very definitely off the beaten track. You'll be fine here, both of you.'

They both glanced at Mimi, but she made no comment.

At that moment they emerged from the trees into a broad parking area and drew up alongside a utilitarian-looking Fiat. As the Mercedes came to a halt, a dense cloud of dust swept over them from behind and Bee hastened to shut her window again as the driver advised them to wait for a few moments before getting out. When the dust finally began to subside, Gayle climbed out of the car, but the driver beat her to it, reaching Mimi's door in time to hold it open for her with an obsequious bow.

'Welcome to Montegrifone, Signorina Robertson.'

He was rewarded by a half-smile and a light touch on the forearm. Bee felt sure she recognised this gesture from last year's blockbuster where Mimi had played the part of the young Queen Victoria. She managed to make it look both regal and sincere, but then, of course, she was royalty herself – Hollywood royalty, but still royalty.

For her part, Bee was still enthusing about the villa. 'I've seen some gorgeous houses in my time, but this is one of the most spectacular. Do we know who owns it?'

Gayle shook her head. 'I'm not really sure. All I know is that you're going to be looked after by an elderly couple who live here. The bad news is that they don't speak much English, so you'll have to act as interpreter.' She shot a glance across at Mimi Robertson. 'Shall we go and see what they're like?'

Gayle led them up the path towards the villa while the driver busied himself unloading the mountain of luggage. As Mimi emerged from the car, Bee saw her tie a scarf over her head. It did little to disguise her and, if anything, with her dark glasses, it made her look even more furtive. Mind you, Bee thought to herself, the only watching eyes probably belonged to the birds in the trees or maybe a squirrel or two. There was no sign of any other human presence anywhere around them.

The villa was truly spectacular. It was three storeys high and almost the length of two tennis courts. The cream-coloured walls were punctuated by huge windows, protected by massive metal grilles on the ground floor, giving it an immensely solid look. Green louvred shutters shielded the upper windows from the baking heat of the sun. Steps led up to a massive arch, housing double front doors, towards which they made their way.

In front of the villa, a flower bed studded with bushes and flowers extended all around the base of the walls, and a meticulously mown and perfectly watered lawn ran back across from there to the parking area. In the middle of the lawn was an ancient well, complete with rope and bucket, half-concealed beneath a luxuriant white rambling rose bush. Bee was further impressed to see two peacocks standing on the grass alongside the well and studying the newcomers with curiosity.

As they reached the front door, it opened to reveal an old gentleman with a smile on his weather-beaten face. As he saw them, he stepped forward and held out his hand in welcome. Bee took a good look at him. He was of medium height, just a bit stooped, with a fine head of steel-grey hair. She reckoned he was probably in his seventies or even early eighties, but he still looked remarkably fit and he had kind brown eyes. He was wearing a crisp white shirt and a dark waistcoat. He had a friendly smile and Bee felt herself warm to him instantly.

'Welcome to Montegrifone, ladies. My name is Umberto. My wife and I will be looking after you during your stay at the villa.'

As expected, he spoke in Italian, and Bee was quick to translate.

Mimi took his hand and shook it, treating him to the same look she had given the driver.

'I'm very pleased to meet you. You do know that I'm hoping to keep my presence here a secret, I hope.'

Bee translated and the old man nodded vigorously.

'Yes, indeed. You need have no concern on that score.'

Bee added her own greeting as she shook his hand. 'I'm very pleased to meet you, Umberto.'

The old man's smile broadened.

'Excellent that you speak Italian, and so well too. I'm afraid my English is next to non-existent.' Bee saw his eyes land on her damaged cheek, but he had obviously been primed in advance. 'I recognise you from your photo in the newspaper, Signorina. I understand both of you have been in an accident and you're looking for somewhere to hide away while you get over your injuries.'

Bee nodded. 'That's right. This looks like the perfect place for us.'

He nodded reassuringly. 'I assure you, you can remain totally anonymous here. Nobody will breathe a word.'

'Thank you so much, Umberto.'

Bee translated what he had said as the driver appeared with the first of the suitcases from the heavily laden car. Only one of them belonged to Bee. All the others belonged to Mimi. While the driver set off back to the car for the next load, Umberto ushered them through the front doors and into the cavernous hallway. This was the size of a small church and the doorways leading off it were tall enough for even a horse and its rider to get through without difficulty. It was wonderfully cool in here after the heat outside and Bee breathed deeply. The floor was centuries-old terracotta and the ceiling, high above, was adorned with a wonderful mural. A magnificent marble stairway curled upwards until it split in two as it led to the floor above. As a historian, it was a fascinating and stimulating place. The idea she was going to be staying here went a long way towards relieving Bee's apprehension about what awaited her.

Umberto led them through a pair of ornate doors into an even bigger room.

'This is one of the sitting rooms. There are twenty-six rooms in the villa altogether, so if you ladies fall out, there'll be ample space for you to get away from each other.'

There was a distinct twinkle in Umberto's eye, but, wisely, Bee decided not to translate the last part of his remark to Mimi. There was no point in tempting fate.

The walls were hung with oil paintings, the floor strewn with wonderful rugs, and there was a monumental fireplace at the far end. It was a spectacular room with windows looking out over a formal garden to the rear of the property. As they made their way in, another figure appeared from a door cleverly concealed in a bookcase set against the side wall, and Umberto was quick to make the introductions.

'This is my wife, Ines.'

Ines was a matronly lady, probably the same sort of age as her husband, and she, too, had a friendly smile. As they all shook hands, Bee noted a distinct look of sympathy as Ines's eyes alighted upon their scarred faces.

'I'm very pleased to meet you ladies and I hope you enjoy your stay here at Montegrifone. I'm sure some good, clean country air will do you both good.'

'Thank you, Ines. You live in a wonderful place.'

'Can I get you some tea or coffee? Or maybe some homemade lemonade. The lemons are from our own trees.'

Cold lemonade sounded excellent to Bee and when she translated she was pleased to see both Mimi and Gayle nod in agreement. Ines scuttled off and Umberto indicated they should sit down while he remained standing with his back to the fireplace. Bee would have dearly liked to study the old oil paintings on the walls, but she knew she would have bags of time for that over the next few weeks. She took a seat on a lovely old sofa alongside Gayle, while Mimi sat down on an identical sofa on the other side of a finely carved coffee table.

'The villa as you see it now was built in the fifteenth century, shortly before Christopher Columbus sailed off to discover the New World, but it replaced a much earlier castle, more of a fortress. Some of the walls date back to the early Middle Ages and are almost a metre thick in places. The earliest record of a building here dates back to 1168, but the experts say it is much older than that. The villa has been in the hands of the same family for five centuries.' Bee translated faithfully. Clearly, Umberto was reciting a carefully prepared speech, but one of his twenty-first century guests had more pressing things on her mind.

'Beatrice, ask him about food. I need to follow a very special diet.' Mimi's priorities were evidently less in the past than the present.

'We've already told them…' Gayle started to answer, but Mimi shook her head angrily and insisted.

'Tell him, Beatrice. I want to be sure everything's quite clear.'

Bee relayed the message and listened in awe as Mimi then reeled off an exhaustive list of things she could and couldn't eat. The list of prohibited items was a lot longer than those she *could* eat and Umberto had to pick up a pad and pen and write it all down. It filled an entire sheet. As far as Bee could tell, her diet consisted principally of egg-white omelettes and celery. Carbs were strictly verboten, as was anything containing sugar. It was clear that staying young, slim and beautiful involved a massive amount of self-denial. Bee hoped Ines and Umberto wouldn't insist that she follow the same diet. Yes, she could maybe afford to lose a pound or two, but she knew that Mimi's diet would have her looking skeletal within weeks.

The lemonade was delightful and came accompanied by a plate of gorgeous *cantuccini*, Tuscany's traditional almond biscuits. These rock-hard biscuits suddenly became wonderfully edible, almost melting in the mouth, when dipped in the lemonade and Bee and Gayle helped themselves to several, while Mimi sat back and watched disapprovingly, or maybe longingly. Bee noticed that Mimi added no extra sugar to her lemonade and wondered idly what the bitter drink might be doing to her digestive system.

After their refreshments, Umberto took them for a guided tour of the villa, from the dining room with a table long enough to seat two dozen people, to the spacious bedrooms above. Bee looked out of the windows on the first floor and it was easy to see why the original builders had chosen this precise spot. The ground sloped steeply away on all sides and it would have been ideally suited to its original purpose of fortress. You could see all the way up and down the valley with its vineyards, olive groves and occasional green fields. As far as the eye could see, the only other building visible was a charming old brick farmhouse just a little way up the valley, the weathered pink roof just about poking out above the olive trees.

As Mimi stood alongside her and looked out, Bee got a glimpse of the irascible diva others on the set of *The Dark Prince* had described.

'Is the other house occupied? I was told we were going to be completely away from any neighbours. Can't you get anything right?' With her clipped English accent, she sounded like Bee's old headmistress. While Bee translated to Umberto, she heard Gayle attempting to pour oil on troubled waters.

'It's all fine, Mimi. We knew about this. Nobody's going to breathe a word. They've all signed on the dotted line.'

Umberto listened to Bee and nodded. 'There are two other houses on the estate, but you can be sure of complete silence about your presence here. Riccardo in the house you can see over there, the *Podere Nuovo*, rarely goes out anyway, so he never really comes into contact with anybody else. He's almost a hermit. The other house, the *Grifoncella*, is a little way down the valley and Luca, the estate manager, lives there. You can trust him implicitly.'

As Bee translated, Mimi looked a little more pacified, if not totally convinced, but even she could see that they had virtually no neighbours. Gayle's 'guys' had been right: this place was about as far off the grid as they could have hoped to find. Apart from these two other houses, there were just fields, olive trees, row upon row of vines, and dense woodland on the hilltops. Once again, the shiver of apprehension ran through Bee's body. What was that line about 'Nobody to hear you scream'?

When they got back downstairs, Bee sat down on the sofa in the sitting room and stretched her legs, resisting the urge to massage her thigh. She looked across at Umberto with a smile on her face.

'This place is wonderful. I feel at home already.'

He and Gayle both smiled back at her. All three of them then switched their attention to Mimi who was standing by a window, staring out into the garden, and Gayle asked the all-important question.

'So, Mimi, what do you think? Are you going to be comfortable here?'

There was a dramatic pause before the actress grudgingly agreed.

'It'll do.'

Definitely not effusive, but nonetheless positive. They all relaxed.

Chapter 4

Either by accident or design, Bee's room was at the opposite end of the villa to Mimi's. The shutters were open,
the bed made up, and her suitcase already waiting for
her when she got there. It was a sumptuous room. There
was an imposing wooden double bed, a massive antique
wardrobe and matching chest of drawers, as well as a fine
old sofa. Leading off the bedroom were two doors. One
led to a large private bathroom, complete with unexpectedly modern bathroom furniture, and the other was
what Umberto referred to as her dressing room. This was
another big room, lined with cupboards. The contents of
her single suitcase looked very lonely in there after she
had unpacked.

Another of Gayle's 'guys' had gone out a few days
earlier at Bee's request and bought her some summery
clothes for when she came out of hospital. These included
several pairs of shorts and some light tops, along with
brand new trainers and sandals. To her surprise, Gayle had
picked up the tab for all of it and Bee had been mightily
relieved. The 'guy' had pretty clearly gone to some very
expensive shops, and designer labels adorned most of the
items. She had very little in the way of smart clothes with
her – just a couple of dresses she had brought with her
from London, one pair of shoes with heels, and a few

other bits and pieces. Somehow, however, she didn't think there would be much call for heels or smart dresses out here in the wilds of the country.

Her bedroom also boasted a fridge bigger than the one in the kitchen of the flat back in London. It was stocked with alcoholic and non-alcoholic drinks, as well as fresh fruit and a mouth-watering selection of chocolates. Bee selected a big bottle of mineral water and poured herself a full glass. Although it was pleasantly cool in her room, the temperature outside was high and, considering it was still only late June, she had no illusions that the next few months here in Tuscany were going to be boiling hot. There was an air conditioning unit above the window, but for now the thick walls of the villa appeared to be doing their work and she didn't need to use it. Interestingly, there was a very fine mesh mosquito net at the window. No doubt, bloodsucking insects were par for the course here in the country.

Her thirst quenched, Bee opened her laptop, delighted to find the Wi-Fi good and fast. She took a quick look at her emails and was suddenly surprised to see one from a very familiar source. She clicked on it immediately.

> Hi Bee. I've just seen the news about your accident. It looked awful. I hope you're all right. Let me know how you are, please. Thinking of you. All my love. Jamie.

Bee looked up from the screen in disbelief.

All my love…?

Of course, she felt pretty sure he *had* loved her. And she had loved him. It hadn't been wild infatuation, but she had genuinely believed it would last, at least in the heady days

45

of their first year together. But, as time passed, they had both slowly come to realise that they were drifting apart. The end, when it had come, had been a low-key affair, more like the dissolution of a partnership than a break-up. There had been no histrionics, no real heartbreak, just a mutual decision to end something that had ceased to have any meaning. Although she had remained in contact with him off and on since then, she was surprised to see him using the L-word. Something he had rarely done in real life.

Seeing his name at the end of the email brought a whole raft of memories pouring back. Why, she asked herself, did these memories all have to be of the last few fraught days and weeks together, rather than the years of happiness that had preceded them? She got up, went over to the window again, and spent a long time staring blankly out over the vines and olive trees but without really seeing them.

Finally, she roused herself, returned to the desk and sent him a bland reply.

> Hi Jamie
> Thanks for asking. I'm getting better now and they've let me out of hospital. I'm just starting a long relaxing holiday in the country with Mimi Robertson of all people. Bee.

She felt a bit guilty to be mentioning Mimi, knowing it would almost certainly wind him up. He was a moderately successful freelance writer, just about managing to support himself from his royalties and magazine articles, but she knew his all-consuming dream had always been to write a screenplay for a Hollywood blockbuster. Following his departure from her life this winter, he had travelled to Los Angeles, no doubt in search of his big break. Knowing that she was now, albeit peripherally, involved in the movie world would be bound to frustrate him. After pressing 'Send', she rather regretted waving this in his face. He was a fundamentally nice guy and he didn't deserve it, but it was too late.

Closing the laptop, she went downstairs for the light early-evening meal they had been promised. Gayle had left in the Mercedes an hour or two before, after assuring herself that Mimi was satisfied with the accommodation. Her whispered parting words to Bee had been, 'Call me regularly. I need to know how you're both doing. And remember, she's a good girl, although I admit she can hide it pretty well sometimes.'

When Bee went into the dining room, she saw that the massive table was set for two people, mercifully side by side, facing out into the formal garden, rather than at opposite ends which would have almost involved shouting at each other to be heard. However, although it was past the agreed time, the other seat remained empty. Umberto appeared and informed her Miss Robertson had decided to skip dinner, so Bee found herself eating alone in a room the size of a badminton court. It was a bit strange, a bit creepy, and could have been a bit lonely. After her communication with Jamie, it would have been easy to slip into maudlin reminiscence and a feeling of loneliness. Fortunately, however, her mood was considerably lightened by the smiling faces of the elderly couple and the abundance and quality of the food on display.

There was a leg of what looked like Parma ham set on a special steel holder from which Ines carved her a few wafer-thin slices. There were olives, sundried tomatoes and tasty local pecorino cheese, along with pots of artichoke hearts, mushrooms and tiny onions, all conserved in thick green-hued olive oil. This was all accompanied by slices of the wonderful unsalted Tuscan bread that Bee had grown to love in the last few weeks. Ines had prepared a mixed salad, within which Bee could see little blue and white edible flowers, quails' eggs and asparagus tips. Alongside was a dish of sliced tomatoes topped with mozzarella and basil leaves, drizzled with thick, aromatic olive oil. The scent of fresh basil filled her head and she breathed in deeply.

If this wasn't enough, there was also a huge wooden board almost groaning under the weight of different salami, ranging from hefty dried sausages the size of Bee's forearm, to little ones the size of her thumb made, according to Ines, of wild boar. Bee took just a little taste of three or four, reflecting that, if she wasn't careful, a few weeks living like this could very easily result in her needing a whole new wardrobe. She resolved to eat sparingly and do her best to get as much exercise as possible.

There was cold mineral water to drink, and Umberto produced a bottle of gloriously cool rosé wine. The label on the bottle announced that it was local wine from the estate: *Tenuta Montegrifone*. As he poured the wine, Bee saw the condensation form on the outside of the glass and run down it like tears. The wine and the food were equally exquisite and Bee felt sorry that Mimi was missing such a treat. They had barely exchanged a handful of words all day and Bee hoped she would loosen up and become a bit more sociable. However, eating alone in these magnificent surroundings was definitely better than

48

struggling to make small talk with a spoiled diva, so Bee took another mouthful of wine and summoned up a smile for Umberto.

'Umberto, this wine is delicious. Thank you so much. Please, why don't you sit down and join me in a glass. It would be nice to have some company.'

Somewhat hesitantly, the elderly man took a seat opposite her and poured himself half a glass of wine. He raised it to his lips, sipped and nodded approvingly.

'I'm delighted you like our local produce. And have you tried the oil?' He pointed to the sliced tomato and basil. 'Here, try one of those.'

Bee did as bid and grunted enthusiastically, her mouth full. Umberto looked pleased.

'The oil's made here on the estate and, without wishing to brag, it's the best oil in Tuscany.'

Clearly, Umberto was not one to hide his light under a bushel.

Bee swallowed before she could answer. 'Thank you so much, Umberto. The tomatoes are delightful and the oil tastes wonderful. It's spicy. I can feel it tickling my throat. It's amazing.'

He looked pleased. 'Excellent. Everything on the table in front of you was produced here, apart from the mineral water, and that comes from just to the east of us in the Apennines.'

'Everything's perfect. I'll have to be careful not to eat or drink too much.'

'Nonsense. Good food never hurt anybody, and wine is as essential as bread or water, when it's good. And, modestly speaking, I have to tell you ours is the best wine in Tuscany.' His old face split into a grin. 'And if it's the best in Tuscany, that means it's the best in the world.'

Bee found herself grinning back.

After her meal, which had concluded with the most amazing *panna cotta* she had ever tasted, Bee felt she really should get some exercise, so she decided to go for a quick walk before night fell. It was still very hot, so she took off the wig and left it behind, slipping a silk scarf into her pocket in case she came across somebody. Outside it was still light, although the sun had almost disappeared below the hills, and the sky was filled with busy squeaking birds, swooping acrobatically through the trees in search of insects. She was pretty sure they were swallows, but her bird recognition skills weren't too hot, so she resolved to ask Umberto next time she saw him. She followed a gravelled path down the far side of the hill and soon found herself on a broad *strada bianca*, marked by the unmistakable imprints of tractor tyres.

She remembered that she had promised her mother a photo of how she looked, so she pulled out her phone. Mustering a smile, she turned her head slightly to the left, to minimise the view of her damaged left cheek, and took a selfie against the backdrop of the villa on its hill. The mobile signal wasn't as strong down here as it was at the villa, so she set off up the valley in search of better reception, the track climbing steadily through the vines.

She passed the house she had seen from the window – the *Podere Nuovo* – on her right, set back a few metres from the track behind a low stone wall. It was a wonderful traditional Tuscan farmhouse with arched doors and windows on the ground floor and an outdoor staircase leading up to the first floor. The windows were framed by old weathered bricks, while the rest of the walls were a mix of bricks and stone, worn by the elements over the centuries. The shutters were the same dusty-green as the villa's, while the roof was made of old pink tiles. All the shutters were firmly closed and the little patch of front garden was overgrown with weeds and burnt yellow by the sun. Presumably the man who lived here rarely came outside. Clearly, Umberto hadn't been exaggerating when he said the man was a recluse. Bee felt reassured.

Although her bruised thigh hurt a bit at first, as it warmed up the pain began to subside and she was pleased to find she could walk, not quite as normal, but reasonably well with only a hint of a limp. This boosted her confidence and she found herself beginning to feel happier about the prospect of making a full recovery, at least as far as walking was concerned.

After a while, she spotted a well-trodden path leading off to her right up through the middle of meticulously tended rows of vines. As she climbed, she studied the vines and saw little bunches of hard green grapes already formed, but not even the size of peas yet. Presumably they would grow and turn black as the autumn approached. She glanced around, her head just emerging above the vines. She was the only human being in the midst of all this greenery and it definitely felt a bit spooky. She was used to noise and bustle, not silence, and she did her best to repress her anxiety.

Suddenly, as she continued to climb, her anxiety levels went through the roof.

There was a sudden movement right in front of her, only a metre or so from her feet, and a sinister-looking yellow and brown snake uncoiled itself and shot off, remarkably quickly, into the next row of vines and out of sight. Bee stopped dead and looked around apprehensively. The idea that she was now potentially surrounded by snakes was seriously frightening. She breathed hard for a few seconds, feeling her pulse beating rapidly, wondering whether to turn tail and flee, before gritting her teeth and starting off again. This time she deliberately stamped her feet on the ground as she walked, keen to scare away any other reptiles before she stepped on them, and she didn't raise her eyes from the dry earth in front of her for one second.

By the time she reached the top edge of the field, she was a nervous wreck and the thought that she would have to retrace her footsteps through snake-infested territory on her way back to the villa was uppermost in her mind. She stopped as she emerged from the vines and took a few deep breaths until she felt her heartbeat starting to slow. She was very relieved to see that she now had three bars of signal on her phone, so she climbed onto a drystone wall after banging it a few times just in case there were more snakes, spiders or other wildlife hiding in the cracks, and sat down to call her mother. On the far side of the wall was an empty field, but a multitude of cowpats testified to it having been used by livestock very recently. Bee was pleased its bovine occupants had now vacated it. The idea of finding herself in a field with a bull did not appeal in the slightest.

She sent the photo of herself to her mother and then called her. First, at her mother's insistence, she dictated her address here at Montegrifone with strict instructions not to pass it on to anybody, and then went on to give her an upbeat version of how she was doing. She assured her mum that she would be back to normal and back to England by the end of the summer and that she was looking forward to a complete rest in the meantime. Her mother definitely approved. It would have been nice to invite her parents to come over, but the problems with her mum's ears meant that wasn't going to be possible. Instead, Bee promised to call them regularly and to send them lots of photos.

Her mother knew her well enough to sense something in her voice.

'How are you finding life in the country? I suppose it's all a bit new to you, isn't it?'

'It'll take a bit of getting used to.' Bee decided not to mention the snake. 'But it's very beautiful. I'm sure I'll be just fine.'

'And what about your famous companion? Your father and I can hardly believe it. Fancy you and Mimi Robertson together!'

'I can hardly believe it myself, mum. To think that I'm here with a household name, it's incredible. I just hope she isn't too much of a pain. She's in a foul mood at the moment.'

'I expect she just needs to relax. As I'm sure you do after everything that's happened.'

Bee hoped her mum was right, otherwise this could turn out to be a very long summer.

After the call ended, she slipped the phone back into the pocket of her shorts and rested on the sun-warmed stone wall, trying to summon up the courage to head back into the snake-infested vines again. She ran her hand over her head, feeling a slight softening of the hair. It was about three weeks now since the accident, so maybe it was beginning to develop into more than just stubble, but she knew it would take a long time before it grew back down to her shoulders or beyond. She let her fingers run gently over her scarred face and wondered, yet again, what she would look like at the end of the summer.

She was suddenly roused from her reverie by the unmistakable sound of footsteps coming up through the vines towards her. If the man got much closer, he would be bound to see her. What if he wasn't one of the people from the estate? If so, there was just a chance he might recognise her from the television or newspapers and reveal Mimi's place of refuge. There was nothing for it. She had to hide.

She swivelled round on the top of the wall and jumped down on the far side. As she landed, her left thigh jarred sending a stab of pain up her injured leg, while her other foot landed in something soft. A glance down revealed her worst fears. She had ended up with one foot right slap bang in the middle of a particularly large, soft, fresh cowpat. With a grimace she withdrew her foot and cursed under her breath.

Ignoring the fate of her sandal for now, she crouched down behind the wall. Her hands flew to her pocket as she scrabbled for the silk scarf to cover her stubbly head, but such was her haste, she only succeeded in dropping that into the cowpat as well and she cursed again. After a few seconds she raised her head gingerly to peer over the wall as the sound of the footsteps on the other side ceased. Unfortunately, as she did so, she must have disturbed a lizard or something as there was a sudden movement right beside her head and she squeaked with fear as the image of the snake in the vines crossed her mind. She recoiled and took a step back, landing in the cowpat a second time and, in so doing, produced a disgusting squelch that gave her away. She immediately heard his voice from the other side of the wall.

'Hello, Miss Kingdom? Is that you? Umberto told me you'd come up this way. My name's Luke, I'm the estate manager. I thought I'd come and introduce myself.'

The amazing thing was that he was speaking in perfect English. So Luca was in fact Luke and, patently, he was English.

She straightened up, feeling very self-conscious, and looked back at the wall. She could see a head peering over the top but, with the setting sun directly behind him, his face was in shadow.

'Hello, good evening. Yes, I'm Beatrice Kingdom.'

She removed her foot from the cowpat for the second time, wincing at the loud farting sound this produced, and rescued the filthy headscarf, holding one corner of it gingerly in her fingers. There was no point trying to put it on now, so there was nothing for it, he would have to see her scars, stubble and all. She took a deep breath and walked along behind the wall until she reached a convenient gate. She stopped there and surveyed her sandal. It was completely covered, along with her foot, and it looked as if she was wearing a single brown ankle boot. To make matters worse, every time she put that foot down, there was a revolting squelching noise. Doing her best to ignore the sensation, she raised the hand not holding the mucky scarf in greeting as he approached.

'Good evening. I'm pleased to meet you. I didn't realise you were English.'

He was tall, with broad shoulders and close-cropped fair hair. He was wearing faded shorts and a T-shirt, and his suntanned legs and arms were muscular and strong. As she raised her eyes to his face, she realised that he was a very good-looking man, although he looked unexpectedly troubled. This melancholic expression instantly endeared him to her.

She felt the colour rush to her cheeks as she saw his eyes on her scars and stubble and she did her best to sound relaxed.

'Sorry about the hide and seek, but I had no idea who you were. You probably know we're trying to keep all this a secret, mainly for the sake of my companion, who's trying to stay out of the public eye.'

As she said the words 'all this', she waved her hand vaguely towards her damaged face and head and saw an immediate expression of sympathy and empathy on his face. He approached the gate and held out his hand.

'Hello, Beatrice, if you don't mind me calling you that. I heard you'd been in the wars.' Bee took his hand and found herself looking up into his light blue eyes. 'And I'm only half-English. My father's Italian, but my mum was from Norwich.'

'Well, you speak perfect English.' And he did.

'Thanks for the compliment, but I know I'm a bit rusty these days. I always spoke to my mum in English as a kid, but then she died and my father packed me off to boarding school in Britain and from there I went to university in Cambridge. I was fluent in English then, but I've been back here now for a while and I don't use it as much as I'd like.'

Bee registered that he would appear to have a good brain. Cambridge university wasn't within reach of everybody, after all. 'Well, the result is that you speak it like a native. By the way, please call me Bee, everybody does. And do you prefer Luca or Luke?'

'Either's fine, Bee. I was christened Luke, but everybody over here calls me Luca. I answer to both. So, how long are you going to be staying with us? Umberto said until your scars heal, but it looks to me as if you're well on the way to recovery already.'

Bee gave him a smile.

'Thanks for trying, Luke, but I've got a mirror at home. I know how bad it looks. I'm afraid it's going to be a long haul but, what the hell? I'm still alive. As for how long I'm going to be here, that's in the hands of my companion. But seeing as she isn't talking to me, or anybody, at the moment, I have no idea. I'll have to start work again in September at the latest.'

'Where's that? In Hollywood?'

'No, I'm a lecturer in medieval history in London. At least that's what I've been doing up until now. The job in Siena was just a temporary—'

She was suddenly on the defensive again as a large black dog came rushing out of the vines behind Luke and charged towards her. Although it was on the other side of the gate, she stepped back apprehensively.

She eyed the dog warily. She had had a bad experience with a big dog back in her childhood and, although it hadn't bitten her, she had been badly frightened by it. Since then, she had always done her best to avoid them wherever possible, even friendly looking Labradors like this one.

'You've not met Romeo yet, have you? He's only a youngster and he's always pleased to meet new people.' Probably noting Bee's hesitation, Luke added, 'He's quite harmless, I promise.'

Gritting her teeth, Bee stepped forward and reached down to pat the dog's head as it poked through the slats. He had a fine set of gleaming white teeth, but the tail at the other end was wagging, so she took this to be a good sign, but she hastily removed her hand and stepped back again once she had touched his cold, wet nose.

Luke leant on the gate from the other side. As he did so, Bee saw both man and dog sniff suspiciously and glance downwards. She shook her head ruefully as she explained.

'In my haste to take cover when I heard somebody coming, I'm afraid I jumped right into the middle of some cow poo. And then, to make matters worse, I dropped my scarf in it as well.'

Luke smiled, a friendly, open smile that took years off him. 'It brings good luck. And, besides, you can't live on a farm without stepping into all sorts of things. Don't worry. The shoe and your scarf will clean up. Let Umberto or Ines have them when you get home and they'll sort them out.'

Bee wasn't so sure that her brand new, very expensive sandal would recover, but she made no comment. Instead, she turned the conversation to more important matters.

'Luke, can I ask you something? On my way up through the vines, I saw a snake. Do you think it was poisonous?'

To her considerable relief, he shook his head. 'No, there are no poisonous snakes around here. Maybe up in the woods, but they're very rare. Was the snake you saw a sort of yellowy-brownish colour?' She nodded. 'It was just a grass snake. Quite harmless.' He smiled at her and, as he did so, she felt herself smiling back. There was no getting away from it: she was enjoying his company, even if the subject was reptiles. 'It was no doubt far more scared of you than you of it.'

'That's what my mum used to tell me about teenage boys.' Bee saw him smile again. 'If that's the case, that snake must have been absolutely terrified, because I was scared stiff. I've lived in the city all my life and I don't really have much experience of nature.'

The dog was still sniffing the air around her foot and Luke looked down at her sandal once more.

'There's a spring a bit further up the hill and a stream runs down the side of these vines. Why don't we go across there and you can wash your foot off in the water?'

'That sounds like a great idea.'

Bee let herself through the gate, keeping a watchful eye on the dog as she did so. Together they walked across the top edge of the vineyard to where a little stream, barely a foot wide, ran down parallel to the rows of vines. The water was clear and remarkably cold, and it soon cleaned the scarf, her foot and her shoe, at least well enough to look less disgusting and to get her back home without squelching too much. When she had finished washing everything as best she could, she sat down beside Luke on the edge of a metal drinking trough to allow her foot to dry a bit. The dog settled at their feet, mouth open, tongue hanging out, panting like a steam train. Bee glanced sideways at his master.

He really was a good-looking man and quite evidently bright, and she couldn't help feeling unexpectedly attracted to him. For somebody who had had no interest in men for a good few months now, this was surprising, inexplicable and really rather annoying. She did her best to transfer her attention from him to her surroundings. Some way below them, she could just make out the pink roof tiles of the villa in the failing light, but otherwise there was little sign of human habitation. She breathed deeply.

'This is a lovely spot, Luke. Tell me, who owns it?'

He had to pause for thought before replying. 'It used to be Baron Cosimo, but he died last year and since then it's become a bit complicated.'

There was something in his tone that made Bee realise she was maybe straying into affairs that didn't regard her, so she changed the subject. 'It's very beautiful and very remote. It's probably going to take me a while to get used to the solitude.'

'But you're not alone, are you? You've got Ines and Umberto, and you've got your friend, the famous film star.'

'Not really a friend. We just both happened to have been involved in the same accident, and so we're hiding out together.' She gave him a wink. 'To be honest, I'm just here to keep her company, if she wants it. Mind you, so far, I get the impression she prefers to be alone, which is probably just as well, as I'm terrified of her.'

'I'm sure the country air will work its magic on her. Just you wait.'

'Who knows!' Bee wasn't convinced.

'Seriously, you wait. Romeo and I come up this way most days. If you sit still and silent, you'll often see all sorts of wildlife. Last week there was a big grey heron just down there on the lookout for frogs to eat or, indeed, one of

60

the brothers or sisters of the snake you just saw. And don't worry about snakes. There really aren't that many of them around. We often see foxes, deer and, of course, wild boar, the scourge of the vineyards.'

'We saw two baby wild boars as we arrived this afternoon. Are the big ones dangerous?'

'It's unusual to see them in the daytime but, yes, they can be, especially if you get between a sow and her offspring. But they're very private and I doubt you'll see any more of them. They can do a lot of damage to the vines, so we do our best to keep them away.'

'But they're the only dangerous animals around here, right?'

She saw him hesitate for a moment. 'Yes, although there are wolves in the hills around us.'

Bee felt her jaw drop. 'Wolves? Here in Tuscany?'

'Yes, but they're very elusive. From time to time we hear them, but it's very rare.'

Bee gulped. Snakes, wild boar and now wolves? This was a far cry from the Tuscany of art galleries, museums and historic buildings she had dreamt of for so long. Maybe she would be better off following Mimi Robertson's example and staying in her room. Seeing her concern, Luke was quick to offer further reassurance.

'Romeo here wanders all over the place and nothing has ever attacked him. And the peacocks at the villa have been there for ten years or more without incident. Trust me, Bee, you're perfectly safe here.'

Bee summoned a smile. 'If you say so, then that's fine.'

She suddenly jumped as the heavy, hairy head of the Labrador landed on her foot. She looked down to find Romeo stretched out on the ground in front of them and she could have sworn she saw the dog wink up at her. The warm head against her skin wasn't an unpleasant sensation, so she didn't move her foot, and she felt rather pleased with herself. She hadn't been in such an intimate situation with a dog since she was a little girl. She looked back up at Luke.

'I suppose Romeo's got the valley all to himself. No wonder he seems to be a happy dog.' As if in agreement, she heard the Labrador give a heartfelt sigh, and his eyes closed once more.

'Romeo is a *very* happy dog, Bee. He roams around all over the place and he's got two homes, so he's never short of company, or food. And, believe me, food is very important to a Labrador. He spends as much time up at the villa with Umberto and Ines as he does with me down at the *Grifoncella*.' Bee smiled at the name that meant 'Little Griffon'. 'Oh yes, he's a happy dog all right.'

They chatted a little more about the valley, the vines and the history of the villa before Luke finally got to his feet and the dog immediately leapt up, tail wagging, raring to go. Bee stood up reluctantly, feeling quite sorry this little interlude was over.

'Anyway, Bee, I've enjoyed talking to you, but I must get on. Come on, Romeo and I'll see you safely back down to the track.'

At the bottom of the field, she bade Luke and the dog farewell and went back towards the villa, reflecting upon the impression Luke had made upon her. One thing was for sure – even though she had come to Tuscany with absolutely no interest in men, she was looking forward to seeing him again.

As she walked back past the *Podere Nuovo*, she got a surprise. She was just level with the front door when she heard a voice, and not a friendly one.

'This is private property, you know. What're you doing here?'

Bee slowed and turned in the direction of the voice, furious with herself that her scarf, while a lot cleaner, was still soaking wet. At first all she could see in the half-light was that a door on the ground floor was now open, and it took a moment before she identified a figure standing in the shadows just inside the door. She stopped and did her best to stay in the shadows herself, pasting on her most disarming smile as she replied in her best Italian.

'Good evening. I'm your new neighbour. I'm going to be spending the summer in the villa.'

For a few moments, there was no response. Finally, he decided to reply.

'What's your name?'

It certainly wasn't the warmest of greetings, but she kept the smile in place.

'My name's Beatrice. My friends call me Bee.'

'And where do you come from, Beatrice?'

She ignored the put-down.

'I'm from London… England. And what about you? Where are you from?'

'This is where I live.' Communication certainly wasn't his thing.

By now, Bee's eyes had adjusted to the shadowy interior of the house and she found she could make him out more clearly. He was tall, with an unkempt mop of shoulder-length grey hair and he might have been in his mid-sixties. The fact that he was holding a full glass of red wine in one hand added to the impression he gave of an ageing rock star. Presumably this was the man Umberto had referred to as Riccardo. She wondered idly who he was and what he was doing here in the middle of nowhere. Maybe he, like herself, was hiding away from the limelight. This thought somehow endeared this prickly character to her, so she redoubled her efforts to be charming.

'Well, you've chosen a wonderful place to live.'

'"… a wonderful place to live."' The mockery was thick in his tone. 'And what would you know about this place?'

'Not very much, I'm afraid. I've only just arrived and I'm beginning to find my way around.'

'Where are you going now?'

'Back to the villa.'

'I see.'

Then, without uttering another word, he took a step backwards and shut the door.

'And a very good night to you, too.' Bee went off, muttering to herself, wondering why he was so grumpy.

The first thing she did upon her return to the villa was to take off her mucky sandal and dump it in a bucket of water she found by the back door. She scrubbed it with her hands as best she could, hoping it would come out all right. She had few illusions, however, as to the state it would be in when it dried out. Somehow, she felt sure it wouldn't return to its original appearance. On impulse, she then soaked the other sandal, so that they would, at least look the same, even if that wasn't likely to be too good, and set both of them on the step to dry.

Once she had finished, she went round to the front door, enjoying the sensation of walking across the soft lawns in her bare feet. A sprinkler was spraying the parched grass with water and she had to wait and then dash past as the wall of water arced away from her. There was no sign of the peacocks, but, in spite of the twilight, she did spot what were presumably peacock droppings and she made sure she avoided them. Clearly, living in the country meant being very careful where you put your feet.

She let herself back into the villa with the key Umberto had given her and padded up the cool marble stairs to her room. As she reached the landing she wondered how Mimi was getting on all by herself and she resolved to try to get her to come out for a walk with her the following day. She wasn't looking forward to a confrontation with her, but she had promised Gayle she would try.

She spent the rest of the evening on her laptop, reading and deleting emails and sending thank you messages to people who had got wind of her accident. There was nothing more from Jamie and she almost felt sorry. Whether this meant she still harboured feelings for him was something her subconscious appeared unwilling to debate. When she had finished, she watched the ten o'clock news out of habit and then climbed into bed feeling unexpectedly tired. As she lay there all she could hear was a distant owl. Otherwise, everything was peaceful. To her surprise, the image playing on her mind as she dozed off wasn't the gorgeous villa, the wonderful surroundings, or even her ex, but the face of Luke, the estate manager.

Chapter 5

Next morning, Bee was woken by the sound of somebody being eviscerated. Or so it seemed. A spine-chilling
series of cries from outside had her out of bed and at
the open window peering through the mosquito screen
apprehensively, wondering what on earth was going on.
To her relief, she discovered that the source of the screams
of distress was none other than the peacocks.

Back in London, the only wildlife she ever saw were
pigeons and occasional urban foxes, both normally scav-
enging among the dustbins for food. Here, there was no
sign of civilisation beyond the formal garden – just rows
of vines stretching out before her and onwards up the
valley towards the distant woods. She pushed the mosquito
screen out of the way, leant her elbows on the sill and
breathed in deeply. The fact that she was at an open
window in her pyjamas should have made her feel uncomfortable but, out here, she had little fear of being observed.

Partway through the night, she had woken up bathed
in perspiration and so had stripped the bed and slept under
just a single sheet, with the windows wide open, but the
mosquito screen closed. As a result, she had stayed cool
and slept soundly, untroubled by flying insects, and now
she felt pleasantly relaxed. She stretched, discovering with
pleasure that the previous evening's walk appeared to have

been good for her sore leg. It was still black and blue and it still hurt, but not as much as before.

The view was charming and the sky a perfect cloudless blue. The villa was very comfortable and the surroundings unspoilt and spectacularly beautiful. It was a lovely, if remote, place to spend a few sunny weeks, even if her companion at the other end of the villa wasn't likely to prove to be the easiest of people to get on with. She listened intently and found she could hear nothing at all. Not a car or plane, no rumble of the underground or human voice. She really was in the middle of nowhere and, to a city girl, this was definitely alien territory with its wolves, snakes and wild boar. To reinforce the point, there was a sudden movement in the vines right in front of her and a high-pitched squeak of terror as some little animal fell into the clutches of a predator. Bee squeaked in sympathy. It was another world out there.

Rousing herself, she went into the bathroom and had a long, luxurious bath, the first since the accident. As she lay in the water, she found herself thinking, once more, of Luke. However convinced she had been that she wasn't interested in any man, he seemed to be occupying an inordinate portion of her thoughts, and she wondered where this might lead. She certainly hadn't come here looking for romance, but she couldn't deny that she found him fascinating and appealing.

She emerged feeling refreshed and ready to face the day, regardless of whether this would involve snakes, Labradors or a grouchy film star. She reflected as she dressed that, however grouchy Mimi might turn out to be, she was always going to be preferable to one of Luke's 'harmless' snakes or a pack of wolves, and this brought a smile to

67

her face. The temperature was already rising, so she put on shorts and a light top and decided to do without the wig. Umberto and Ines would just have to get used to her appearance.

Downstairs she found Ines in the dining room, but there was no sign of the film star, grouchy or otherwise.

'Good morning, Ines. Any sign of Miss Robertson?'

'Good morning, Signorina.' If Ines noticed Bee's stubbly hair and scarred head, she gave no sign. No doubt, she and her husband had been forewarned. 'I've just had a call from her. All she wants is a glass of freshly pressed orange juice. I'm just about to take it up to her.'

'Please call me Bee, rather than Signorina.' An idea came to Bee. 'And why don't I take the orange juice up to Miss Robertson? I want to speak to her anyway.'

'Well, if you're sure… Bee.' Ines hesitated. 'She did sound a bit bad-tempered. I don't know if something's happened…'

Bee gave her a little smile. 'She's probably just grumpy. I believe these film stars can sometimes be a bit temperamental.' This was an understatement if half the stories she had heard on set were to be believed. 'I'll give her the juice and stand well clear.'

'That's very kind. When you come back down, if you don't see me, I'll be in the kitchen. It's down at the end of the corridor. Here's the orange juice. Thank you for doing my job for me.'

Bee took the little silver tray from Ines and carried it back upstairs. As she passed the paintings on the walls alongside the staircase, she took a quick look at each of them. Part of the research for her doctoral thesis had been on medieval and Renaissance art and she had become pretty good at recognising really old paintings from fakes. As far as she could tell without studying them in greater detail, the paintings hanging on either side of her were all old and no doubt fairly valuable, but at first sight it didn't look as though there was any masterpieces among them. Tuscany had been home to some of the greatest artists of all time, from Leonardo da Vinci to Michelangelo, but the artists on display here, while competent, were definitely not in that league. Nevertheless, she resolved to devote some serious time to studying the most interesting paintings carefully, just in case. The idea was rather stimulating.

When she reached Mimi's suite, she stopped, took a deep breath, and knocked on the door.

'Miss Robertson, it's me, Bee. I've brought you your orange juice.'

'Just leave it outside.' No please, no thank you, and the tone was definitely grumpy – or worse.

Bee suppressed a feeling of annoyance and did as instructed, before having one last try at establishing communication.

'I wondered if you felt like coming for a walk this morning.'

'No.' There was a silence and then she heard a grudging, 'Thank you.'

Nobody could accuse Mimi Robertson of wasting breath on unnecessary words, but Bee took heart from the 'Thank you'. Maybe the country air was beginning to work its wonders on the film star.

'Fine, well, goodbye then.'

There was no response and Bee left her to it.

After a morning on the internet, looking fruitlessly through a host of websites for a possible change of job,

Bee decided she would go for a longish walk. She wanted to do things properly so she asked Ines to prepare a little picnic for her. After dissuading her from providing enough food to feed a starving family, Bee settled for a cheese and salami sandwich, some apricots from the garden, a bottle of water, and the remains of last night's rosé from the fridge. She put everything in her little backpack and set off, this time heading down to the river, determined to follow it back upstream to its source. She chose trainers instead of sandals, deciding not to risk walking any distance in her cowpat sandals. Besides, they were still wet. Ines informed her she had found them on the back doorstep and had washed them twice more in the hope of returning them to something approaching their former glory, but Bee had fears that Dolce & Gabbana sandals and cow poo wouldn't mix.

For the walk, she left her wig behind, but tied her freshly laundered scarf over her head, knotting it on the left so it acted as protection, and camouflage, for her scarred cheek. On top of this she set a wide-brimmed straw hat Ines had found for her. Apart from offering shelter from the sun, this combination would hopefully be useful if she should come across anybody, although she had worked out that this was highly unlikely. It was an unsettling thought that here in the valley there were, in all probability, more wild boar than people.

Once she reached the river, she was unsurprised to see that it consisted of little more than a tiny trickle and an occasional handful of shallow pools of clear water. Nevertheless, the croaking of frogs and lush green vegetation at the edges was testament to the fact that there had been water there not too long ago. She walked upstream until the fields and vines gave way to woodland. Remembering what Luke had said about poisonous snakes, she kept her eyes peeled, but saw nothing more sinister than a lone squirrel surveying her from the branches of a tree and, at one point, a never-ending line of large black ants trudging across the path. She hopped carefully over them and carried on upwards as the path she was following became ever steeper until she decided to call it a day. Her thigh was aching a bit by this time, so she set down her bag and took a good look round. It was a delightful, if isolated, spot.

A rocky outcrop above her forced the stream into a little waterfall, below which a pool had formed. The water was crystal clear and quite deep, and she could even see little fish darting about in it. Around her in a half-circle, low tree-capped cliffs cut her off from the outside world and a large, flat stone provided a perfect picnic table. She opened her little backpack, poured herself half a glass of wine, and reflected on the beauty of her surroundings.

The place was like something out of a fairy tale, some-where beyond the real world. It felt as though Little Red Riding Hood or the Three Bears were about to appear at any moment. She sipped her wine as she settled back on her elbows and stretched her legs. It was a bit spooky to be here in the woods all by herself, but she was gradually beginning to get used to the solitude.

Then suddenly, she realised with a start that she wasn't alone after all.

She sat bolt upright as she heard the sound of some-body, or something, crashing though the undergrowth towards her. An image of an enraged wild boar crossed her mind, and she was starting to scramble to her feet,

71

looking for a tree to climb, when the intruder broke out of the bushes and came running towards her, tail wagging.

'Romeo!'

Bee wasn't sure whether to be relieved or dismayed. Although not a wild boar, the sudden appearance of a hefty black dog was sufficiently scary to make lose her grip on her glass and tip the remains of her wine into her lap.

The dog skidded to a halt in front of her, mouth open, revealing his intimidating set of teeth. Looking further along his body, though, Bee couldn't miss the fact that Romeo's tail was wagging furiously. He definitely looked pleased to see her. Hesitantly, she held out one hand, knuckles first, and he rubbed his face against it, giving little happy canine grunts as he did so. Reassured, she scratched his ears and within seconds he sank down and rolled over onto his back, all four legs in the air, tail still wagging. Bee was very impressed, both with him and with herself.

'*Buongiorno*, Romeo, how're you today?'

The dog didn't seem to object to the mixture of languages and wagged his tail so hard, the whole rear portion of his body wagged with it.

She pulled out a tissue and dabbed at the pink wine stain on her shorts, looking down at the dog with mock severity.

'Look what you made me do, dog.'

He made no reaction to this remark, but her next question definitely got his full attention.

'Would you like a bit of salami sandwich?'

As she spoke, she reached into her backpack and brought out the plastic bag containing the food. The dog immediately rolled back over onto his front, tongue hanging out, and it looked very much as if he nodded. Clearly, to a Labrador, this had been a rhetorical question. Romeo was definitely in no doubt that he would like a bit of sandwich, if not the whole thing.

Bee broke off a big bit of bread and salami and handed it to the dog who took it very gently from her fingers. As she watched him wolf it down – it barely touched the sides – she looked around to see if his master was with him, but even though she called out, there was so sign of any other humans. Evidently, Romeo was out for a walk by himself and she couldn't help a little twinge of disappointment that she wasn't going to see the handsome Luke.

She finished the salami sandwich under the unblinking gaze of the Labrador and subsequently discovered that this particular dog also like sponge cake, and even apricots. In fact, she seriously questioned whether there was anything he wasn't prepared to eat. By the end of the meal, he was lying at her side, his nose resting on her thigh, and she found she didn't mind in the slightest. In fact, she realised she rather liked the fact that she wasn't all alone after all.

When she decided it was time to return home, the dog trotted happily along with her, occasionally running off into the trees or vines to bark at some real or imagined animal, but he always came back to her and his presence was reassuring.

She got back to the villa feeling hot and tired, but secretly rather proud of herself that she had managed to navigate the vines and woods without getting lost or attacked by wild animals, and the dog followed her in through the back door. There was a bowl full of water ready for him and she saw him drink gratefully, splashing a considerable amount of it over the kitchen floor as he did so. She removed her sunhat and scarf, ran her fingers across her head, and followed the dog's example, helping herself to a glass of cold mineral water from the fridge and drinking it all in one go. But not so messily.

She was just swilling the glass under the tap when she heard footsteps outside and saw the dog sit up, head cocked, listening intently. She reached for her scarf, but barely had time to remove it from her pocket. By now Romeo's tail had started wagging, thumping as it hit the floor. The back door opened and Umberto came in.

'Good afternoon, Umberto. How are you?' She returned the scarf to her pocket.

He didn't bat an eyelid as his eyes alighted upon her scarred head. 'Fine, thank you. I see the dog's deserted me for somebody younger and prettier.' He gave her a grin. 'I don't blame him. Have the two of you been for a walk?'

Bee told him where she had been and how the dog had suddenly materialised out of the trees. Umberto wasn't surprised.

'He spends most of his time down by the river at this time of year. I can't say I blame him. It must be really hot underneath all that fur.' He scratched the dog's head with one hand. With the other, he produced something from a drawer.

'Here, Bee, you might find it useful.'

It was a very old and very detailed map of the valley, showing field boundaries, contour lines, paths and tracks. The date on it was 1903. Bee thanked him warmly and resolved to use it to guide her on walks around the estate.

He looked pleased. Turning back to the door again, he bade her farewell. 'I'm off to take a look at the vines down by the river.'

Unsurprisingly, the dog trotted off with him, no doubt looking forward to going for a swim.

Chapter 6

A week later Gayle came to visit them one last time before flying back to LA with the rest of the crew and she commented on how fit and healthy Bee was already looking as a result of the regular walks in the fresh air she had been taking. Bee agreed that she was feeling good and that her sore thigh was now pretty much back to normal. Gayle disappeared upstairs and spent a quarter of an hour with Mimi before emerging once more with an expression of relief on her face. Taking Bee by the arm, she led her out into the garden and round to the opposite end of the villa from the film star's room. When she deemed they were sufficiently far away not to need to whisper, she told Bee what had transpired during her brief conversation with Mimi.

'It sounds as though she's given up on the idea of a lawsuit for negligence. Mind you, she's still not too happy.' She caught Bee's eye and grinned. 'Somehow I don't think anybody at Pan World will be getting Christmas cards from her this year. But she's calming down. I don't know if it's your influence or this gorgeous place, but she's definitely sounding and looking a bit more relaxed than she was.'

'It can't be my influence. I've barely spoken to her all week. She hasn't come out of her room as far as I've seen, and the most communication we've had has been through her door when I bring her a cup of tea.'

'Well, whatever it is, I reckon it's working. I'm off back to the States later on today, but do stay in touch.' She tapped Bee's arm. 'I was thinking. If you like, I could spread the word that there's this red-hot historical expert looking for a job. You never know...'

Bee beamed at her. 'Gayle, that would be amazing. Please do. There are precious few lecturing positions in my field on offer at home in the UK at the moment and the more I think about it, the idea of going back to my old job appeals less and less.'

'Didn't you enjoy it?'

'Oh, I enjoy the teaching and the research. It's the fact that Professor Touchy-Feely got off with barely a rap on the knuckles that sticks in my craw.'

'Couldn't you take the lot of them to an industrial tribunal? Or go to the police? That's what I'd have done.'

'That's not me, Gayle. I'm terrified of anything like that. Can you imagine me standing up and describing how I felt when he stuck his hand up my dress? I'd die of embarrassment.'

Gayle looked sceptical. 'I'd have him hanging up by his heels... or his balls.'

'Yes, but you're you, Gayle. You're a whole lot tougher than I am.'

'Don't do yourself down, Bee. You're tough, all right. The way you've come through this whole accident business has been impressive. Anyway, like I say, I'll spread the word about you. You never know...'

When the time came for Gayle to leave, Bee thanked her again and was sorry to see her go, but she didn't feel abandoned. She was definitely beginning to become acclimatised to her home in the country.

However, the fact that life in the country could be substantially different from city life was brought home to her only a few days after Gayle's visit. Bee had hand-washed some delicates the previous evening and hung them outside on the line by the kitchen door to dry overnight. When she went out mid-morning to bring her things back in, she got a big surprise. As she stepped out of the back door, she realised that she wasn't alone and she stopped dead. Standing by the washing line was a large brown and white goat with the collar of her rather nice real silk blouse in its mouth. This was one of her favourites and, annoyingly, the goat was doing its best to tug it down from the line.

Her first thought was that goats in the flesh were a hell of a sight bigger than her distant memories of goats in the children's section of London Zoo. Her second was that the light blue blouse in this one's mouth had been bought for her by Jamie two years earlier in a Parisian boutique, and it hadn't been cheap. She hurried back into the villa for reinforcements, but there was no sign of Umberto or his wife so she went back out again and stood there for a few moments, eyes fixed on the goat, watching its jaws rhythmically chewing at the delicate fabric, before natural indignation kicked in. She clapped her hands and shouted as firmly as she could.

'Leave that alone, goat! Bugger off back to where you came from!'

She paused and then, for the avoidance of doubt, repeated herself in Italian.

The goat showed no sign of comprehension or of wanting to leave her clothing alone. She clapped her hands again, before nervously taking a couple of tentative steps towards it. A glance downwards revealed that this was very definitely a male goat and, somehow, this made the invasion of her privacy even greater. She also noticed a couple of sharp-looking horns on his head. His expression had by now moved from stubborn to confrontational and her resolve deserted her. Not wishing to discover how a toreador feels when he drops his cape, she retreated into the kitchen and took refuge behind the half-closed door.

Undaunted, the goat gave a final tug and dislodged the blouse from the line, sending the clothes pegs flying. He then turned and trotted off towards the gate in the far corner of the garden, bearing his trophy in his mouth. Bee waited until he disappeared and then slipped back outside and hastily collected the surviving clothes from the line. Then she went over to ensure that the gate was firmly barricaded, reflecting that the old saying about locking the stable door after the horse had bolted was no doubt based on fact.

A bit later on, after checking her emails, she decided to put on her sunhat and set out for another walk. The fact that this might give her the chance to see Luke again was something that didn't escape her. It had been a week since she and he had talked and she knew she missed his company. It was overcast this morning, but dry and still very warm, so she decided to go for a longish walk, following some of the paths on the map Umberto had given her. Seeing as she had gone up the valley the previous day, she decided to go the other way this time. As she came back downstairs, she thought she had better report the presence of a marauding ruminant in the garden and went through to the kitchen. Inside, she now found Umberto, sitting at the table with a cup of coffee and a newspaper. The table was covered in shopping bags. As he saw her, he pushed back his chair and started to get to his feet, but Bee hastened to reassure him.

'Please don't get up, Umberto. I'm just going for a walk and I thought I'd better let you know that there's a big brown and white goat on the loose. I found it in the back garden.'

Umberto looked unsurprised. 'That would be Berlusconi. He's a real escape artist. He should be in the field down by the river with the others, but he's always getting out. Luckily, like his namesake, he's quite a one for the ladies, so he always goes back.'

'Well, he also likes silk. I found him trying to eat the clothes on the line.'

'That's Berlusconi. I'm so sorry, I should have warned you about him. Ines and I have been out doing the shopping and I'm afraid I didn't check the gate. If it makes you feel better, he ate a pair of my trousers a while ago.'

'He really ate them?' Any lingering hopes Bee might have harboured of maybe getting her French blouse back evaporated.

'Ines managed to get one leg back from him, but the rest just went down his throat.'

Bee decided there was nothing to be gained from asking what state the trousers had been in when they emerged, assuming they had emerged. Instead, she changed the subject.

'Anyway, Umberto, I wondered if Romeo might like to come with me again. We've been walking together a good few times now and I really like his company. Is he here?'

'Not here, but I wouldn't mind betting he's not far away. He'll have heard us come back in the car and he'll be round for his mid-morning snack any time now. Wait a minute.' He rose to his feet and went over to the back door. Slipping two fingers between his lips, he gave a piercing whistle and then stood back to wait.

It didn't take long.

Less than a minute later, Romeo appeared, tail wagging furiously. This time Bee found she didn't feel in any way intimidated by him and she managed to stroke his head and ruffle his ears without any qualms.

'He never says no to a walk.' Umberto dissuaded the happy dog from jumping all over both of them. 'Well, you've got a lovely day for it, not too hot. So, where are you thinking of going today?'

'Last time I went for a longish walk, I went up the valley, so today I thought I'd head down the valley. How does that sound to you?'

'Good idea. You can't go wrong – specially with Romeo as your guide. Turn up left once you reach the barns at the *Grifoncella* and you can circle back through the vines and the woods. Romeo knows the way.'

Bee wondered if he really did, or if she would end up lost in woods full of dangerous animals, but her mind was made up and she nodded.

'That sounds perfect, Umberto. Thank you. And I've got your map with me anyway.'

The dog appeared to enjoy these walks and she definitely liked the feeling of companionship she got from walking with him. Although he was a big dog, with a fine set of gleaming white teeth, she could sense that he presented no threat to her. Indeed, she found herself stopping to stroke him on numerous occasions. She was definitely making excellent progress as far as her fear of dogs was concerned. As far as her actress companion was concerned, however, the same could not be said. As she had told Gayle, she had barely exchanged a handful of words since arriving at the villa and most of these had been through the door of Miss Robertson's room. Bee felt sure it would do the actress a lot of good to come for walks with her and the dog but, so far, her efforts to get her out had fallen on deaf ears. Still, she thought to herself, better the company of a happy dog than a grumpy actress.

The *strada bianca* was well maintained, although from time to time there were ruts made by massive tractor tyres. As she walked, she looked around, breathing deeply, relishing the clean country air and the relative cool of the morning. It was peaceful and almost completely quiet, apart from the sound of her new trainers crunching on the hard, dry surface of the track, but she was beginning to get used to the silence by now and it was no longer so scary. In fact, if she listened hard, she realised that what she had interpreted as silence was in fact full of a multitude of little sounds. In the background she could hear the twittering of birds, the buzzing of bees in search of nectar, and the almost imperceptible sighing of the breeze in the vine leaves. She found herself feeling remarkably relaxed. The sense of loneliness she had felt when she had first arrived here in the valley was definitely waning, and the company of the big dog was definitely helping.

The *Grifoncella* was made of weathered old brick with a sun-bleached red tiled roof. It was less grand than the villa and a good bit smaller, but she took an immediate liking to it. There was a rambling rose climbing across the front of the house and there was also one of the most massive and luxuriant wisteria vines she had ever seen. The scent of the flowers was heady and she stopped and savoured it. The garden was alive with bees, busily dipping into the blooms for pollen. Big yellow and orange butterflies fluttered from blossom to blossom and shimmering blue-green dragonflies zipped about. It was an idyllic spot.

Bee toyed with the idea of knocking on the door and saying hello to Luke, but an almost teenage sense of angst held her back. He knew where she was staying, after all, and he hadn't made any move to come to the villa to see her, so it was pretty clear he was keeping his distance — for whatever reason. And, of course, she reflected with a sigh, the reason might be her damaged face. This wasn't a happy thought and she did her best to banish it.

She set off again to look for the path leading up the hill. Just after the barn, a narrow path led away to the left and Romeo set off up it without being told. Umberto had been right when he had said the dog knew his way around.

The path climbed steadily and, as it did so, it narrowed considerably. On one side were the serried ranks of the vines and on the other a gulley with the remnants of a tiny stream trickling down it. From the width of the gulley, she could see that this most probably became a roaring torrent at the height of the rains, but certainly not now. The path was bordered by wild flowers and thorny bushes. Bee in her shorts had to take care as she squeezed past the biggest of these. Romeo the dog had no such qualms. By now she was getting used to the sight of lizards rushing for cover as she passed, and with Romeo in the lead, she felt much more confident that any bigger reptiles, particularly those without legs, would also be frightened off before she stumbled upon them.

She soon found herself in thick woodland and the path wound on up through a confused mixture of fir trees, bushes and bigger, deciduous trees. The ground was studded with occasional clumps of wild flowers and, as she climbed higher, she started seeing mushrooms. She was no expert, but the bright red ones with white spots looked – and no doubt were – deadly poisonous. Foraging for food, she decided, would definitely have to wait until she was accompanied by somebody who knew what was or wasn't likely to kill her. The irony of surviving a serious head wound, only to be struck down by a humble mushroom, didn't escape her.

She finally emerged from the trees onto a bare patch of hilltop. On her map, this place was marked with a fan-shaped symbol and the significance of this was imme-diately evident.

The panorama before her was indeed worthy of a special symbol on the map. She sat back on a big boulder and rubbed her thigh, more out of habit than necessity. It was barely aching at all after what had been a fairly hard climb, and she felt relieved and encouraged. It was now over a month since the accident and this part of her, at least, appeared to be pretty much back to normal. As for her face, she could see that it was also improving day by day, although she knew there was still a long way to go and no way of knowing what the final result would look like.

She removed her hat, ran her hands through her stubbly hair, and settled down to enjoy the view. Although she was perspiring from her exertions and the dog beside her was panting like a steam train, it had definitely been worthwhile. She found herself looking straight out over a series of hills, some quite steep, all crowned with dense woodland and covered lower down by row upon row of vines or olive groves. Altogether, it was stunning and once again she breathed deeply, feeling glad to be alive. She heard a heartfelt sigh and saw Romeo flop down at her feet, his tongue hanging out. He too, looked happy to be here.

'Not a bad place, eh, dog?'

He grunted in reply and stretched, pressing his paws against her feet. The grunt turned into a half-whine, half-howl and she found herself smiling down at him. If any of her friends had told her, even just a month earlier, that she might find herself going for walks all alone in the countryside with a big black dog and enjoying herself, she would have laughed in their faces.

She had been sitting there admiring the view for a while when Romeo suddenly jumped to his feet, nose pointing down the path up which they had climbed. As he did so, Bee heard the sound of footsteps approaching, and approaching rapidly. It sounded as though somebody was running up the hill towards her. In a panic, she scrambled across to the far side of the rock and crouched down, desperately hoping to keep out of sight.

She was only just in time.

The footsteps grew nearer and nearer and then stopped, and there was silence, during which she suddenly realised that, in her haste, she had left her sunhat in plain sight on the rock. She cursed silently and scrabbled in her pocket for her scarf, waiting to see what would happen. She didn't have long to wait.

'*Ciao*, Romeo, you're a bit far from home. Bee, is that you? You can come out. It's me, Luke.'

Bee felt a sudden movement beside her, immediately followed by the touch of a cold wet nose against her cheek. She uncurled herself from her foetal position and found herself looking straight into the Labrador's face. She emerged from her hiding place, wagging her finger at the dog as she did so.

'You're useless at keeping secrets, Romeo. I told you I was hiding. You weren't meant to give me away.'

Romeo ignored the rebuke and stood on his hind legs, stretching his front paws up against her, tail wagging happily. She stroked his head as she looked across at Luke, a warm sensation coursing through her body at the sight of him. He was wearing tight running shorts and a singlet and he looked very appealing. She swallowed hard.

They stood and chatted for a few minutes, and there was no disguising the fact that she thoroughly enjoyed his company. Whether he felt the same was hard to judge. Although he was charming and friendly, he didn't smile very often and she couldn't miss the stress lines around his eyes. Clearly something was bothering him and she would have loved to help but, for now, all she could do was to try her best to be cheerful and hope it would transmit across to him as well.

After a bit he glanced at the watch.

'Anyway, Bee, I'd better get back. I just came out for a quick run. I like to come up here when I can. It's always been a special place for me.' He smiled almost shyly. 'Ever since I was a little boy.'

'It's a lovely place, as is the whole area. I love this valley.'

'Do you? Do you really?' He sounded really pleased.

'And the villa, and your lovely *Grifoncella*. I love it all. Were you brought up here in the valley?'

He hesitated for a second. 'Pretty much. I know it like the back of my hand and I wouldn't ever want to leave. Anyway, I'm sure we'll meet up again before too long. And remember, anything you need, just ask Umberto. I'll leave you Romeo. He'll steer you home safely. Romeo, stay!' He stroked the dog's head affectionately. 'He's getting a bit more obedient. Let's see if he stays with you or if I find him running back down behind me.'

'Thanks, so much. He's great company. And Umberto and Ines have been ever so helpful and friendly. Goodbye, Luke. I've enjoyed seeing you.'

He turned and left and, to her surprise, the dog made no attempt to follow him. As Luke disappeared, try as she might, Bee found it impossible to keep her eyes off his retreating back – and not just his back. The running shorts really did stretch very tightly across his bottom. As he disappeared back into the trees once more, she sank down on the rock, her hand still absently scratching the ears of the dog who didn't appear in the least worried that his master had deserted him.

'Blimey, dog, that is one very handsome man.'

Chapter 7

Bee found herself doing a lot of thinking on the way back to the villa. She was still in a state of mild shock at the strength of the impression Luke, or Luca, was making on her. She even found herself wondering if this lovely valley was somehow enchanted. First, she had developed an unexpected connection with a big dog, of all things, and now suddenly this man had appeared and she could almost feel his spell being cast upon her. It was hard to comprehend, not least for somebody who, so recently, had sworn off men for the foreseeable future.

She had had a number of boyfriends before meeting Jamie, but none of them had ticked all the boxes. At first, she had truly believed she had found in Jamie her partner for life, but this, of course, had turned out not to be the case. But none of them, Jamie included, had made such an inexplicable first impression on her as Luke had. It would have been nice to talk this new experience through with somebody, but as her companion here was apparently only interested in herself, Bee felt sure Mimi wasn't going to be any help. She discussed it with the dog as they walked back down through the vineyards, but he provided little in return.

She spent that afternoon on the computer and then walked round the villa, studying the paintings on the walls. Her impression that many of them were very old was confirmed, but, regrettably, she didn't discover any of great value. The reason for this was explained by Umberto over a cup of tea and a slice of Ines's wonderful home-made sponge cake.

'The villa belongs to the Negri family. When Baron Cosimo Negri died last year, he left the estate heavily in debt. He was a wonderful, generous man, but he didn't have much of a head for business. There are things he should have done to reduce the amount of tax to be paid upon his death, but he didn't think that far ahead. To be honest, that's why we're renting out the villa, to raise some extra money. After the baron's death, we got experts in from Siena University to give us a valuation of the artworks in the villa and any really valuable ones were sold at auction.'

Bee nodded. 'And did you manage to raise enough to pay the bills?'

Umberto shook his head. 'Alas, no.' He gave her a rueful grin. 'But we live in Italy, so we did a deal. The people at the bank weren't very happy, but they've given us a loan and ten years to pay it off.'

'And if you don't?'

'I shudder to think. I suppose if the worst comes to the worst, the estate will have to be sold.'

He hesitated, but then evidently decided not to say more. Bee decided not to press the point. It was, after all, nothing to do with her.

'So, you're responsible for looking after the villa and Luke – Luca – for running the estate? You must both be very worried for the future.' She reflected upon the strain she had seen on Luke's face.

89

Umberto's wry grin reappeared. 'It probably won't bother me too much. In ten years' time I'll be ninety-two – that's if I get that far.'

'Wow! So, you're eighty-two. You look so much younger.'

His grin broadened. 'Thank you, Bee. But I'm more worried for Marco, my boy. He works here on the estate and it's his future, as well as Luca's, of course.' He looked up and caught her eye. 'So, you've met Luca, then? You used his English name.'

Bee told him how the two of them had met up the very first night and then again on the hilltop today and Umberto nodded.

'I'm pleased. It'll be good for him to have the opportunity to speak English again. He's hardly spoken a word for quite a while now.' He caught her eye. 'To be honest, he hasn't done a lot of talking to anybody.'

'I think he said he's been back here for some years.'

'That's right, three years now. And he's been doing a great job. The baron was very fond of him and so am I, as is Ines. He's brought in a lot of innovations and there's no doubt the quality of the produce has gone up and the estate is starting to make a decent profit again. That rosé wine you like, for instance, that was his idea. Traditionally we've always only made red – excellent red, but just red. Now he's even talking about trying his hand at making sparkling wine.'

'I saw his lovely house, the *Grifoncella*. Does he live alone?' As she asked the question, Bee found herself wondering what had prompted it, although her subconscious knew full well what the reason was.

'*Now*, yes.'

There was a finality in the old man's tone that made Bee realise she would appear to have overstepped the mark again. She was quick to apologise.

'I'm very sorry, Umberto. This has nothing to do with me.' She tapped his arm. 'I promise I won't be so inquisitive next time we speak.'

He laid his hand on top of hers for a second. 'It's all right, Bee. It's a sad story, but it's no secret. Everybody round here knows about it, so it's probably just as well you hear it from me first.'

'Only if you want to, Umberto.'

'Luca went off to live in Australia for a number of years after finishing university. While he was there, he met a girl. Dawn was… is her name. Nice girl, and very pretty too. But then a few years ago, after his first heart attack, Baron Cosimo asked Luca to come back and take over the role of estate manager. Luca immediately agreed and Dawn came with him, but it didn't last.' The expression on his face darkened. 'Everything seemed to be going well for the first year or two. They got engaged and were even planning the wedding, but then, a year ago now, the baron had his big heart attack and died. It all went downhill between Luca and Dawn after that.'

Bee had been listening closely, fascinated. 'But why? What happened?'

'Ines and I don't know exactly what triggered it, but Dawn decided she wanted to go back to Australia. Maybe this was because Luca was suddenly so very busy. Previously, although he had effectively been running the estate, he had always had the baron to support him. With all the awful complications brought about by the baron's poor financial planning, Luca found himself working all hours

91

and I suppose Dawn felt abandoned. I did my best to help, but he really has been at the sharp end of it all, going through the accounts for days on end, visiting the bank time and time again, talking to lawyers, and dealing with the crippling bureaucracy we have here in Italy. And I don't just mean for a week or two, or even a month or two. It's been dragging on and on for the best part of a year and it's still ongoing. It would have been a really tough time for him anyway, but with Dawn's departure, it must have been unbearable.'

'But surely she could see that? Why couldn't she stay with him to give him her support?'

'I don't think it was a sudden decision. Things had been strained between them for some time before the baron's death. She was a city girl from Sydney and she'd been finding being stuck out here in the middle of the country-side really tough. She'd been doing some part-time work from home on the computer, but it was pretty obvious she felt as if she was out on a limb here. She had very few friends around here and I think being left all alone at home day after day while Luca dealt with everything was the last straw.'

Bee nodded slowly. *Yes*, she thought to herself, *this was just about as far away from the bright lights as you could get in a populated country like Italy, but surely Dawn must have realised this was on the cards when she agreed to marry Luke?* She looked up at Umberto.

'And Luke – Luca – didn't want to go back to Australia with her?'

'He couldn't, Bee. He was responsible for looking after this place and he had promised the baron he wouldn't leave.' The old man paused for a sip of his now cold tea. 'Poor Luca found himself with an impossible choice to make – break his promise to the baron or follow his fiancée. And apart from the promise, the fact is that he's from here and he's got the valley in his blood. Reluctantly, last autumn they decided she would go back to Australia for a few months as a trial separation, and then, early this year, the inevitable happened. Word came through from her that she had decided to break off the engagement and stay in Australia. I've done my best to help, but he's been all on his own. It's been tough for him.'

Bee had to bite her lip to stop herself from asking more, but she managed to restrain herself. Little wonder Luke had been looking troubled. Having lost his fiancée only a few months ago and with the prospect of maybe even losing his job on the estate, it wasn't surprising he was feeling the pressure. She could well understand that.

Umberto swallowed the last of his tea and stood up remarkably nimbly for an octogenarian. 'Anyway, I must get on. In case you're interested, I've got to take a consignment of our wine up to Florence tomorrow morning. It's only just over an hour's drive. Would you maybe like to come with me?'

That sounded interesting. 'I'd love to, if I wouldn't be in the way. I visited Florence when I was a girl and I fell head over heels in love with the place.'

'It's a wonderful city, all right, but it's going to be full to bursting with tourists. I suppose that's something you should consider.'

Bee hesitated. 'Mm, you're right, of course. I wonder if it *is* such a good idea. What if I'm recognised? That could lead back to Miss Robertson. Maybe it's best if I stay here. I'd better go and see what she thinks.'

Umberto suddenly glanced at his watch and turned towards the kettle. 'It's four thirty. I need to take Miss Robertson her afternoon tea.'

'You make it and I'll take it up to her, Umberto. It's awful to see her stuck in her room all the time. I'll see what she says about Florence and, if she's not up for that, I'll have another go at getting her to join me for a walk around here in the fresh air.'

He gave her a sceptical look, but made no comment as he boiled the water and prepared Mimi's green tea in a charming little Japanese teapot. When it was done, he glanced at Bee.

'Do you like green tea?'

She nodded. 'I've had it a few times. I quite like it.'

'Then I'll put two cups on the tray just in case she lets you into her room.'

Bee smiled at him. 'Yes, let's think positive. And have you got a couple of *cantuccini* biscuits by any chance? I wouldn't mind one, even if her diet prevents her from joining me.'

Umberto filled a dish with biscuits and Bee took the tray up to Mimi's room. Balancing it in one hand, she tapped on the door and waited. A few seconds later there was the usual terse reply.

'Yes.'

'It's me, Bee. I've brought you some green tea.'

'Oh, right. Well, come in.'

Pleasantly surprised to have been granted access to the inner sanctum, Bee opened the door and the first thing she saw was the film star's bottom. Clad in yoga pants, Mimi was head down, bottom up, legs and arms dead straight, her body forming a perfect triangle with the floor as she held herself up on her outstretched hands and bare feet. Bee had done a bit of yoga herself and recognised the position immediately.

She walked in and set the tray down on the side. Mimi remained motionless in the same position without speaking. After a brief pause, Bee risked saying a few words.

'*Downward Dog?* I always find it hurts my wrists.'

Slowly, Mimi dropped back onto her knees and then stood up, stretching as she did so.

'So, you do yoga too?'

'Just a little. I'm not in your league, Miss Robertson. You did that perfectly.'

To her relief, she saw Mimi smile.

'If you like, I can give you a few lessons while we're here.'

'I'd love that, thank you, Miss Robertson.' *Wow*, she thought to herself, *this is progress.*

'Call me Mimi. We're going to be here for a while and you can't go on calling me Miss Robertson.' Mimi glanced across at the tray. 'Thank you for bringing this.'

'You're welcome… Mimi. I got Umberto to give you a few biscuits as well in case you're hungry.'

To her surprise, the actress turned back towards her and smiled – a real, genuine, open smile.

'*In case* I'm hungry? Beatrice, I'm always hungry. I've been hungry for the past twenty years of my life.'

Bee found herself smiling back, delighted to see this softer side to her. She risked a personal question.

'So, out of interest, Mimi, what've you had to eat today so far?'

'Breakfast was a glass of orange juice.'

'Just orange juice?'

Mimi nodded ruefully. 'Afraid so. No bacon and eggs for me.'

'But, not even toast?'

'Sometimes I might have a slice of dry toast with a cup of green tea, but I'm trying to cut back.'

'And for lunch?'

'I skipped lunch.'

'Wow. Have you always eaten so little?'

Mimi perched on the end of her bed and nodded. Although Gayle had indicated she was well over forty, she really didn't look any older than Bee herself. Even like this, without a hint of makeup, she was stunningly beautiful and her body was as toned as a teenage gymnast. However, by the sound of it, this hadn't been achieved without considerable sacrifice.

'I've been eating like a mouse ever since I got into this business. And what about you, Beatrice? Have you always been slim?'

Bee nodded. 'Pretty much. Plus the last few months have been a bit stressful for me so I've lost a bit of weight. And of course, I've been exercising a lot since arriving here at Montegrifone.'

'Exercise is the key, Beatrice.'

'Would you like to call me Bee? All my friends call me that. Beatrice always sounds so formal.'

'Of course, Bee.' Mimi glanced down. 'I see Umberto has put two cups on the tray. Do you drink green tea?'

'I drink anything – except for strong coffee last thing at night.'

'I haven't had a cup of coffee in ten years, maybe more.' Mimi stood up and went across to the tray. She picked up the teapot by its bamboo handle and poured tea into the two exquisite little cups. 'I've read that coffee's poison, you know. People say it's right up there alongside alcohol as one of the worst things for your body.'

'Please don't tell me alcohol's bad for me. I couldn't bear it – seeing as we're living in the middle of a vineyard.'

Mimi actually smiled as she handed Bee a cup and then took the other herself. She sat down on the sofa and indicated that Bee should join her. As Bee did so, she brought the dish of biscuits with her and set it down between the two of them.

'Have you tried these, Mimi?'

'Not for a long, long time.'

'Well, I'd like to dip one in my tea and eat it, but I won't have one unless you join me.' She caught Mimi's eye. 'Your call.'

She saw Mimi hesitate before coming to a decision.

'Just one. Because I didn't have lunch.'

They each took a biscuit and Bee watched as Mimi dipped the tip of hers into her tea and nibbled it.

'Good?'

'Wonderful.' The smile on her face said it all.

As Bee sipped her tea and ate two biscuits, she remembered what it was she had come up to say. 'Talking about exercise, I've been going for lovely walks up and down the valley over the past few days and I think the country air's really doing me good. I feel relaxed and I've been sleeping like a log. Anyway, I was wondering if you felt like coming for a walk with me some time. It's a beautiful area, you know.'

Mimi nodded. 'I can see. The view from my window's marvellous. Yes, I'd like to come for a walk, but not today,

I'm afraid. I've got a ton of things to sort out this afternoon and evening now that the US has woken up. I've got my PA, my accountant, my agent, my lawyer, my real estate agent and God knows who else, all desperate to talk to me. I think I'll stay in and do a bit of yoga when I can between phone calls. They all want to do videoconferencing, but I've refused until I'm looking more normal. But, maybe we could go for a walk tomorrow or the next day. That would be nice.'

'Talking of tomorrow, Umberto tells me they need to deliver some wine to Florence. Would you like to come along?'

Mimi shook her head decisively. 'Definitely not, Bee. All it would need would be for one tourist to see me and that would be it. As soon as somebody posts a photo of me in Florence looking like this on social media, the secret would be out. No, you go if you like, but make sure you stay covered up. And don't let any paparazzi follow you back.' She snorted. 'They're like leeches, you know.'

'Well, I might go, if you're sure you don't mind, but I won't get out of the car. Surely you could do the same. Nobody would spot us inside a vehicle.'

'It would be wonderful, but it's not worth taking the chance. No, Bee, you go by all means and I'll try to join you for a walk around here the day after.' She beckoned with a finger. 'Lean towards me a bit more, Bee, would you?'

Bee did as requested. Mimi took Bee's chin gently in her hand and turned her head towards the light, studying her injured face closely. Then she pulled Bee's head forwards and scrutinised the scars among the stubble. Finally, she released her and sat back.

'I'm afraid you came out of the accident a lot worse off than I did. You had lovely long hair, didn't you? But your scars all look as though they're healing up really well. Are you in any pain?'

Bee shook her head. 'Not now. I had a splitting headache for a few days after they brought me out of the coma and then my skin all got very itchy, but it's settled down now. The doctor said I should be more or less okay again by the end of the summer. Here's hoping. But, I must say, you're looking pretty good already.'

Mimi screwed up her face. 'Not in High Definition, I don't. That picks out every single line and wrinkle.'

As she spoke, Bee realised that – apart from the cuts on her cheeks – there wasn't a single wrinkle on Mimi's face. Her skin was as smooth as silk. She was about to comment, but Mimi carried on, now with an expression of distaste on her face.

'You know what I got yesterday? An email from a director I've worked with in the past. He says he wants to cast me as a zombie. The guy even tactfully suggested my "facial disfigurement" would add credibility to the role.' She paused to take a long, calming breath. 'The movie business is full of arseholes.'

Bee smiled supportively. 'Not just the movie business. One of these days I'll tell you about my own experiences.' She leant towards Mimi's face. 'Really, your skin's looking good. If I look like you do now by the end of the summer, I'll be well pleased.' This was an exaggeration, but she knew by now that the movie world lived by exaggeration.

'That's very sweet of you to say, Bee. But you're young and you're fit. You'll heal quickly, I'm sure.' She finished her tea and Bee was quick to follow suit. 'Now, I'd better finish my workout and get on the phone. But I've enjoyed talking to you, and I promise I'll join you for dinner tomorrow.'

Bee came out of Mimi's room and had to stop and pinch herself at the thought that she had just been having tea with a global superstar. Somehow since arriving at the villa she had got used to being alone or just accompanied by the dog, with an occasional conversation with Umberto, Ines or Luke. She had almost forgotten about her reclusive housemate. Now, as it appeared that Mimi was beginning to mellow and had turned out to be unexpectedly good company, Bee was awed at the thought that she might strike up a real friendship with somebody from such a different realm. And she was beginning to see that Gayle had been right about Mimi having a softer side. She found herself smiling as she went downstairs to tell Umberto that she would be delighted to accompany him to Florence in the morning, but without Mimi.

That evening before dinner, Bee took a short walk up the track and back again, without the dog this time, and she was returning home past the front of the *Podere Nuovo* when she heard her name.

'Good evening, Beatrice. It is Beatrice, isn't it?'

He sounded far less confrontational than the previous time she had spoken to him, so she stopped and looked for him. There was no sign of him by the open doorway, so she searched among the bushes and weeds of the overgrown garden, finally spotting him sitting on a bench under a particularly gnarled old olive tree. Clouds on the horizon obscured the sun this evening and there were few shadows under the tree, so she could definitely see him better than before. And, of course, he would no doubt be able to see her and her scars quite clearly this time.

'Good afternoon. And yes, it's Beatrice, or Bee.' She decided to keep it formal, but she did her best to smile at him. 'And your name is Riccardo?'

'That's right. So, what happened to your head?'

His tone wasn't unkind, but there was certainly no attempt at tact.

'I had an accident.'

'I can see that.' There was a pause, during which she spotted a glass of red wine in his hand. Seeing her interest, he raised the glass in her direction. 'Can I offer you a glass of wine? It's the local stuff and it's very good, you know.'

Bee hesitated for a moment. On the one hand, she was curious to find out more about this strange man. On the other hand, she had no intention of sitting down with somebody who was going to be rude to her. Curiosity finally won out and after a brief internal debate, she decided to accept his offer.

'Thank you, that would be very kind.'

'The bottle's here, but you'll have to fetch yourself a glass. Inside, end of the corridor. Kitchen. Loads of glasses there.'

His tone was abrupt, but she bit her tongue and went up the steps to the front door and followed his instructions anyway.

The inside of the house came as a considerable surprise to her. Somehow, she had been bracing herself to find a filthy, chaotic mess but, instead, she found the hall and passage clean and tidy, and the kitchen spotless. There wasn't a single dirty dish to be seen anywhere and the floors looked as if they had been freshly washed. It was a fine big kitchen, dominated by a huge traditional Tuscan fireplace. In the middle of the room was a massive farmhouse table, an equally hefty sideboard, and the biggest old wooden dresser she had ever seen. On the open shelves of the top portion of the unit there were glasses and cups, while plates were stacked in a solid wooden rack. There was a narrow larder in one corner of the room and through the open door, she saw the shelves loaded with bottles, some full, some empty. Clearly wine was an important part of Riccardo's life. She helped herself to a glass and went back outside.

As she walked out into the open again, she noticed there had been an unexpected smell in the house and it was only now that she realised what it had been. There was no doubt about it. It was oil paint, and it was very familiar to her. Her grandmother's hobby had been painting in oils and there had always been that smell lurking in the background every time she went to visit her gran, while she was growing up. Even now, every time she visited an artist's studio, she would find herself transported back to her grandmother's little cottage.

She made her way through the weeds to where Riccardo was sitting.

'You have a lovely house.'

He ignored her remark. 'Red all right for you?'

'Yes, thank you.' She held out her glass and saw him pick up the bottle at his feet. This was a massive two-litre bottle with a metal cage-like opening device that reminded her of the old lemonade bottle her father kept in the shed full of white spirit. Fortunately this bottle didn't contain white spirit and was almost full of red wine. It was no doubt very heavy and, as he filled her glass, he managed to spill some on her sandals. Whether this simply indicated that he was a bit clumsy or that he'd had too much to drink was difficult to assess. As for the sandals, the wine could hardly make them worse, after their baptism in the cow poo the previous week.

He was sitting on a bench, but there was what looked like an ancient well opposite him so she perched rather primly on the stone surrounding it, rather than take a seat beside him. Although there was no longer any direct sunlight, the stone was still warm beneath her.

She took a good look at him as he bent down to replace the bottle on the stone slabs at his feet. It was hard to tell his age. He was probably in his mid–sixties, but if she were to discover that he was five years older or younger, it wouldn't have surprised her. His mass of grey hair looked even more unkempt than the previous time she had seen him, but he was wearing clean jeans and a fresh white T-shirt. If he was an alcoholic, it didn't appear to be affecting his ability to keep the house and himself smart. Maybe he just liked a drink in the evening. She raised her glass towards him, the smile still plastered on her face.

'Cheers, and thank you.'

He nodded briefly, but made no attempt to raise his own glass to his lips. Instead, he studied her closely before speaking.

'You're here with the famous film star, aren't you? Robertson, Mimi Robertson.'

Bee's heart sank. She had been hoping he didn't know the full story.

'That's right. She's back at the villa. We were both involved in a nasty accident a few weeks ago and we're trying to hide out until we get over our injuries.'

'This is a good place for hiding out.' She felt his eyes on her scarred cheek. 'I'm sorry you had the accident. It must have hurt.'

She took a better look at him and it became immediately clear from the lines on his face and the black rings under his eyes that he had known his own share of suffering. In spite of his prickly attitude, she felt an immediate sense of kinship. She realised that she was in the presence of a fellow-sufferer, somebody who had experienced trauma, just like she had. The smile on her face became less forced.

'Thank you, Riccardo. I'm getting better, but it's a slow job. Anyway, the thing is that nobody's supposed to know that we're here. Do you think you could be kind enough to keep our secret and not reveal the fact that we're here to any of your friends?'

He smiled, but it wasn't a happy smile. 'My friends? You need have no worries on that score. I haven't got any friends.'

'Are you in hiding as well?'

She didn't really know why she asked him that. Maybe she just sensed something in him. She took a big mouthful of wine, preparing herself to get up and leave in a hurry if he reacted badly to the question. In the end, she didn't have to.

'I suppose I am in a way.' This time it was his turn to take a big mouthful. 'But it might be from myself.'

Puzzled, she wanted to ask him more, but she sensed that this wasn't the right time. From his expression, he was as mystified as she was that he had opened up to her. Instead, she returned the conversation to the banal.

'Does Romeo the dog come and visit you, too?'

He shook his head. 'Nobody comes to visit me.'

His tone was as gloomy as his expression. Rather than dig the hole any deeper, Bee drained her glass and rose to her feet.

'I'll bring Romeo round one of these days. He's a sweetie. I'm sure you'll love him. Anyway, thank you for the wine, I'd better be going, but I'll be happy to come and visit you again, if you like.'

There was a long pause, during which he slowly raised his eyes from his feet to her face. When he finally replied, she was relieved to hear him sounding less dejected.

'I'd like that.'

Chapter 8

The trip to Florence turned out to be unexpectedly enjoyable. This was not so much because of the delightful Tuscan scenery they passed on their way there, nor was it the sight of Florence itself with the magnificent duomo and Giotto's bell tower rising from the middle of the mass of pink roofs. The reason was the driver.

When Bee came down at eight o'clock, armed with a bag containing her dark glasses, scarf, wig and sunhat, ready to set off with Umberto, to her surprise she found Luke waiting in the hall. He gave her a little smile and she found herself beaming back at him.

'Good morning, Bee. I gather from Umberto that you're coming up to Florence with me this morning.'

'Hi, Luke. I thought Umberto was doing the driving.'

Luke dropped his voice, even though they were speaking in English. 'He's marvellous, but he's in his eighties now. He's not as fit as he could be and I don't like the idea of him driving any great distance. So, if you don't mind, you've got me as your chauffeur.'

Bee was still smiling. 'Of course not. In fact, if you're busy, you could give me the address and I could drive if you like.'

He shook his head. 'That's very kind, but I think it might be a bit soon for you to be seen in public, don't you?'

'That's what Mimi said. I suppose you're right. Well, I promise I'll do my best to keep you from falling asleep at the wheel.'

Outside, Bee found a businesslike and fairly battered pickup truck with a pallet wrapped in plastic film tied down in the back. This was piled high with dozens of cardboard boxes, presumably containing wine. She climbed up into the big vehicle and slid onto the bench seat beside him. The truck felt huge at first and she was glad he had turned down her offer to drive. As promised, she did her best to chat to him during the trip but, in spite of her considerable curiosity, she decided not to press him on his personal life and the conversation stuck to fairly neutral topics.

She enjoyed looking out at the Tuscan scenery as they drove past Siena and onto the main highway heading north. He pointed out the magnificent hilltop town of Monteriggioni off to their left with its perfect medieval walls and towers. She was already familiar with this partic-ular architectural gem as some of the filming of *The Dark Prince* had been done against that stunning backdrop, but it was good to see it again. A bit further along he told her the lush green hills to their right were the famous Chianti hills, home to some of Italy's very best wine. It was a busy road and she didn't want to disturb him with too much chat, so she just admired the view and enjoyed being here with him. Although she barely knew him, she felt very comfortable in his company. There was definitely something about him that attracted her greatly.

They delivered the wine to a wholesaler in the busy modern outskirts of Florence and it was the work of barely a few minutes for a forklift truck to lift the pallet off the back of the pickup. Bee stayed inside all the time with her scarf covering her head and cheek, and made sure nobody noticed her. Then, as Luke climbed back into the cab again, he made a suggestion.

'There's no point trying to drive into the city as the whole *centro storico*'s pedestrians only, but it would be nice to give you the chance to do a little bit of sightseeing at least. I was wondering, have you ever been to San Gimignano?'

'No, but I've heard it's fabulous.'

'It certainly is, but even more than that, the countryside all around there is quintessentially Tuscan. I don't need to be back at Montegrifone till lunchtime so, if you like, we could take the scenic route home and go past or even stop off at San Gimignano on the way.'

He negotiated his way out of the sprawling surrounds of the city and they climbed into the hills once more, gradually losing the worst of the traffic until he turned off onto even narrower roads where they met virtually nobody apart from a few brave cyclists toiling up the ever-steeper slopes in the mid-morning sunshine. The sky was a bit cloudier than in previous days and Bee wondered if there was a change in the weather on the way. Certainly, the dry grass at the roadside looked as if it and the rest of the countryside could do with some rain. All around them now were olive groves and vineyards and delightful, weathered, old red brick and stone farmhouses, almost all of them with one or more cypress trees nearby. Gradually, the hills became steeper and the buildings fewer and further between. From time to time the narrow road reached a crest and ran along a ridge for some way, affording stunning views back towards Florence behind them and out over row upon row of wooded hills ahead.

After a short while, San Gimignano appeared on the hill right in front of them and Bee was fascinated by the silhouette it produced against the skyline with its collection of stunning high towers, built over half a millennium earlier, soaring up from the roofs of the houses below. All around the town were more of the ubiquitous cypress trees, like towers themselves, and the overall impression was unlike anything she had ever seen before. As Luke had said, it couldn't have been anywhere but Tuscany. As they approached the town, he slowed and looked across at her.

'What do you think? Are you going to stay in the cab or risk getting out?'

Bee hesitated. 'I'll let you be the judge of that. If you can find somewhere to park, I'll get into my disguise and you tell me.'

Luke only just managed to squeeze the big vehicle into the overflowing car park outside the walls of the medieval town and Bee didn't need him to tell her it was going to be crowded inside the city walls. She pulled out her wig and placed it carefully over her head. Setting the sun hat on top, she slipped on her sunglasses and turned towards him.

'What do you think? Will I do?'

This was the first time he had seen her in the wig and he looked mightily impressed.

'Absolutely. You look completely different and the hair covers a lot of your damaged cheek, even if the scarring's not that visible anyway. I say you'll do just fine. You look great.' He hesitated for a moment, clearly debating whether to say more, but then he turned away and got out. Bee wondered what had been on the tip of his tongue. A compliment, maybe?

He led her past a row of parked tourist buses and into the historic little town through a narrow gateway set in the ancient stone walls. There were people everywhere and virtually every shop was selling souvenirs ranging from the expensive and stylish to the decidedly tacky. Bee decided it might be a nice gesture to buy something for Mimi, but then found herself confronted with the problem of what to buy for a multi-millionaire. A lovely leather purse would be something she herself would love to have, but she felt pretty sure Mimi – assuming she carried money, and from what Gayle had said that was unlikely – would never use it or would already have some amazingly expensive designer purse. There were all manner of biscuits and sweets on offer, along with wines, liqueurs, salami and cheeses, but for somebody restricted to such a Spartan diet as Mimi, they would be a most unfair present. In the end, Bee decided to go for the one thing Mimi would never buy for herself in a million years. In one shop window she spotted a totally tacky plastic model of San Gimignano inside a snow globe. It was so hideous, it was almost attractive in a decidedly retro way. Bee pointed it out to Luke.

'What do you think? A little present for a billionaire film star?'

He stopped and stared and then burst into laughter. It was the first time she had seen him laugh so freely and it transformed his face. Bee found herself smiling back at him. Yes, he really was a very, very good-looking man.

'I thought the only thing you should give somebody who's got everything was Penicillin. Are you sure she hasn't already got one of these priceless gems?'

Bee shook her head and took a ten euro note out of her purse. 'I wonder if you'd mind going in and buying it?'

He was still smiling. 'This has nothing to do with your desire to stay incognito, has it? It's because you're too ashamed to be seen buying something like this.' He assumed an air of resignation as he took the banknote from her. 'Well, all right then. I haven't got any pride.'

As he went in to do the deed, Bee reflected how very good it had been to see him with a genuine smile on his face and to hear him joking. From what Umberto had told her, this hadn't been happening very much of late.

Armed with her new purchase, Bee walked up the road with him and into the maze of narrow streets, squares and alleys that made up the little town. Seen close up, the towers were even more impressive. Many of them were barely the width of a big room, but they shot up ramrod-straight for a very long way. Some had birds nesting in the niches, one even had a healthy-looking tree growing out of the top, high above the crowds. Everywhere they went, they had to push their way through a mass of people and Bee had to agree that Mimi had definitely been right. It would have been all too easy for somebody to recognise her here.

After a while, Luke pointed across a small square to a café with tables outside, sheltered from the sun by the buildings all around it.

'How about a coffee, Bee?'

'Something cold, I think, but a sit-down would be welcome.'

He scrutinised her closely. 'The first time I saw you, you were limping. It looks to me as if that's all sorted out now. How are you feeling?'

As they sat down at the last table of the line, as far away from prying eyes as possible, Bee gave him her answer. Her sore thigh was feeling better and better, and she knew the fresh air and exercise were doing her good. There weren't any scales in her room, but she didn't need them to tell her that all this exercise was definitely keeping her trim.

'I've still got some bruising, but the pain in my thigh's virtually gone. All the walking I've been doing with your lovely dog has definitely helped.'

'And your face looks like it's healing nicely. I reckon you're well on the way to recovery.'

'Thanks, Luke. I certainly hope so.'

He gave her a little smile. 'So, still enjoying your stay in the valley?'

'I love it. The first couple of nights were a bit strange. I heard owls and little animals out in the vines – no wolves, I'm glad to say – but absolutely nothing else. At first it felt almost intimidating just how quiet it is around here, but I've definitely got used to it now. By the time I go back to work, I'll probably find my flat too terribly noisy for words.'

'So your plan is to go back to London?'

'Not necessarily. I'm actively looking for another job at the moment. In fact, for all sorts of reasons I think I might well try to find somewhere outside London.' She paused for a moment, before voicing her most intimate fear. 'My main worry at the moment is that if I end up looking like a freak, nobody'll want to employ me and that'll end my career. I don't know what I'd do if that happened.'

'Don't be so silly. Apart from anything else, they wouldn't have a legal leg to stand on. That could never happen. It's your brain that counts, even though you look good as you are.' She felt her heart give an involuntary leap, even though she sensed he was just being nice. 'We live in enlightened times. So you end up with a little bit of scarring... so what? You'll still be accepted as you.'

'I hope you're right, Luke. I really do. As for the whole "enlightened times" thing, I'm not convinced. I don't think much has changed. I'll bore you with my tale of woe some other time.'

'But you're staying here in Tuscany until the end of August?'

'I hope so.' As she said it, she realised she really meant it. 'Relations with Mimi back at the villa have started to thaw, so I'll see what she thinks. If the doctors are right, I'll hopefully be back to something approaching normal by the middle or end of August, or as close to normal as they can manage. The question is just what the new normal's going to look like.'

'If it helps, Romeo will think you're beautiful regardless.' She saw him hesitate, remembering his manners. 'And so will I, of course.'

She watched him run his hand through his short-cropped hair. As he did so, she found herself idly calculating that it was less than an inch long. Presumably her own hair would be about that length in a month or so. It looked good on him, but it was a far cry from her pre-accident long head of hair.

As he drank his espresso and she slaked her thirst with an ice-cold mineral water, they chatted some more and by the time they got up to leave, she felt she knew him a good bit better. Although he still hadn't shared much about himself, he had spoken in such affectionate terms about Umberto and Ines that she could sense the warmth he felt for them and for their beloved valley. No wonder he had been so torn when his fiancée had faced him with having to choose between the valley and her.

They got back to Montegrifone at just before one o'clock and he dropped her off outside the villa.

'Thanks for keeping me company, Bee. It was a fun morning. I haven't had too many of those recently. Thank you. I mean it.'

She very nearly gave him a kiss on the cheek but, instead, she just reached over and touched his forearm with her hand.

'Thank *you*, Luke. It was lovely and I enjoyed your company. A lot.'

She jumped down from the cab and slammed the door, turning to give him a wave as he set off again down the drive in the direction of his house. She walked into the villa and to her surprise found Mimi in the dining room. This was a very good sign. The film star was wearing shorts and a T-shirt, her trademark mane of hair just tied in a loose ponytail, and her face bore no trace of make-up. She looked quite normal and relaxed, and it suited her. Bee went over to her and produced the snow globe from her bag.

'Hi, Mimi. Here's a little souvenir for you. We went to San Gimignano and you were dead right. There were so many people there it would have been madness for you to risk being recognised.'

Mimi's reaction to the present was similar to Luke's when he first saw it. She hooted with laughter and then jumped to her feet to give Bee a hug.

'Marvellous, thank you, Bee. So I get to see San Gimignano after all.' She turned it upside down. 'And in the winter as well.'

Bee sat down opposite her as Ines appeared with a big mixed salad that appeared to have every possible ingredient in it from olives to onions, nuts to nasturtiums. Alongside it was a plate of slices of tomato with mozzarella, dressed with basil and olive oil. It looked wonderful. As they ate, Bee recounted the events of the morning and queried Mimi about this afternoon.

'So, are you coming for a walk with me this afternoon?'

She was disappointed to see Mimi shake her head. 'I really can't I'm afraid, but I'll be down for dinner and I promise I'll come for a walk with you tomorrow.'

At three o'clock, Bee put on her sunhat and went down to the kitchen to collect Romeo who was dozing there and together they set off down the valley. To her delight, she ran into Luke again before she had gone very far. He was in the pickup and he slowed to a stop as he saw her. A cloud of dust swept over them as he did so. The ground was still terribly dry, even if the vines continued to be a healthy green colour. He leant out of the window as the dog stood up on his hind legs against the door to be petted.

'*Ciao Romeo.*'

Like Umberto and Ines, Luke pronounced the dog's name the Italian way, with the accent on the 'e'.

'Hello, Bee. Sorry about the dust. What's that saying about mad dogs and Englishmen out in the midday sun? Is it hot enough for you?'

'Hi, Luke. It's good to see you again and, yes, it's definitely hot.'

It really was but for the first time she could also feel moisture in the air. What he said next confirmed her impression.

'Enjoy your walk today. There's rain forecast for tomorrow and it'll all be a bit sticky and muddy round here for the next few days after that.'

'I thought I could feel a change in the weather coming along. I bet you farmers could do with a bit of rain, though. Everything's so dry, isn't it?'

He nodded. 'Yes, the well in front of the villa's half-empty. That's our normal way of judging how dry it all is. So where are you headed for your walk?'

'I thought Romeo and I could try going up into the woods again for today's walk.'

'Well, if you do, keep your eyes open for mushrooms. It's a bit early, but you never know what you'll find, especially with the weather on the change.'

'I saw a whole lot of mushrooms the other day, big red and white ones. They looked poisonous to me.'

He smiled again, and it lit up his face. 'And they were. No, the ones to look out for are porcini. Do you know what they look like?'

Bee shook her head hesitantly. 'Sort of. I've eaten them and they taste lovely. I think I'd recognise them, but I've never seen them in the wild. I suppose I could google them.'

'Not down here. The signal's rubbish.'

She saw him turn his attention to the interior of the truck. After a moment his hand emerged holding a battered ballpoint.

'I don't suppose you've got a piece of paper on you?' Bee shook her head. 'I could draw on your hand if you don't mind.'

Bee held out her hand to him and he took it gently, opening her fingers so he could draw on her palm. The sensation this created in her was nothing short of erotic. She felt a wave of desire sweep over her and she almost had to steady herself against the door mirror. Apparently oblivious to the turmoil he had created in her, he drew a little picture of a round-topped mushroom with a tapered base. When he finished, he released her hand and she stared at it stupidly, still the prey of powerful emotions.

'As long as the top's darker than the base, and the underside of the top is sponge, not gills, you should be all right. But just to be on the safe side, if you do find some, take them to Umberto or Ines. They'll be able to tell you if you've got the real thing or not, and Ines will be able to prepare them for you.' He glanced at his watch. 'Anyway, I'd better get going. Enjoy your walk.'

As he drove off, Bee looked down at the Labrador who was sitting in the middle of the track, scratching his ear with his hind leg, apparently unmoved by the departure of his master.

'Blimey, dog, that really is one very handsome man.'

Bee's mushroom hunt that day turned out to be unsuccessful. Although she saw a good number of the poisonous ones, there was no sign of the porcini Luke had drawn on her hand. However, in readiness for her next foray, she looked them up on the internet when she got back home and studied the pictures until she felt pretty confident she would be able to distinguish them from other more sinister mushrooms. It was with real regret that she finally washed Luke's sketch off her hand.

–

That evening, Mimi was true to her word and appeared in the dining room at seven o'clock as agreed.

Umberto was waiting with a bottle of Prosecco in an ice bucket. Bee went over to greet her as she came in, and at her heels she heard a clicking of nails on the marble as Romeo roused himself from his snooze at the arrival of a new face. For a moment Bee was worried Mimi might object, but the opposite turned out to be the case. As soon as she spotted the Labrador, Mimi crouched down and proceeded to make a terrific fuss of him. Within seconds, the dog was lying on his back having his tummy tickled, grunting happily to himself and sweeping the floor with his tail.

Bee made the introductions.

'Mimi, this is Romeo.'

Although Mimi was crouched down, she launched into full Thespian mode. Bee smiled as she heard the words of Shakespeare echoing around the room.

'Romeo, Romeo, wherefore art thou, Romeo? Deny thy father and refuse thy name.' She gave the dog a final stroke and stood up again, smiling at Bee. '*Romeo and Juliet* was my first ever acting role. It was at school and they gave me the part of Lady Capulet because I was tall. I didn't have many lines, but I loved every minute of it and from that moment on, I was hooked.'

'Have you ever played Juliet herself?'

'Only once, but I'll never forget it. It was a one-night special at the Globe in London for charity. You know it's an open-air theatre? Well, it bucketed down with rain all evening. You could hardly hear yourself think, the audience and even most of us on stage were drenched, but the critics loved it.' She grinned. 'I was in bed with a stinking cold for days afterwards, but it was worth it.

'Prosecco, Signorina?'

Umberto nodded towards the ice bucket and Bee was surprised and pleased to see Mimi accept.

'Yes, please.'

As he busied himself opening the bottle and filling the glasses, Mimi glanced at Bee and pointed down at the dog, still sprawled on the floor at their feet.

'So, does this big fellow here come for walks with you, Bee?'

'That's right. Romeo and I are getting on like a house on fire.'

She went on to tell Mimi how proud she was of herself for managing to make friends with a big dog after years of fear. Mimi gave her an answering smile.

'How could you not? I love dogs, and anybody can see this one's a big softy. I've always wanted one, but how can I? I spend half the year out on location and it wouldn't be fair to the dog. Before *The Dark Prince* I spent two months in deepest, darkest Yorkshire in a freezing cold stately home, playing the part of the unfaithful wife of a brave soldier fighting on the Western Front during the First World War. Before that I was in Washington, putting on an American accent as the first female president of the United States. Sometimes I forget where I am. A dog would just get very confused.'

Umberto handed them glasses of ice-cold Prosecco and retired to join Ines in the kitchen, leaving Bee and Mimi to chat. Bee told her about her walks and Mimi filled her in on the developments with *The Dark Prince*.

'I heard from Amos that it's gone to post-production, so that's good.'

'That means editing?'

'Editing, special effects, sound effects, CGI.' Seeing the blank look on Bee's face, she translated. 'Computer-generated imagery. You'd be amazed how much gets added to any movie these days.'

'So does that mean it'll be out soon?'

Mimi shook her head. 'Post-production can take months. I believe the plan is to get the movie out before Christmas, but I'm not holding my breath. The premiere of the Yorkshire one's planned for October, I think, so I'll have to be back in the UK for that.'

Umberto returned with the news that dinner was served and the two of them took their seats at table. Ines brought in a plate of grilled lamb chops and chicken breasts and another one of her wonderful mixed salads. Earlier on, Bee had managed to convince her that neither she nor Mimi needed a pasta course as well, but clearly from the mountain of meat on the plate, Ines had decided to ensure the two of them didn't go hungry. Mimi helped herself to a small piece of chicken and some salad and Bee couldn't help reflecting, yet again, how her lifestyle, idyllic in the eyes of so many people, came with some serious disadvantages. She certainly didn't pity Mimi, but she was beginning to appreciate that Hollywood made serious demands upon its chosen few.

As they ate, they chatted, and Bee soon found herself telling Mimi about Jamie. Mimi listened with interest.

'So it just sort of fizzled out? But you're still talking to him?'

Bee nodded. 'I suppose we both realised the relationship wasn't really going anywhere. He was... is... so set on his career. I always came second to that.'

'And his career is?'

'He's a writer. In fact, a few weeks after we broke up, he went out to Hollywood. He's desperate to get one of his screenplays read.'

To her surprise, Mimi laughed, but then hastily explained.

'Sorry, Bee, I'm not laughing at what happened to you. It's just that everybody in LA has got an idea for a movie, if not a full screenplay in their bag. Everywhere I go, people are thrusting them at me. I've had several pushed through my car window, one even dropped into my garden from a drone, and I can't tell you how many my PA gets through the post every week. He'll have his work cut out to get his screenplay read.'

It was a very pleasant evening and the conversation flowed, particularly from Mimi. It was as if she was trying to make up for all the lonely hours spent in her room. By the end, Bee felt she knew, and liked, the famous film star a lot more. Prompted by Mimi, Bee told her about her own career and how she had ended up in Tuscany.

'The very late Middle Ages and early Renaissance are my period really. Pretty much anything in the two-hundred-year period from around 1300 to the discovery of America – by Columbus, not the Vikings. When I saw the advert for a Historical Consultant position based in

Siena, it looked too good to be true. After all, Tuscany was the birthplace of the Renaissance and all around us there are so many amazing historic places. Today's visit to San Gimignano has inspired me. In a week or two, as soon as I feel up to it, I've been thinking about renting a car and doing a bit of driving around.'

Mimi looked up from her salad. 'That sounds wonderful – once we are a bit more respectable. Why don't we do that? I'd love to come with you if you don't mind. That way, I'd have my own personal guide.'

Bee thought for a moment. The idea of touring some of Tuscany's hidden gems really did sound good and it would be nice to have company.

'I'd love to do that, Mimi. Why don't I go ahead and book a rental car for later in the month? Neither of us particularly wants to be seen in public at the moment, but from the anonymity of a car, we'd still be able to see lots of wonderful places.'

Mimi's eyes were shining. 'Oh, yes, please do and, of course, I'm paying.' She stopped for a moment as she had a better idea. 'Or rather, Pan World can pay. They owe us. I'll call Gayle and get her to rent us a nice comfortable car.'

Bee shook her head slowly. 'I'm all for Gayle paying for it, but I think we'd be better off with a small, unostentatious car so we don't draw too much attention. Besides, the roads can be pretty narrow round here. I've rented a Fiat Cinquecento a few times before. Why don't you ask for one of them. I'm happy to drive if you don't want to.'

'You know, Bee? I've seen those little Fiats and I've always wanted to try one. Yes, let's get one of those. Leave it to me. I'll call Gayle tonight.'

Bee went to bed feeling delighted at the evident change in Mimi's mood. Whatever problems had been troubling her since arriving here, they seemed to be fading away, to reveal a charming, friendly and unexpectedly normal person. Clearly, Gayle had been right all along. Underneath the daunting façade, Mimi was a sweetie.

Chapter 9

Later that evening the heavens opened and it rained right through until the following day. This was real heavy rain and Bee could hear it beating down outside her open windows. Next morning, looking out, she could see the vineyards running with water and the vine leaves bent under the weight of rain that had fallen.

Mimi was still in her room, so after breakfast Bee returned to hers and checked her emails. To her surprise, there was another one from her ex. Its contents were, to say the least, perplexing.

> Hi Bee
>
> Glad to hear you're doing well and getting better. Are you still in Italy? By coincidence I'm going to be in Tuscany in late July. Maybe we could meet up for old times' sake. I'd love to see you again.
>
> x
> Jamie

Although his upcoming visit to Tuscany was a surprise, the far bigger surprise was the tone of his message. Could it be he was missing her, maybe even hoping he and she could get back together? The thing was that, now, after her inexplicable reaction to meeting Luke, Bee knew that Jamie was definitely history. Whether Luke was the least bit interested in her, or any woman apart from his lost fiancée, was highly debatable, but the one thing she now knew for sure was that he had made far more of an initial impact upon her than Jamie ever had. On that basis, what would be the point of meeting up with Jamie and maybe encouraging him if, indeed, he really was trying to get her back? She now knew she wanted more from love and from life. The other thought going round in her head was that this was much more likely to be an attempt by him to wangle a meeting with Mimi. And that wasn't going to happen.

After a period of introspection, she decided the best thing would be to pour cold water on Jamie's suggestion.

> Hi Jamie
> I'm afraid I've signed a non-disclosure agreement and can't reveal where we are. Besides, it's the middle of nowhere and I wouldn't know where we could meet up. Enjoy yourself in Tuscany. B

She closed her laptop. Looking out of the window, she was pleased to see the rain finally abate and patches of blue begin to appear in the sky above the villa. When she went down for lunch, she was delighted to find Mimi already there and, even better, with a broad smile on her face.

'Hi Mimi. Joining me for lunch again? That's good. And you're looking cheerful.'

'Yes, indeed. I've just had some really good news. I've been offered the part of a sort of Bridget Jones look-alike in a romcom to be set in LA.'

'A romantic comedy sounds fun. And you could live at home.'

'Yes, but that's not the best part. The really good news is they want me to go up a dress size for the part, so you know what that means…?'

Bee grinned at her. 'Food?'

'Food! Maybe you'd be kind enough to break the news to Ines.' She was beaming. 'I can eat! Whoopee!'

Bee smiled back, delighted for her. 'That's great news. And I can't recommend Ines's cooking highly enough. It's exquisite, and almost entirely local. You'll love it.'

Bee broke the news to Ines over lunch and they were promised a slap-up dinner that evening to celebrate. Mimi also gave Bee some other news.

'I spoke to Gayle last night and I got an email from her just a few minutes ago. She's booked us a little Fiat and the rental company are going to deliver it the last week of July. Hopefully we'll both be looking a good bit more normal by then.'

'Terrific. I'll give some thought to the best places to go. The sky's the limit around here, but I know where I'd like to start. Have you ever heard of the sword in the stone?'

'The Disney cartoon or King Arthur?'

'Neither, or at least only indirectly. The fact is there's a real twelfth century sword in a stone not that far away from where we are now. It's housed in a little chapel about thirty kilometres away. Maybe you might like to start your tour of Tuscany there.'

'I can't wait.'

Bee remembered Luke's question to her the previous day. 'By the way, Mimi, how long do you plan on staying here?'

'I've been wondering that myself. The way things are going, I would hope my face will be back to normal by, say, the end of July or early August. The fact is, though, I'm not needed back in the US until September, so I'm thinking about maybe staying on a bit longer and making a real holiday of it, say until the middle or end of August. What about you?'

'The doctor wants to see me again at the beginning of August and he seemed to think I should be reasonably presentable again by the end of the summer, so I'm more than happy to stay as long as you want.'

'Terrific. There's just one favour I have to ask of you. I'm going to have to learn my lines for a new movie over the summer. Would you maybe be prepared to give me a hand? You know, read the other parts to me.'

'Yes, of course. That sounds like an interesting way to spend the summer.' A thought occurred to her. 'But isn't there anybody waiting for you back in LA?'

'A housekeeper, a pool boy and a sort of general factotum, that's all.' She met Bee's eye for a moment. 'As far as men are concerned, the answer's no.'

Bee was surprised, but she made no comment, knowing that it wasn't her place to pry. Instead, she just waved vaguely towards the open windows. 'This is such a gorgeous place. I can't think of anywhere nicer to spend a summer.'

Mimi nodded. 'I feel the same way, and it's the whole change of pace that's so wonderful. It's like I've taken a trip to another world. No stress, no early starts, no sneaking about avoiding paparazzi, no spending ages on my appearance. Do you realise? For the first few days I was still putting on make-up and dressing up as if I was going to be meeting God knows who. Then the penny finally dropped and I started to relax. I feel better and better with each passing day now and I can sense the tension just dropping away.'

'So, are you up for a walk this afternoon?'

'Definitely.'

'It'll be muddy, so wear old shoes.'

From the look Mimi gave her, Bee could tell that Hollywood film stars didn't have old shoes. Remembering the fate of her expensive sandals, she feared for whatever designer footwear Mimi would choose to wear. Still, it was great that Mimi had finally agreed to leave the sanctity not only of her room, but now of the villa walls as well. Much as she enjoyed walking with the dog, his conversation skills were sorely lacking and she knew it would be wonderful to have somebody with whom she could chat.

–

That afternoon, Bee and Mimi, accompanied by their canine companion, went for a walk down the valley. By now, the sky had cleared, the sun was out, it was baking hot once more and Bee had no doubt the puddles would soon dry up. In the meantime, however, on Umberto's advice, they stayed on the main track and thus avoided almost all of the mud. Or rather, Mimi and Bee stayed on the track while Romeo disappeared into the vines, to emerge two-tone – top half black and lower half a rich brown. Mimi was quick to comment.

'I'm sure artists must have a name for the brown of the mud round here.'

'How about *umber* or *burnt Siena*? They sound suitably arty, although I seriously doubt whether Michelangelo ever had to scrape his paint off a Labrador.'

When they got down to Luke's house, they were in for a surprise. As they walked past, the front door opened and Luke appeared, raising his hand in greeting. He came walking towards them and Mimi stopped apprehensively, pulling her sunhat down over her face. Bee immediately leapt in to reassure her.

'It's all right, Mimi. It's Luke, the estate manager. He knows all about us and he's signed the non-disclosure agreement.'

She saw Mimi begin to relax, although the brim of her hat remained pulled down.

'Good afternoon, ladies. The weathermen were right about the rain, weren't they, Bee?'

'Hi, Luke. Yes indeed, and when it rains round here it really rains! Please let me introduce you to Mimi Robertson.'

'Miss Robertson needs no introduction.' Luke held out his hand gallantly. 'I would have recognised you anywhere.'

Mimi raised the brim of her hat and looked up as she took his hand and gave him a smile in return. Bee couldn't miss the fact that this smile went a whole lot further than the greeting she had given Umberto and Ines. It was clear she really was pleased to see him. As she spotted the expression on Mimi's face, an unexpected feeling ran through Bee's body. Could it be she was jealous?

'Luke, good afternoon. I'm very pleased to meet you.' Mimi definitely looked as if she meant it.

'I hope you're enjoying your stay here at Montegrifone. Are Umberto and Ines looking after you well?'

As Mimi and Luke chatted, Bee did her best to analyse her feelings. There was no doubt in her mind that the sight of the beautiful film star smiling and chatting to the hunky farmer had produced the sort of sensation in her that normally only comes when you have strong feelings for somebody. Did this mean she was developing strong feelings for Luke? She liked him. She felt sorry for him after the rough hand he had been dealt, but she could see full well that he wasn't interested in her or any woman at present. Would that change if a beautiful film star suddenly appeared in the mix?

As she was still mulling it over, her phone whistled. She pulled it out and checked the message she had just received. It was from Gayle and it was disconcerting.

> Hi Bee. A quick heads-up. I've heard from my guy in Siena that Joey knows where you are and he says he's coming to visit. No idea how he found out, but be warned. Gayle.

'I was just saying to Luke he should come and have dinner at the villa some time. Bee? Bee, are you listening?'

Bee roused herself at the sound of Mimi's voice.

'Sorry, yes. Did you say dinner? Great idea.'

In fact, although the idea of a quiet dinner *à deux* with Luke definitely did appeal, the thought of having to sit and watch as he and Mimi flirted most certainly didn't. But, of course, there was nothing she could do about it so she mustered up a big smile as she slipped her phone back into her pocket.

'Whenever you like, Luke. You're the one who's got to work.'

'That's very kind of you both. Well, maybe Saturday night? How would that suit you?'

They both nodded and, after a bit more chat, he bade them goodbye and drove off in his pick-up. After he had left, Bee decided to risk taking Mimi up the steep path into the woods, hoping it wouldn't be too soggy underfoot. This meant they had to walk one in front of the other so they weren't able to talk, and Bee was dying to hear what sort of impression Luke had made upon Mimi. She felt pretty sure she already knew and it did nothing for her mood. Apart from this, there was now the complication of Joey, the Hollywood heart-throb, supposedly coming to visit her. And she didn't need to be Hercule Poirot to have a pretty good idea what he would be hoping to get out of the visit.

Bee's spirits were raised by the discovery underneath what might have been a chestnut tree – her tree recognition skills weren't much better than her bird recognition talents – of a little family of mushrooms that exactly fitted Luke's description. Although long-since washed off the palm of her hand, Bee had memorised his sketch as well as more detailed descriptions from the internet, and felt pretty sure these were the legendary porcini mushrooms. Not having her little backpack this time, she took off her scarf and used it as a makeshift bag to carry them. A bit further on both she and Mimi found several more, one partly nibbled by some animal, so by the time they got back to the villa, they had a decent collection.

They went round to the kitchen door and found Ines picking roses in the garden. Bee showed her the mushrooms and the old lady was full of praise for the two of them.

'What lovely porcini! Well done. Now, what are you going to do with them?'

'Would you like them? I gather they're considered a delicacy.'

'They certainly are, but you found them, so they're yours. If you want a suggestion, I'd say eat a couple of the little ones raw, sliced with a bit of grated Parmesan, and drizzled with olive oil. Or slice them, dip them in egg and breadcrumbs, and fry them. And you could use the others to make a wonderful pasta sauce. Why don't I prepare a few of them for tonight as a starter, before the roast lamb?'

'Wonderful, Ines.' Mimi glanced at her watch. 'Now if you'll excuse me, I have to rush back and check my emails. Thanks for the walk, Bee. I really enjoyed it.'

'Leave me your muddy shoes and I'll clean them, Signorina.' Ines pointed to the step. 'Just leave them there.'

As Mimi went off barefoot, Bee glanced across at the two-tone dog who was rolling in the grass, grunting to himself.

'Talking of mud, Ines, I'm afraid Romeo's going to need a bath. Why don't I take him down to the river for a splash about?'

She and the dog headed down to the bridge. After the rain, the river was considerably fuller than before and the dog wasted no time leaping into a pool and swimming enthusiastically, if fruitlessly, after the stones Bee threw into the water for him to fetch. The net result was that by the time he came out again he was, once more, a clean black Labrador. As they walked back up the hill to the villa, Bee scrupulously keeping him to the path, she found her head buzzing with thoughts of no fewer than three men. There was the farmer for whom she felt attraction, but who didn't appear to want her; the actor who probably only wanted her for sex, but she didn't want; and the former boyfriend who also maybe wanted her, but she no longer wanted. It was very confusing and, for somebody who had decided she had no interest in men, it was annoying.

As she reached the corner of the villa, she heard somebody calling her name and she looked up. Mimi was leaning out of her window on the first floor.

'Bee, I hope you don't mind, but I've just had a call from Joey... Joey Eagle. He's coming to pick me up in a couple of hours and he's taking me out for an early dinner. He promises it's somewhere we won't be seen. So, please could you tell Ines. Thank her very much, but I'm afraid Joey always does things at the last minute.'

'Of course, Mimi. Have a good time.' Bee took a deep breath. 'And give Joey my love.'

She found Ines on the back step, scrubbing Mimi's trainers.

'Let me have your shoes, Bee, and I'll do them at the same time.'

Bee protested that she could clean her own shoes, but the old lady was adamant and she ended up giving in and slipping off her trainers. As she did so, she passed on Mimi's news and apologies. Ines looked totally unphased to hear that her meal plans had just been shot down in flames.

'No problem, Bee. The roast hasn't gone into the oven yet so we can have that tomorrow, unless you're feeling very hungry tonight.'

'Absolutely not, Ines. I know, why don't you just do some porcini mushrooms this evening? Maybe with a salad?' She had a thought. 'In fact, when you're preparing the mushrooms, could I come and watch?'

'Of course.'

Leaving the dog rolling once again on his back in the grass alongside Ines, Bee went back upstairs and analysed the latest developments.

So, it appeared that Joey was not, after all, coming to the villa for her sake, but for the sake of the beautiful actress. While a considerable relief, it was also just a tad annoying to find herself second best. This same beautiful actress had also invited the man Bee rather liked to dinner in two days' time. This, too, was a tad annoying. Which left her with… Jamie. Not, she told herself angrily, that she wanted any of them. Or did she?

She found herself thinking ruefully that her nascent friendship with the glamorous movie star should have come with a health warning: *Can seriously damage your relationships*.

Chapter 10

Ines sliced the mushrooms into strips, dipped them in raw egg and breadcrumbs and then quickly fried them to produce mushroom fritters as a starter. Bee stood beside her with a glass of wine and watched. At her side, eyes trained on the pan, was Romeo. The fact that a dog might be interested in eating mushrooms came as a bit of a surprise, but just underlined the omnivorous nature of this particular dog's appetite.

As Ines was preparing the food, Bee heard a high-pitched howl from outside that managed to draw even the dog's attention away from the food. It was a car's engine, but no car Bee had ever heard before. Leaving the dog in the kitchen, she went along the corridor to the entrance hall to investigate. Peering through a side window, she saw a spectacular long, low, yellow sports car pull up outside. The driver's door swung upwards like a bird's wing and the unmistakable shape of one of the most famous actors in the world climbed out. Reassured, she opened the door to him, even though she wasn't wearing her wig. To her surprise, as he caught sight of her, he came jogging across and took her in his arms, lifting her off the ground and spinning her round apparently effortlessly.

'Hey, Beatrice, honey. How great to see you.'

He set her down again, but kept hold of her shoulders, looking intently at her injured face and head. Then, apparently reassured, he kissed her on her good cheek and pronounced judgement. 'You look a million dollars, Beatrice. And here I was, getting all worked up that you'd no longer be the most beautiful professor I've ever met.' He kissed her again for good measure. 'I'm so pleased for you.'

'Hello, Joey. It's good to see you, too.' And it was. Womaniser or not, he was a nice guy – as Hollywood legends go.

'Joey, darling, how nice of you to come.' Mimi had also heard the car and had appeared behind Bee.

Joey transferred his attention to Mimi, but didn't sweep her into his arms. In fact, Bee couldn't miss the almost shy expression on his face as he went over to her.

'Hi, Mimi. I'm so pleased to see you looking as good as new.'

Mimi was looking stunning. A hint of make-up had almost completely concealed the remains of her scratches, and the light summer dress she was wearing was a dream. She looked as if she was about to float away. She bestowed an equally light kiss on each of Joey's cheeks, and Bee could have sworn he blushed.

'So, would you like to come in for a drink or are we going straight off?'

'I've only got the Lambo for a few hours, so shall we head straight off? The place we're going's only a short drive from here.'

Before returning to the car, he caught hold of Bee again and gave her another kiss.

'So long, professor. See you again soon, I hope.'

'Bye, Joey.'

As the sexy sports car nosed its way back down the drive, Bee returned to the house. Umberto, alerted by the unmistakable howl of the engine, was waiting on the doorstep.

'What's a Lambo, Umberto?'

He gave her the sort of look school teachers normally reserve for their very slowest pupils.

'You've never heard of a Lamborghini, Bee?'

Comprehension dawned. Bee had indeed heard the name, but this was the first time she had seen one in the flesh.

'Got it. So, the perfect low-profile car if you're taking a film star who doesn't want to be recognised, out for dinner.'

'My thoughts entirely. We can only hope he wasn't tailed by the paparazzi.'

They went back through to the kitchen where Ines had just finished frying the mushroom fritters. She pushed the plate across the table towards Bee.

'Want to try them?'

Bee picked up one of the still-warm slivers of mushroom and nibbled it. It was exquisite. She looked across at Ines and her husband who were watching her curiously.

'Come on, you two, do have some. They're wonderful.'

The elderly couple helped themselves to pieces of the porcini and nodded approvingly. Umberto gave Bee a smile.

'There's nothing better than eating something you've grown yourself or found by yourself.'

Bee nibbled a few slices, loving the crispy texture of the outside compared to the soft inside, and then had an idea.

'Have I got half an hour before dinner, Ines?'

'Yes, of course. Are you going somewhere?'

'I thought maybe I could take a few of these mushroom fritters down to Riccardo in the *Podere Nuovo*.' She saw them both look up in surprise. 'I've met him a couple of times now and I said I'd go back and see him again.'

Umberto and Ines exchanged glances.

'He's been talking to you?'

'Yes, he was a bit grumpy at first, but he's gradually softening up.'

Ines's expression changed from surprised to pleased.

'That's very good news, Bee. We've barely been able to get a word out of him for ages.'

'Years...' added Umberto.

'Who is he? Is he hiding away like Mimi and I are doing?'

The elderly couple exchanged glances again, before Umberto answered.

'Riccardo Negri is the son of Baron Cosimo Negri, my former employer and lifelong friend, who died last year.'

Now it was Bee's turn to look surprised.

'So Riccardo is now Baron Riccardo?'

Umberto shook his head. 'Not really. Italy's been a republic since just after the Second World War and aristocratic titles have no validity here any more. Some people still use them, but Riccardo's not one of those. No, he's just plain Signor Negri these days.'

'And he now owns the estate?'

Umberto hesitated. 'Not exactly. It's complicated.'

Once again, Bee got the impression she was intruding on personal matters so she hastily changed the subject.

'Well, if you don't mind, I'll just pop out for half an hour with a few of these bits of mushroom.'

She toyed with the idea of putting on her wig, but, given that Riccardo had already seen her without it, she stayed as she was. It was a hot evening and she was much more comfortable without it, even though she still felt a bit self-conscious about the stubble on her head. Armed with the plate, she walked the few hundred yards to his house and was delighted to see him sitting under the olive tree once more. She went up to the gate and called out to him.

'Riccardo, good evening. I was wondering if you wanted to try some mushrooms I found this afternoon?' As she spoke, she kept her fingers crossed that he would be in his friendlier, rather than his irascible, mood. Luckily it was the former.

'Good evening, Bee. Do come in.'

She went across to where he was sitting and set the plate down on the bench beside him. He looked down with interest.

'Porcini?'

'That's right. Ines prepared them and I got her to check them first. I promise I'm not trying to poison you.'

For the very first time she spotted what might have been an attempt at a smile from him. He reached down with his fingers, picked one up and tasted it.

'Absolutely excellent. Thank you. Will you join me for a glass of champagne while we eat these wonderful mushrooms together? You know where the glasses are.'

'Thank you, Riccardo, that would be nice.'

Bee left him there and let herself into the house. As she walked down the corridor to the kitchen, the smell of oil paint was even stronger than before and, on an impulse, she paused by a half-open door and glanced inside. She found herself looking into what was quite evidently an artist's studio. There were canvases stacked around the wall, but the painting on the easel in the middle of the room stopped her in her tracks. It was a portrait, head and shoulders, of a woman.

And the woman, without question, was her.

He had painted her with a magnificent head of long brown hair, piled up in an intricate pattern, held together by old-fashioned pearl-tipped pins. Around her neck was the vague outline of what would probably become a necklace. There was still a lot of work to be done before the painting would be finished, but the likeness was already remarkable. She stood there, rooted to the spot. It was more than a bit creepy that a man she barely knew should have chosen to paint her – and so remarkably accurately as well. At least, she told herself, he had painted her with her clothes on, but still… Why or how he had chosen her was beyond her, and she would have loved to stay and study it more closely, but she didn't want him to know she had been spying, so she hurried into the kitchen and helped herself to a wine glass.

Back outside, she took her usual seat on the edge of the well and watched as he removed the champagne bottle from a bucket at his feet and poured. As he replaced the bottle in the ice, she wondered about querying his choice of subject for his latest painting, but decided to bide her time and queried his choice of wine instead.

'So, is this a special occasion, or do you drink this stuff all the time?'

She saw him hesitate, before responding. 'To be totally honest, it's my birthday today. I normally don't remember, and nobody else does, but remarkably this year I did, so I thought it merited opening something a bit special.'

Bee couldn't miss the expression of regret on his face, so she leant forward and clinked her glass against his. 'A very happy birthday to you, Riccardo. I'm glad I could share it with you.'

'And thank you for the mushrooms. It's been a long, long time since I tasted porcini – a birthday present!'

They sat and sipped their champagne and ate the crispy mushroom fritters. The sun had dropped below the hilltop behind them and it was very pleasant sitting there, looking up at the swallows as they swooped over them, collecting insects on the wing. The birds produced rowdy high-pitched screams as they did so and their aerial antics were like watching fighter planes involved in a dog-fight. Against the deep blue, almost purple, of the evening sky, it was a compelling spectacle. After a bit, Bee decided to risk doing a bit of digging.

'So, I see you're an artist.'

She had to wait quite a while before she got a response. Finally, he looked across at her and his eyes caught and held hers.

'So, you've seen it?'

Bee flushed. 'Yes… I'm sorry, I wasn't snooping, honestly. The door was open and I just glanced inside.' She took a mouthful of wine and felt the bubbles fizz on her tongue. 'It's really, really good. But why me? Did you work from a photo or what?' Maybe he had got hold of a copy of a newspaper with her picture in it.

He shook his head. 'I've been blessed, or cursed, with a memory for images. I painted from memory.'

'After seeing me so briefly?' Bee was amazed. 'Are you famous? Should I have heard of you?'

He ignored the question. 'So you like it?'

'I love it, Riccardo. You've got me to a T. But I still want to know why you chose me.'

He dropped his eyes to his wine glass and just mumbled. 'It still needs a lot doing to it, but I'm glad you like it so far. As for why I chose you, that's easy. I've always loved beauty, in whatever form I can find it.'

'Looking like I do, I would hardly call myself beautiful.'

'Superficial.' He didn't raise his eyes from his glass. 'The scratches on your face are superficial. They'll soon pass, but your underlying beauty will remain.'

Bee was amazed. She sat there for a minute or two, wondering what might be going on in this elderly man's head while he stared blankly downwards. At a loss for words, finally she repeated her question.

'The world's full of loads of women who look much better than me – scars or no scars – so why me?'

He must have realised by this time that she was sounding alarmed and he looked up, a benevolent and apologetic expression on his face.

'Beauty isn't just on the outside, Beatrice. It may surprise you to know that you're the first person in a very long time who has spontaneously taken an interest in me. The fact that you've come here this evening with the mushrooms just confirms I was right in my initial assessment of you. You are a beautiful person, whatever your mirror may tell you at the moment. But look, if you like, I can paint over it. It was just something I felt compelled to paint, but I wouldn't want to make you feel uncomfortable in any way. Just say the word and it's gone. *Sic transit gloria mundi.*'

'Of course not, Riccardo. You can't destroy something as wonderful as that. No, please finish it.' She reached over with her glass and clinked it against his once more. 'Thank you. Seriously, I take it as a really huge compliment.'

'Only if you're sure.'

He lapsed into silence once more. Bee gave him a minute or two to say more, but finally realised she would have to make the running in this conversation.

'Do you think I might be able to see the rest of your work some time? Would you mind? I'd really like to.'

She had another long wait before he answered.

'If you want to. There's not a lot of new stuff. To tell the truth, that portrait of you is the first new canvas I've started for months.' The note of regret was back in his voice, but she saw him rally. 'But you really need to see them in daylight. Why don't you come back some time when the sun's out?'

Bee told him she would drop by to make an appointment in the coming week.

'I'm really looking forward to seeing your paintings.'

And she meant it.

–

Dinner was delightful. Along with the mushroom fritters, Ines had prepared a salad of raw porcini and Parmesan, accompanied by slices of freshly carved ham and, of course, the wonderful Tuscan unsalted bread. Afterwards,

Bee couldn't resist some of Ines's homemade meringue ice cream, which was amazing. After dinner, she settled down in the lounge to watch a DVD from the collection on the shelves in there. She deliberately avoided any of the numerous films starring Mimi Robertson and opted for an old black and white movie starring Marilyn Monroe instead. It was about three quarters of the way through when she heard the howl of the Lamborghini outside. She glanced at the clock and was surprised to see it was barely ten o'clock. Seconds later, she heard the front door and a few moments after that, the sound of the car departing. Mimi appeared at the lounge door. Alone.

'Hi, Bee. What's this? *Some Like It Hot*? I love this movie.'

She took a seat on the sofa alongside Bee and they watched the end of film together, laughing at the comedy and marvelling at Marilyn's amazing dress. As it finished and the credits rolled, Bee looked across at Mimi.

'So, did you have a good time in the Lamborghini?'

'Yes, surprisingly good. In fact, I was quite sorry he had to shoot off again so early. You know what he did? He knew I didn't want to be seen, so he took me for a picnic. He had a wicker hamper, a blanket, even a tablecloth. He drove up to an observation point on one of the higher hills and we sat under a couple of umbrella pines, drank champagne, ate cold lobster and watched the sun go down over Tuscany.'

'How romantic!'

Mimi avoided commenting. 'You know what I was thinking? How wonderful it would be to live here.' She saw the expression on Bee's face and elaborated. 'Not all the time, of course. For work reasons, I'd still have to be based in LA, but can you imagine having a little place hidden away in the backwoods like this? A bolthole to disappear to.'

Bee nodded in agreement, although Mimi's application of the adjective 'little' to this place was a stretch, and she couldn't resist doing a bit of stirring.

'Maybe with a handsome film star or a hunky farmer waiting for you?'

Mimi looked across at her and grinned. 'Like your hunky farmer?'

'*My* hunky farmer?'

'It's pretty obvious you've got the hots for him.' Mimi laughed out loud at the expression of stupefaction on Bee's face. 'And I get the feeling he might well feel the same way about you. Why d'you think I invited him to dinner?'

'You invited him to dinner for *me*?' Bee was floundering, trying to make sense of what she was hearing. 'But I thought you and he were getting on rather well.'

'And we were, but he's not for me. Apart from anything else, you saw him first and I'm not the sort of woman who gets involved with other people's men. But the main reason is because people like me always tend to stick to our own.'

'Your own?'

'Showbiz folk. It's so much easier. Ours is a funny life, quite surreal in many ways. Non-showbiz people find it hard to adjust to and, of course, there's the whole financial side of it. Nothing makes a relationship go sour faster than money, and too much is as bad as too little. And in my case, it makes things really hard. They say I'm one of the richest women in Hollywood, and that's an awful lot for a prospective partner to handle.'

Bee nodded. This was one complication she knew she would never have. Alongside her, Mimi stretched her legs and rested her head back against the sofa as she continued.

'From my point of view, there would always be the nagging doubt that he was into me for my money rather than for myself. And, of course, for him there'd always be the problem of having to come to terms with the fact that I make so much more than him. Some men find that hard to handle.' She gave Bee a wry smile. 'I don't expect you to feel sorry for me – poor little rich girl – but trust me it's complicated.'

Bee was genuinely surprised. Somehow, no doubt like the majority of the rest of the world, she had assumed that people like Mimi had it all. In practical, financial terms she did of course, but the complicated ramifications of this wealth for her private life were something Bee had never thought through before.

'And Joey? He's from your world, after all. How about picking him for a partner?'

Bee saw Mimi hesitate, but only for a moment.

'If you'd asked me that only a few hours ago, I'd have laughed in your face. But, I have to admit, after tonight, I'm warming to him. Underneath the bravado, he's a nice guy.'

'I know he's got a bit of a wild reputation, but I like him, too.'

'Well, I'm glad you do, Bee, because you're seeing him again on Saturday night. I invited him to join us for dinner. Along with your hunky farmer.'

Chapter 11

The meal on Saturday night went very well. Joey arrived first, this time in an anonymous-looking Ford, no doubt after being advised by Mimi to keep a lower profile. He was followed a few minutes later by Luke and the dog. Romeo had been specially invited at Mimi's request.

It was a lovely evening, so they sat outside in the garden and chatted as the shadows lengthened, the Labrador lay sprawled across the flagstones at their feet and the peacocks strutted around in the background. Joey was wearing a pink polo shirt that showed off his muscular biceps, while Luke wore a white linen shirt, beneath which Bee could see the outline of his rugged body. Mimi looked gorgeous in one of her designer dresses that revealed a whole lot more than Bee would have felt comfortable revealing. For her part, Bee had opted for a short summer dress with a floral print that went well with her suntanned legs and arms. She felt pretty sure she looked quite good in it, apart from her face. Given that they had all seen her without her wig, she decided not to bother. It was now quite a few weeks since the accident and the scars on her head, even the large one with all the stitches, were gradually becoming hidden by her ever-softer hair, although her cheek still had a way to go. All in all, though, she was starting to feel more and more comfortable about her appearance as the days passed by.

They chatted about the area and their walks around the estate, and the fact that she and Mimi were gradually getting more and more familiar with life in the countryside. Bee told them about Berlusconi the goat, the snake and the mushrooms, and Mimi revealed that she had found a black spider the size of a walnut in her bathroom. Swift work with the toothbrush glass had captured the arachnid which had then been released into the wild via the window. Joey was clearly on his best behaviour and played the role of sober grown-up really remarkably well. Just as Mimi had claimed to have been able to see that Bee liked Luke, so Bee could see that Joey liked Mimi. A lot. Mimi, however, was much harder to read.

Luke sounded quite animated and interested to know if they were enjoying living out here in the country, spiders and snakes aside, compared to their previous urban lifestyles. Mimi was the first to answer and Bee got the feeling it was with total sincerity.

'I'm amazed at just how much I've come to love it here in such a short time. It's so peaceful, so beautiful and so restful. Do you realise, this is just about the first time since my career took off that I've been away from work for so long? I was worried before coming here that I might be bored stiff. But nothing could be further from the truth.'

At that moment, Umberto appeared with a second bottle of champagne, followed by Ines with a plate of *fettunta*, the local name for slices of toasted bread, rubbed with garlic, and drizzled with the thick local olive oil and salt. Bee had already had this local speciality and she loved it. Besides, she told herself, she could safely eat garlic tonight. After all, she wasn't going to be kissing anybody.

They ate outside by candlelight. It was warm, it was sociable, and it was really rather romantic. Or at least, it could have been if Bee had managed to pick up even the slightest hint of a vibe from Luke. Alas, although he looked and sounded interested in what she had to say, she had to conclude there was nothing romantic going on in his head. Sadly, he appeared to want to be friends, nothing more.

On the other hand, Joey couldn't have been clearer about his intentions. In fact, Bee felt pretty sure that Umberto, Ines and even Romeo the dog had managed to work out that the handsome film star was making a play for his beautiful opposite number. Mimi, on the other hand, was playing it very cool indeed. She smiled at him, laughed at his jokes and occasionally touched his hand or arm, but Bee got the feeling she was far from falling into his muscular arms any time soon.

The meal was a delight, starting with local ham and salami, followed by *pappardelle ai funghi porcini*, the sauce for the broad strips of pasta made from the mushrooms they had found. The main course – by which time Bee and Mimi were both beginning to flag – was roast goose with lovely roast potatoes cooked with rosemary and thyme. For dessert, Ines had made a strawberry tart and more of her homemade ice cream to go with it. The result appeared to go down very well with Mimi in particular, who surprised everybody by coming back for a second helping. From the floor, the dog's eyes definitely indicated his approval as all the lovely smells percolated down to him. Ines had deliberately baked an odd bit of pastry specially for him and when they gave it to him at the end of the meal, it disappeared without trace, leaving Romeo with a big canine smile on his face.

Afterwards, the two men had coffee, while Bee and Mimi settled for small glasses of *vin santo*, a gorgeous dessert wine made there on the estate. By now it was quite dark apart from the flashes of countless fireflies under the trees. Out in the vines a couple of owls were hooting at each other. It was a delightful, warm, peaceful evening.

'You know something?' Mimi glanced across towards the others. 'I had never really appreciated silence until I came here. If you think about it, our lives are all about noise: talking, acting, travelling about, and always with a background hubbub. Coming here and experiencing what silence is all about has been a real revelation to me. I'm sure it's going to be the thing I miss most when I leave here.'

Bee nodded in agreement. The valley really was a magical spot.

Finally, at around midnight, the party broke up and the two men made their exit. Mimi kissed both of them on the cheeks before they left, but Bee couldn't see any difference in intensity between the attention she lavished upon either of the two of them. For her part, Bee also kissed them both, but if she were called upon to indicate which woman's touch Luke had enjoyed more, the film star would have won the prize. Luke's reaction was cordial, but nothing more. It was with a sensation of regret that Bee stood on the doorstep and watched him head off into the night with his faithful dog at his side.

As Joey's Ford set off down the drive, Mimi turned to Bee and smiled.

'So, did you have a good time?'

'Absolutely. And you?'

Mimi nodded. 'Very definitely. Did you know? Joey told me he flew over from the States this week specially to see me.'

'He certainly seems keen. I definitely got the feeling he's hooked. Are you going to take it any further?'

'I'm not sure. He's off to LA tonight, but he said he'll be back.'

'He's flying to the States tonight?'

'Yes, he's rented a private jet so he'll be able to sleep on the plane. I do the same thing if I have to travel. It's comfortable and you can be sure you aren't going to be woken up by a bunch of fans holding autograph books.'

Bee was suddenly jolted back to reality. This evening she had almost forgotten she had been in the presence of two of the most famous faces in the world. The conversation had been relaxed and they had chatted like normal people. Suddenly, with this revelation, she was reminded that she had strayed into waters where she was a very small fish indeed. But, before she could react, Mimi turned the conversation from executive jets to farmers.

'Luke was looking good tonight, less stressed than the last time I saw him.'

Bee nodded thoughtfully. 'I thought he looked better as well, but the worry lines are still there if you look hard enough. Apart from anything else, I think he's really worried for his job.' She went on to tell Mimi what Umberto had said about the debts the estate had to repay and the possibility of the villa having to be sold if they couldn't keep up the annual payments.

Mimi nodded sympathetically, but couldn't help adding. 'I tell you this, Bee. If this place ever came up for sale, I'd buy it like a shot.' She grinned. 'And, of course, I'd keep him in his job. Maybe I should tell him. That might set his mind at rest.'

'It might indeed.'

'That way you could marry him and live here happily ever after.' Her grin broadened.

Bee felt her cheeks blushing. 'Not much likelihood of that, Mimi. Somehow, I get the impression he isn't interested.'

Mimi caught her eye for a moment. 'You're really not very good at reading the signs, are you?'

'The signs?'

'As well as yoga lessons, maybe I should start giving you lessons in how to read men. They aren't anything like as complicated as we are, you know. And take it from me, Luke the farmer likes you a lot.'

Bee wasn't so sure.

Chapter 12

The following week, Bee dropped in on Riccardo to make a date to view his paintings and found herself invited straight in. It was a sunny, scorching hot afternoon and there was certainly no lack of light. He appeared at the door with a paintbrush in one hand and beckoned her inside where it was pleasantly cool in comparison. He looked remarkably bright today and, apart from his tousled mane of hair, he was, as ever, very smartly turned out, his T-shirt without a single paint stain. Somehow she had been half-expecting him to be wearing a scruffy old smock, coated with decades of oil paint, but that was definitely not the case.

As he ushered her into his studio, she saw that he was walking with difficulty, leaning heavily on a stick. This no doubt explained why she had been sent to fetch her own wine glasses on previous occasions. It hadn't been a sign of inhospitality and she felt sorry for misjudging him. Inside the studio, she saw a different painting on his easel. She glanced around, but there was no sign of her portrait this time.

'What do you think?' He extended an arm towards the new canvas. 'I only started it this morning, so there's still a long way to go.'

Bee scrutinised it for a moment before recognition dawned. It was a still life of a heap of old, gnarled vine stems, their twisted trunks intertwined, giving the overall effect of human bodies writhing together. The closer she looked, the more figures and shapes she could make out. What really surprised her, however, was that he wasn't copying from a staged pile of old vines. In front of him, on a little table, was a single vine stem, just one. She turned back to him in surprise.

'I think it's marvellous. I can see men wrestling, somebody taking a bath, and pretty clearly two people bonking their brains out, all through the medium of a few lumps of wood and your imagination. I don't know how you do it.' She hesitated, spotting something in the picture. 'Wait a minute, I make that three, no four people bonking their brains out.'

He laughed, the first time she had heard him laugh and she was pleased for him. 'And you talk about *my* imagination? I can't see anything of the kind.'

She couldn't work out if he was kidding her. The more she looked at the painting, the more human bodies she could make out. She wondered for a moment if these really were just the product of her overactive, and possibly frustrated, imagination. No doubt Freud would have had a field day with her psyche if it really was just a painting of some vine stems. Luckily, Riccardo didn't let her dwell upon her inner thoughts. He slowly led her around the room, picking up canvases from the floor and leaning them against walls or bits of furniture until she was surrounded by them. One thing was patently clear: he was a very talented artist. She repeated her question from the other evening.

'These are amazing, Riccardo. So, are you famous? You should be.'

For a moment it looked as though he was about to shrug off the question once more but, finally, he relented.

'I used to sell quite a bit of my work, but the fact is, I've hardly painted anything for ages now.'

'Why not?'

For a moment she got the impression he wasn't going to answer, but, after a pause, he did. But it didn't shed any light on the question.

'Life… Stuff happens.'

Bee didn't insist, but resolved to check him out on the internet. Riccardo Negri shouldn't be too hard to find. His voice interrupted her train of thought. She glanced up and saw that he was holding his portrait of her. As she looked on, he rested it on another easel and she could see that it had moved on a good bit from the last time she had seen it. The green dress was now quite clearly fashioned out of lace, in the most amazing detail, but her face, neck and shoulders still needed to be completed.

'I wonder if I could ask you a favour, Bee.'

'Of course, anything.'

'I wonder if you might be prepared to give me an hour or two of your time one of these days to sit for me.'

'What, to model for you?'

'Yes, please. It's all right. I'm not asking you to take your clothes off or anything like that. No, it would just help me immensely if you could sit while I try to finalise your face in this painting I started the other day. Like I told you, I paint from memory, but you can't beat the real thing.'

Reassured, she gave him a smile. 'Of course I will, but you'll have to use your imagination as far as the left side of my face is concerned.'

She read sympathy in his eyes.

'That won't be a problem. You're very kind. Any day or time to suit you. You choose.'

'I'm free pretty much any day.' A sudden thought occurred to her. 'But, in return, I'd like you to promise that you'll come up to the villa for dinner one of these days. Will you do that?'

His eyes dropped, and she saw him shake his head, suddenly serious.

'I can't do that.' His voice was low.

Bee remembered what Umberto had said about the ownership of the estate being 'complicated' and realised she was probably on thin ice here. Maybe he hadn't inherited from his father, after all, and the new owner didn't want him there. She tried again.

'You don't even need to come inside if you don't want to. The other night we ate outside in the garden. How would that be?'

There was a long silence that she finally decided to break. There was no point flogging a dead horse.

'Anyway, you think about it, Riccardo. And, of course, I'll be happy to model for you any time.'

He looked up, an expression of relief on his face. 'I promise I'll think about your kind invitation, but it's complicated.' That word again. 'And thank you for agreeing to sit for me. Just one thing, though. When you come, could you find a top that reveals your throat and maybe even your shoulders? I'd really like to get the skin tone dead right and the dress I've put you in has a wide neckline.'

'No problem. I'll dig out something suitable. By the way, why the old-fashioned costume? From the style of the dress it looks Renaissance?'

'It's a period of history that's always fascinated me. You've probably noticed quite a few of my paintings are in that style.'

'Any reason?'

'Maybe because some of the greatest artists who ever lived were active then. And quite a few of them were working not so very far from where we are now. Just think, Botticelli painted his *Birth of Venus* just down the road in Florence. Let's just say it's my very humble attempt to pay homage to the greats.'

'So you don't like doing modern stuff?'

'The present day is so much sadder than the past.'

From the expression she could see on his face, Bee felt quite sure he was referring not only to painting, but to his own life.

–

That evening, before dinner, Bee checked out Riccardo Negri on the internet and got a major shock. The Wikipedia entry was long and informative, but not only about his art career. As well as charting his professional life from humble art student to international fame resulting in a number of his paintings being exhibited in galleries around the globe, it also included a biography of him. This was a real eye-opener and Bee read it with rapt attention.

Riccardo Negri was born in 1955 at Montegri-fone, the only child of Baron Cosimo and Margherita

Negri. In 1980, he married an Englishwoman, Elizabeth Greensleeves, who sadly died of cancer some years later. After his wife's death, Riccardo went through a bleak period of depression, reflected in his paintings of the time. Ironically, this more sombre turn to his art was what brought him to the attention of the critics and saw his career leap forward. The general consensus was that his work after the death of his wife was on an altogether superior level compared to his early work. However, his productivity of late had gradually dwindled to a trickle and he had now almost disappeared off the radar.

But none of that was as unexpected or as astonishing as the fact that the article recorded the birth of his only son. The boy was born some ten years before the death of his wife and his name was Luke.

Bee sat back in amazement. So Luke, the estate manager, was in fact Riccardo's son. The breath whistled out of her lungs. Why, she wondered, was Luke maintaining a pretence of being just a hired hand when he would presumably inherit the estate, and the redundant title of baron, in due course? What had Umberto meant when he had said the inheritance was 'complicated'? Why was Riccardo living here alone and claiming he never spoke to anybody? And did that include his son?

Bee knew she needed to talk to somebody about this and the obvious choice was Umberto, who clearly knew all there was to know about Montegrifone. She glanced at the time and saw that she still had an hour before dinner so she went down to look for him. She found him sitting in the shade outside the back door with the dog sprawled out at his feet.

'Umberto, I wanted to ask you something, but if it's too personal or a secret, just say so and I'll forget it. It's none of my business anyway.'

She saw him turn towards her, the sad smile on his face indicating that he had been expecting this.

'You've been talking to Riccardo again?' Bee nodded. 'And you want to know why we have a father and a son in two different houses a few hundred metres apart, who don't talk to each other?'

Bee nodded once more. 'But only if you feel like telling me. I don't want to intrude.'

'It's no secret, Bee. Have you ever spoken to Luca about his father?'

She shook her head. 'No. I only discovered they were related a few minutes ago.'

'The simple fact of the matter is that Luca loved his mother and she loved him. When she died, it was a terrible blow for a young boy of only ten. He turned to his father for love and support and got nothing in return.' Umberto's eyes were gazing out over the vines, a pained expression on his face. 'Riccardo had always been solely focused on his painting until he met his wife, and there's no doubt he loved her dearly. He had some sort of breakdown after her death. We could all see that. He sent Luca off to a boarding school in England and retreated into himself. He virtually barricaded himself in the *Podere Nuovo* and we saw less and less of him. When Luca came home for the holidays, his grandfather, along with Ines and myself, looked after him. He and his father spoke less and less, and by the time Luca went on to university they weren't communicating at all.'

'How awful! And then Luke – Luca – went off to Australia.'

'That's right. It was his grandfather's idea. The Australians have been at the forefront of all sorts of innovations in winemaking and Baron Cosimo suggested he go over there to learn what they had to teach him… and also, to put as much distance as possible between him and his father.'

'How very sad – for both of them. And then Cosimo died and Luca came back to run the estate.'

'He came back a couple of years before his grandfather died to take over from another old man who had been running the estate until a heart attack forced him to cut back.'

'Who was that, Umberto?'

He turned towards her with a gentle smile on his lips. 'That would be me, Bee.'

'I'm so sorry to hear about your heart. Are you all right again now?'

'Never been better. My pacemaker and I go everywhere together and I feel fine. Anyway, as you know, last year Baron Cosimo died and that's where it all gets very complicated. You see, by Italian law, half had to go to his only son, Riccardo, while he left the other half to Luca. He could see that Luca, rather than his arty father, represented the future of the estate.'

'I see. So Luca and Riccardo have ended up joint owners of the estate, but are unable to talk to each other.'

'Yes, but it's worse than that. Like I told you before, the baron failed to ensure his affairs were in order before he died and there was a big tax debt to pay. The problem was that neither Riccardo nor Luca had the money to pay it. I don't think Riccardo cares where he lives any more and he'd be happy to sell up, but Luca's desperate to avoid that, and it's been worrying him sick. He really loves this place and all the people who work here. It would be a tragedy for him and for them. Add to that losing his beloved grandfather and then his fiancée and you can see why life's been pretty tough for Luca over the past year.'

Bee sat back and did her best to digest the tale she had just heard. What was it Mimi had said about money causing all sorts of problems?

'And there's no chance of getting them back together?'

'Not so far. We've all tried. After the baron's death, Ines and I both did our best to get Riccardo and Luca to talk, but to no avail. I think Luca might be prepared to give it a try, but Riccardo has just refused point blank. He's been shut away in that self-imposed prison of his for so long, I seriously doubt he'll ever come out again.' Rousing himself, he caught Bee's eye. 'Although I must confess I'm amazed he's started talking to you. That's got to be a good sign.'

–

A few days later, Bee was out for another walk. Romeo was nowhere to be found and Mimi was tied up with more phone calls, so she went by herself. The sun was already dropping behind the hilltop, but the air temperature was still high and she was soon perspiring. As usual she made a point of stamping her feet as she walked up through the vines, but mercifully didn't run into any snakes this time. She remembered she had promised to call her mother, so she headed for her original spot, perched on top of the drystone wall, and phoned home.

Her mother sounded delighted to hear from her. Bee started by telling her about her life here in general terms, but before she could bring up the subject of Mimi, Joey, Riccardo or his son, it turned out that her mother had news of her own.

'Bee, you'll never guess who dropped in to see me the other day.' She didn't wait for a reply. 'Jamie.'

'Jamie? He came down to Newbury to see you and dad?' Bee was stunned, and immediately very suspicious.

'Yes, indeed, although your father wasn't here. He was on the golf course. Jamie came in and it was such a lovely day, he sat with me in the garden. I've always liked him, you know, even if you and he had your little problems.'

'A bit more than little problems.' Bee could hear the frustration in her voice and her mother can't have missed it.

'That's all water under the bridge now though, isn't it? Anyway, we had tea together. Luckily, I'd baked some of my scones that morning.'

Choking back her annoyance, Bee listened patiently to her mother's account of the lovely afternoon she and her ex had spent together before finally jumping in.

'So, what was the reason he came down to see you, mum?'

'No reason. He said he was just passing through.'

'So, it was just a courtesy call?' This was so foreign to Jamie's normal modus operandi that Bee could hardly believe it was the same man.

'Yes, just to say hello, he said. Oh yes, and did you hear somebody stole his phone?' Again, she didn't wait for a reply. 'You see, he said he lost it in London and, along with it, he lost all his phone numbers and his address book.'

'But surely everything would have been backed up…?'

'I don't know, but I had to give him your number again and your address in Italy. He'd lost it, you see.'

Suddenly the scales fell from Bee's eyes. Of all the people to have got hold of her address – and Mimi's – Jamie was just about the worst she could imagine. What if he passed the information to people in Hollywood or, even worse, the media? That was the kind of thing he might do. And as for losing his phone…! She had no doubt nothing of the sort had happened. It had almost certainly all been a ruse to get her address. She took a deep breath before answering as sweetly as possible.

'I'm glad you had a nice afternoon.'

'Oh, I did. It's such a shame things didn't work out between the two of you. He's such a nice boy. You never know though. Maybe you'll get back together again.'

Bee sat there seething. One thing was for sure, she wasn't going to mention anything about the people here. The less her mother knew about where she was and with whom, the better. She felt like screaming at her mother, but she knew, from long experience, that it would do no good. In the end she limited herself to a plea from the heart.

'Please, please, mum, don't give that address to anybody else. You maybe don't realise it, but you've put me in a terrible position. Legally. Do you understand?'

'But, seeing as it was Jamie…'

'What's done's done, mum, but please, never again. All right?'

As she finally rang off and returned the phone to her pocket, she was still fuming internally. So Jamie now knew where she was. It wouldn't surprise her in the slightest if he just suddenly appeared. And if he did? Would he expect her to invite him in? She really didn't want to encourage him and, with a start, she realised that she really didn't want Luke to meet him. No sooner did the thought cross her mind than she found herself wondering just why that might be. There was nothing going on between her and Luke, after all, so why should it matter?

She was still mulling this over as she set off back down the hill again. She wasn't sure whether she should speak to Gayle first or to Mimi. As she emerged from the bottom edge of the vines, her thoughts were interrupted by the appearance of a familiar figure trotting along the track towards her. She dropped to her knees, realising as she did so that her thigh no longer hurt at all, and held out her arms, the sight of the dog helping to restore her good spirits.

'*Ciao*, Romeo, and how are you today?'

She made a fuss of him and then they walked back to the villa together. In the kitchen, she found Umberto who suggested she might like an *aperitivo* and went to fetch a bottle of cold rosé. Bee decided she had better speak direct to Mimi so she called her and told her she would be in the garden if she felt like joining her and Umberto. As he was opening the wine bottle, she filled the dog's bowl with water and watched him drink eagerly. It really was very hot indeed, clammy hot. This evening, although the ground was dry as dust, it felt as if there was moisture in the air and dark clouds had appeared at the horizon.

Umberto led her out into the garden and handed her a glass of wine. She persuaded him to sit down and join her for a drink at the table, with the dog sprawled at their feet. Although now in the shade, the wooden tabletop was still warm beneath her bare arms.

'Do you think it's going to rain?'

He nodded grimly. 'They're talking about possible thunderstorms over the coming days. We need the rain, but I'm always worried about hail.'

'What, at this time of year?'

'It's happened before. Some years we get hailstones the size of golf balls, and not nice smooth ones. They're great jagged lumps of ice. They can do a serious amount of damage to the vines. A few years back, we lost half our crop. It just tore the leaves and the young grapes from the vines.'

'How awful. I do hope that doesn't happen this year.'

They chatted a bit more while the dog lay at their feet, mouth open, panting noisily as he tried to cool down. A few minutes later, Mimi appeared and immediately made a fuss of Romeo. She looked relaxed and happy and accepted a glass of rosé willingly. Bee did her best to relegate the conversation with her mother to the back of her mind for now and smiled back at both of them. It was a very lovely evening, after all.

However, as soon as Umberto had left them, Bee wasted no time in breaking the news to Mimi about her mother's faux pas with Jamie. Mimi was visibly taken aback but, to Bee's relief, she took the news phlegmatically.

'If he should turn up, or if any journalists turn up, I'll make sure I stay out of the way and you'll have to tell them

165

I've already left.' A thought occurred to her. 'You can tell them I hitched a lift with Joey in his jet.' She caught Bee's eye and grinned. 'Make sure you tell them I only did it reluctantly, or they'll start trying to guess whether we're getting together.'

'Are you?'

Mimi just smiled.

Chapter 13

Three days later, the storm finally broke, bringing with it deafening claps of thunder, torrential rain, strong winds and... Jamie.

Fortunately for the vineyard, there was no hail but, as far as Bee was concerned, hailstones the size of golf balls would have been preferable to the sight of her ex. She was in her room that evening after dinner, sitting at the computer with the rain lashing the windows, cowering back every time a lightning flash lit up the room, when the phone at her bedside rang. It was Umberto and he sounded suspicious.

'I'm sorry to bother you, Bee, but there's a man at the gate and he's asking for you, in English.'

'Oh, crap!'

Umberto might not have understood the word, but, from her tone, he couldn't have missed how this news made her feel.

'Do you want me to tell him to go away?'

Bee paused for thought. What she had been dreading had now happened. What should she do? Conscious that Umberto was waiting for a response, she made a snap decision.

'Don't do anything for the moment, Umberto. I'll come straight down.'

As she went down the stairs, her mind was racing.

She could get Umberto to tell Jamie there was nobody of that name here and send him away, but, from past experience, she knew that wouldn't satisfy him. When he wanted, he could be as tenacious as a little terrier. He would sniff around and, quite possibly, give away Mimi's hiding place at the same time. Her only option was to let him in and sit down and talk to him, trying to appeal to his better nature.

She met Umberto in the hall, standing beside the intercom linking the villa with the gates. As she approached, he moved to one side and, reluctantly, she lowered her mouth towards the grill.

'Who is it, please?'

'Bee, it's me, Jamie.' There was relief in his voice. 'It's absolutely pouring down out here. Please, can I come in.'

It didn't bother Bee in the slightest if he got soaked, but there was no point in delaying the inevitable. She pressed the button to open the gates and straightened up, catching Umberto's eye.

'It's my ex-boyfriend. He's found out where I'm staying. I'll wait for him at the door if you could go and tell Mimi to stay out of sight. Just say, "Bee's boyfriend is here". Your English is good enough for that, isn't it?' He nodded. 'The last thing I want is for him to see her. If he asks, I'm going to tell him she's gone away.'

Umberto nodded his agreement and set off up the stairs. Bee went over to the front doors and opened one half. As she did so, a lightning flash illuminated the whole scene for a fraction of a second and she recoiled. By now, the track outside had turned into a muddy stream and she could hear the engine revving as the car drove up the hill and the wheels slipped in the mire. As she looked on, a little Ford appeared, snaking from side to side as the tyres struggled to find some grip. At the wheel, staring out from behind the windscreen wipers was Jamie, and Bee's heart sank.

As he reached the parking area, he must have turned the wheel too sharply, as the car suddenly slid sideways off the gravel, the right-hand front tyre lodging in a flower bed, crushing part of a massive oleander bush in the process. She heard the engine race and saw mud being flung up, but to no avail. He was stuck. Finally, he turned it off and all she could hear was the continuous drumming of the rain on the ground, a cascade of water coming from the overflowing gutters high above and deafening claps of thunder.

Heaving a deep sigh, she stepped a bit further forward. As she did so, the car door on the driver's side opened and Jamie sprang out. Seeing her standing in the light, he hurried along the path towards her, doing his unsuccessful best to keep the rain off his head with his holdall.

'Hi, Bee. How good to see you, but what appalling weather!' His shoulders were running with water and he shook himself like Romeo emerging from the river. 'It's absolutely foul!'

'Hello, Jamie. I wasn't expecting to see you here.' In fact, she had been, but he didn't need to know that.

She could hardly leave him out in the rain so she stepped aside and beckoned him in. Closing the door after him she turned to see him smiling winningly at her. His hands were held out towards her, but her heart had hardened. She made no attempt to take his hands or fall into his arms, and he couldn't fail to notice. Letting his hands drop back to his sides, he studied her closely before passing judgement.

'I'm so pleased to see you looking a lot better than I expected.'

While not the most gushing compliment she had ever received, it was so unusual for him to comment favourably on her appearance that it made her stop and think. Why was he being so nice? Was he just thinking of his damn screenplay or were his motives more personal?

'That's good to hear. Now, tell me, to what I owe this visit.'

'You don't sound very pleased to see me.'

'I'm glad you've worked that out.'

'Why? What've I done?'

There was a suit of armour in the corner of the lobby, with a vicious-looking spiked steel ball and chain gripped in its gauntlet. The idea of picking it up and swinging it at Jamie had distinct appeal, but she restrained herself. For now.

'What've you done?' She had to work hard to avoid shrieking at him. 'Do you realise that by taking advantage of my mum so deceitfully and now coming here, you've put my job, my future, everything in jeopardy.'

'Of course I haven't. I just wanted to know where you were so I could see you again, Bee.'

'After I'd specifically told you I was legally prevented from revealing my whereabouts to anybody, as well. It's just the same old you, isn't it? Thinking only about your-self as usual.' She stopped and took a very deep breath. 'So, once again, why are you here?'

'To see you, of course.' From the expression on his face, even he could hear the insincerity in his words this time.

She just looked at him. His eyes met hers for a second before dropping to the floor as he made a final attempt to bluster his way out of it.

'Come on, Bee, I've just driven all the way down here from Pisa in a hurricane. You could try to be a bit nicer.'

'You could try answering my question honestly.'

'Like I said, I wanted to see you so badly. I've been missing you.'

'Well, you could have saved yourself the trip. It's all over between us. We agreed that months ago. We both know that.' She subjected him to another searching stare. 'So, try again and, this time, make it the truth.'

She saw his shoulders drop as he realised the moment had arrived. Out of the corner of her eye, she spotted Umberto lurking protectively at the top of the stairs, a concerned expression on his face. She shot him a reassuring glance as Jamie finally confessed. What he told her came as no surprise at all.

'It's Mimi Robertson. You see, if only I could get her to read my screenplay, I'm sure she'd love it. And if she loves it, I'm made!' She saw him look around for the first time. 'Is she here?'

'You could have saved yourself the trip. She left three days ago for the US. You could have stayed in LA and waited for her.'

She saw his face fall.

'She's gone?'

He ran a weary hand across his wet forehead, sweeping the hair out of his eyes. She found herself registering that he was still a good-looking man, but any feelings she had had for him were long gone.

He didn't meet her eyes, just stared down at his feet. 'I'm not in LA any more.'

'So where are you living these days?'

'I'm back in London. In fact, that's the other reason I wanted to see you. I'm having terrible trouble finding a flat I can afford and I wondered if I could maybe move back in with you.'

Bee was genuinely dumbstruck. It took her several seconds and a lot of self-control before she could answer.

'After splitting up with me, you now want to come back?'

'Yes, you mean a lot to me. But, if you don't feel the same way, I could just be your flatmate.' He adopted his most persuasive tone. 'You'd be out at work all day and I could look after the place, water the plants and stuff. In the evenings and weekends I could disappear. You'd hardly ever see me.'

Bee took three long, slow, calming breaths.

'No, Jamie. It's all over. Right? So, no, it wouldn't work.'

He actually looked quite hurt and for a few seconds she felt a twinge of remorse.

'It would if we worked at it.' He was making one last try.

'I've moved on, Jamie. I know it wouldn't work.'

'Moved on? Have you found yourself somebody else?'

'No... I mean, maybe. Oh, I don't know. Anyway, apart from anything else, I don't even know if I'm coming back to London yet.'

As she said it, Bee found herself wondering yet again exactly what she was going to do once this lovely interlude in Tuscany finished. Doing her best to shrug the thought away, she opened the front door again and peered out. If anything, the rain was falling even more heavily. She closed it once more and turned back towards him.

'Anyway, for now, I presume the fact that your car is stuck in the mud means that you're going to have to stay overnight?' She didn't wait for his response. 'I'll get Umberto to make up a bed in a spare room. But, Jamie, I want you out of here first thing in the morning.' Before he could object, she added. 'They've got tractors here on the estate. I'll get somebody to tow you out of the flower bed as soon as it's light.'

–

When Bee woke up next morning, the rain had stopped and the sun had returned. A few residual white clouds on the horizon were all that was left of the storm, apart from the mud on the track and in the vineyards, and a sad-looking Ford Fiesta with its front wheel buried under the beautiful oleander covered in pink flowers. She opened the mosquito screen and leant out, breathing in the relatively cool morning air, certainly a lot less sticky and humid than before the storm. It was a gorgeous morning and if it hadn't been for Jamie in a bedroom along the corridor, she would have felt really quite happy.

Seeing him had given her mixed feelings. It had revived memories of their time together – some good, some not so good, some awful. For a while she had reflected on what they had had and what she had lost, but not for long. Seeing him again had reinforced her conviction that there wasn't anything, and there could never be anything, between them any more, even if he had sounded as if he was willing to give it another try.

Downstairs in the kitchen, she found Umberto and Ines. By now, she had got them to stop going to all the trouble of setting out breakfast every morning in the echoing dining room and had finally convinced Ines that some toast, butter and jam and a cup of tea in the kitchen was all she needed. As she walked in, Umberto gave her some good news.

'I've spoken to Marco, my boy, and he'll be up shortly to tow your boyfriend's car out of the flower bed.'

'Thank you so much, Umberto.' She gave him a big smile as she helped herself to a slice of toast. 'And he's very much my ex-boyfriend.'

'Do you think he suspects Miss Robertson's still here?' Ines sounded worried.

Bee had spent quite some time thinking the same thing the previous night.

'He's no fool, so I think he probably suspects she is. Before he goes off this morning, I'm going to have a serious talk to him.' Although just what she was going to say remained to be seen.

Just then, they heard a powerful engine and they trooped out of the kitchen to find Umberto's son, Marco, heading up the hill on a massive tractor. As he saw Bee, he stopped and leant out of the cab.

'Good morning, Bee.'

'Good morning, Marco, it's very kind of you to help. Your father's probably already told you. I've got a bit of a problem with a car.'

She saw his eyes light up. 'Not another Lamborghini?' He grinned at her. 'I spotted the yellow one last week. You couldn't miss it.'

'No, just a little rental car this time.'

'Pity, seeing as I drive a Lamborghini myself.'

Bee was amazed. Besides, she hadn't seen any other flashy sports cars round here. Marco gave her a broad grin and pointed along the bonnet of his enormous vehicle.

'I'm driving the Lambo now, in case you hadn't noticed.'

For the first time Bee registered the badge on the front of the tractor – a powerful bull, lowering its horns to charge – and the magical name below it.

'Lamborghini make tractors?'

'That's how they started. The sports cars came later. Anyway… where's the car?'

'A friend came to see me yesterday at the height of the storm and he skidded off the track. The car's stuck in the mud round at the front of the villa. Could you give it a pull back onto the track?'

'Of course. You'd better get him to come out and start the engine first.'

'I'll go and talk to him.'

While Marco sat down in the kitchen for a coffee with his parents, Bee ran upstairs and knocked on Jamie's door. She heard his voice from inside and turned the handle. She found him ready to go, standing in the middle of the room with his bag in his hand. From the look of it, his jacket was still damp from the previous night's downpour and she almost felt sorry for him. Almost.

'The tractor's here, Jamie. If you're ready, I would really like you to go.'

For a moment she almost felt sorry at the sight of the forlorn expression on his face, but only for a moment. As she turned back towards the door, she heard his voice.

'Bee… are you sure Mimi Robertson's gone?'

Bee did her best to keep a straight face.

'I've already told you she's gone.'

'You never were a very good liar, Bee. She's still here, isn't she?'

'I tell you she's gone.' He was right. She wasn't used to lying and she wasn't very good at it.

'Look, Bee, you know what I want. Just give her this, would you?' He reached into his briefcase and pulled out a bound A4 document. 'Just ask her to read it. Please...?'

Bee delayed replying for a moment. Maybe he had just presented her with the only argument that would keep his mouth shut and the secret of their whereabouts intact. Hesitantly, she took the manuscript from him and stepped closer so she was looking him square in the eye.

'If I do that for you, I want you to promise me you won't breathe a word to anybody about my being here? If the press get wind of it, there'll be all hell to pay – for me... and for you. Mimi's a powerful figure in the movie business. If even so much as a postcard arrives here with her name on it, I'll ask her to ensure that your name is blacklisted forever by everybody in Hollywood. Any chance you might have had of getting one of your scripts read would be gone forever.' She had no idea whether this was even possible, but she was pleased to see him flinch as the threat registered. 'Do I make myself absolutely clear?'

For a moment, she thought he was going to kiss her. Instead, he just held out his hand. As she shook it, he at least had the decency to apologise.

'Absolutely. Of course. Thank you so very, very much. I'm sorry, Bee. It was an underhand thing to do. It's just that... you know...'

She knew all right. All the time she had known him, he had been fixated on this one thing – getting one of his screenplays read by somebody in the movies. His writing had always meant more to him than anything or anybody else, herself included.

'And remember this; you'd not only be screwing up your own chances, but mine, too. I signed a legal agreement not to disclose Mimi's whereabouts and you've dropped me right in it.' He managed to look a bit chastened. 'But I'm not making any promises, Jamie, other than to see that she gets it. Let me make that clear: I'll make sure that Mimi gets the screenplay, but if she chooses to throw it straight in the bin – and from what she's told me, that's the most likely outcome – that'll be your hard luck, Understood?'

'Absolutely. Thank you, Bee. Thank you. You know how much this means to me.' He caught her eye. 'This is a new screenplay. I've only just finished writing it. I'm sure she'll love it. I think you might, too.'

'No promises, Jamie. Clear?'

'Clear. And, Bee, I meant what I said about giving it another go. I really do miss you, you know.'

She managed to summon a little smile.

'It wouldn't work, Jamie. You'll find someone else. Move on.'

'Is that what you've done?'

'To be totally honest, Jamie, I have no idea.'

She led him downstairs and saw him out to his car. The tractor arrived a minute later and Marco made short work of attaching a sturdy rope and then, with a minimum of effort, tugging the car back onto the gravel. As the rope was disconnected, Jamie jumped out and went over to thank Marco and to apologise for damaging the shrub. Marco brushed his apology away, telling him the oleander would grow back in no time. As soon as Jamie got back into the car, Bee didn't hang about. She stepped forward, leant down to the open window, and addressed a few final words to her ex.

'I'm counting on you, Jamie. Don't let me down.'

'I promise, Bee.' He smiled. 'And I meant it when I said you were looking good. I'm so very pleased for you.'

Bee waited until she saw his car emerge onto the road beyond the river and the electric gates close behind him, before turning and heading straight up to Mimi's room where she knocked on the door.

'Hi, Mimi, it's me. Jamie's gone, so the coast's clear again.'

'Come in, Bee.'

Bee opened the door to find Mimi on the phone. She hesitated, but Mimi beckoned her in. She closed the door behind her and went over to the window and surveyed the now familiar view over the garden and the vines beyond. From behind her she could hear Mimi's voice and it was immediately apparent that the person on the other end of the line was Joey. She did a bit of calculation and worked out that it must be about one o'clock in the morning in California so Joey was clearly still very keen. The conversation – at least from Mimi's end of the line – was definitely cordial and friendly, maybe more. Bee felt happy for her. They made a nice couple.

No sooner did that thought cross her mind than she had to stop and shake herself. Here she was in the presence of a Hollywood idol, privy to news that could set the gossip columns of the world alight – and no doubt make her a wealthy woman in the process – if she ever chose to leak it out. In the same breath came the realisation that – irrespective of any agreement she had signed – she would never do that. Mimi was fast becoming a friend, and a precious one at that.

When the call ended, Bee explained the deal she had extorted from her ex. 'I put the fear of God into him and told him that if he even so much as breathes a word about us being here I'll make sure he never works again.'

Mimi smiled broadly. 'I bet you had him shaking in his shoes. You're normally so sweet. I wish I'd seen you laying down the law.'

Bee smiled back. 'You can't teach students without developing a certain amount of experience at reading the riot act. Normally it's making them aware that getting drunk is not a valid excuse for not handing in their assignments on time.' She indicated the manuscript in her hand. 'Anyway, I told Jamie I'd see you got this, but I made no other promises. From what you've told me, you get so many screenplays it'll most probably end up in the bin.'

Mimi took it from her, glanced at the title and grinned. 'I see he's called it *A Big Mistake*. That doesn't bode well.' She dropped it onto her bed. 'Mind you, he might be lucky. I really haven't got much to do at the moment so you never know, I might even take a look at it.'

'Do as you will. Like I say, I told him no promises.'

Chapter 14

A few days later their little Fiat was delivered by the car rental company, and Bee and Mimi decided to risk setting out on the first of their tours of Tuscany.

Bee was delighted Mimi had taken the news of Jamie's arrival and departure so remarkably well and relations between the two of them didn't appear to have been soured by the episode. She couldn't help wondering whether the star's reaction would have been so understanding even just a few weeks earlier. Evidently, their stay in this little piece of paradise was having a beneficial, calming effect upon Mimi and, if Bee was honest with herself, on her as well. Even Jamie's clumsy eruption into her life hadn't annoyed her as much as she had feared. He was one-track-minded and completely obsessed with his writing, but his arrival had at least given her the confirmation that their relationship had run its course. There would be no going back.

She prepared today's route with an eye to historical, but also scenic, interest. This part of Tuscany, to the south of Siena, was dotted with picturesque hilltop towns and villages, one more charming than the other. Their first stop, as promised, was to be the sword in the stone at San Galgano and, to get there, they would have to negotiate a series of narrow country roads.

Bee took the passenger seat and acted as navigator with a detailed map borrowed from Umberto, while Mimi was happy to drive, both of them concealed behind dark glasses and Bee's head covered by her wig. Mimi revealed to Bee that back home in California she owned four cars, ranging from a Bentley to a Porsche, but rarely used them, preferring to be chauffeured around in an anonymous saloon with tinted windows. The last time she had driven anything as small as a 500 had been in her teens, back home in Britain. This stirred childhood memories in both of them and they chatted amicably as they picked their way through the narrow winding roads across to their first destination of the day.

Both of them were surprised at how sparsely populated this part of Tuscany was. Compared to the bustle of Siena, or the claustrophobic crowds of tourists in Florence, it was remarkable how few buildings they came across as Bee navigated them over the heavily wooded hills towards San Galgano. It was only when they started to drop down into the river valley to the west that they began to see houses and villages again. The houses were often surrounded by cypress trees, like dark fingers pointing into the sky to mark the fact that humans now occupied this space. And almost without exception, the villages were always set high on hilltops.

'Presumably they built up there for protection, Bee?'

Mimi was trying to drive and, at the same time, glance up at a little town perched on the hilltop high above them.

'Very definitely. This area was in a state of almost continuous warfare in the Middle Ages, mainly between the Pope and his cronies fighting against the lords of cities like Florence and Siena. Most of them employed the services of some very unsavoury bands of mercenaries who would think nothing of pillaging anywhere they came across on their travels. Hilltops made it harder for them and, where the locals could scrape up the money, walls around the town made things even more secure.'

She followed the direction of Mimi's eyes.

'That's Chiusdino. Let's go there after we've seen San Galgano, shall we? The view from up there must be amazing.' She returned her attention to Mimi. 'This area's all new to me. I visited Tuscany as a kid, but only saw the main cities. What about you?'

Mimi shook her head.

'Believe it or not, the two months on set in Siena and now these few weeks at the villa are almost my only experience of Italy. I'd only been to Rome before, but that was for an award ceremony and I just flew in and out in a day.' She glanced across at Bee ruefully. 'You wouldn't believe how often that's happened to me. The places I've visited would rival, or outdo, almost anybody's bucket list, but most of the time all I ever see is the airport and the inside of a limo or a helicopter.' Bee saw her grin. 'Poor little rich girl, right?'

Bee grinned back. 'What about when you were younger? Before you became famous? Didn't your parents take you anywhere nice on holiday?'

Mimi's face became more serious again, not just because a tractor and trailer had suddenly appeared from a side turning, forcing them to slow almost to a standstill.

'My parents took me and my sister on holiday most years, but it was always package holidays to seaside resorts, mainly in Spain. Of course, that was for financial reasons. Dad didn't make an awful lot of money working for the council and we were always struggling to make ends meet. As kids, Meg, my sister, and I were perfectly happy with beach holidays but, looking back on it now, I wish we'd been a bit more adventurous.'

'I didn't know you had a sister. What does she do? Is she in movies as well?'

Mimi shook her head. 'She used to be a professional tennis player, but now she's a full-time mum. She's got three lovely kids and a husband who adores her.'

Bee couldn't miss the note of envy in Mimi's voice. She did her best to offer encouragement.

'Good for her, Mimi, if that's what she wants. Personally, I've been concentrating on my career.'

'You wouldn't like to settle down? Start a family?'

'I suppose I will do one day, but not yet. I mean, Jamie and I got on pretty well and we lived together for a couple of years, but the idea of kids never occurred to me.' She glanced across. 'And you, Mimi? I imagine your career is all-important to you, isn't it?'

Mimi didn't answer immediately. This gave Bee time to check the map and point out a turning ahead.

'See that sign? Take a left there and we should be at San Galgano in a couple of minutes.'

Mimi did as instructed and they soon saw another turning to the left, signposted to the abbey. They found themselves on a straight road, lined with cypress trees, with cars parked on the verge on both sides.

'Shall we stop here? I don't like the look of that.'

Mimi pointed along the road ahead to where a small bus was attempting to do what looked like a thirty-three point turn across the road and a queue of traffic had already formed either side of it.

'Good idea.'

Mimi pulled off the road and they bumped to a halt. Bee checked her wig in the mirror. She had worked out by now that if she put it on slightly squint, the hair on her left side did a pretty reasonable job of hiding her damaged cheek. The cheek itself was looking better day by day as the scars healed and the colour changed back from angry red to a normal pink. She had been told to avoid the sun, so she stuck her sun hat on top as usual. As a result, her face was substantially paler than her arms and legs, but all in all she didn't look too bad, at least to a casual passer-by.

Mimi's sunhat and dark glasses, coupled with the same foundation she had applied for dinner the other night with Joey, almost completely hid her remaining scarring. All considered, the two of them, dressed down in baggy tops, sensible shorts and trainers, would hopefully not attract attention.

As they climbed out of the car, Mimi finally answered Bee's question, but she prefaced her answer with a request.

'I enjoy talking to you, Bee. I really do. I don't have many close friends and it's a real joy to be able to talk about all this stuff. Just promise me one thing, will you, please?'

Bee smiled at her. 'I know what you're going to say and I promise. I'm enjoying spending time with you, too, and you can be sure I'll never betray your confidence. What happens in Tuscany stays in Tuscany.'

Mimi reached across and squeezed her hand.

'You're a sweetie, Bee, you know that? I really mean it. Anyway, the answer to your question is that the idea of a family and kids really, really appeals to me. The problem has been finding the right man and, I suppose, finding the time.' She released Bee's hand and smiled conspiratorially. 'Besides, I'm forty-two and if I'm going to do it, it had better be sooner, rather than later.'

They walked along the tree-lined avenue past a No Entry sign that a number of cars had ignored, either by accident or design, towards the abbey itself. Although Bee knew what to expect, the sight of the building came as a considerable surprise to Mimi, who turned towards her in amazement.

'But there's no roof.'

The huge abbey church was now just four walls open to the sky. The façade with its three arched doorways and two simple windows above looked like something left over from a bombing raid, bleak and bare. It was a very big building and in its heyday it must have been a site of serious importance. But now, as they got closer, all they could see of its former magnificence were the sculpted lintels over the doorways, featuring flowers and plants. Slipping into her role of guide, Bee added a few words of explanation.

'The abbey was built by the Cistercians in the thirteenth century. Cistercians always sited their abbeys in valleys with flowing water and good agricultural land nearby. They weren't rich, ostentatious monks like some of the other religious orders. They believed in the simple life with no frills and they worked the land, trying to be as self-sufficient as possible. It must have been a pretty Spartan lifestyle.'

Mimi smiled across at her. 'I know where they were coming from. Since coming to Montegrifone, I've been finding that it's really good to get away from all the glitz.'

Buying tickets to enter the ruined church produced the first test of their precious anonymity. While Mimi lurked in the background and studied the vaulted ceiling of the Scriptorium, Bee went over to the desk and bought two tickets from the friendly girl behind the counter. She kept her battered cheek slightly averted and she noticed nothing untoward on the other girl's face. Returning to Mimi, she whispered in her ear.

'So far so good. The disguise seems to be working.'

As they walked around the inside of the eerie, empty church, Bee explained how famine first and then the Black Death in 1348 had driven the monks out, leaving the magnificent abbey to fall into rack and ruin. It was an impressive but rather gloomy place, and they were both glad when they got back out again and began the short walk up the hill to see the sword in the stone.

The sword in the stone, allegedly planted there by Saint Galgano himself, occupied the very centre of an ancient stone and brick construction on the top of a hillock. The original building was an early medieval chapel, totally circular, formed of alternating rows of light grey local stone and red brick. Over the years, other bits of building had been added, along with a parking area and little garden. A very chatty old couple looked after the place and the gift shop alongside it. Bee led Mimi into the chapel and pointed to the sword in the stone. Protected beneath a clear plastic cover, all that was visible was the rusty handle, protruding from a boulder. Alas, the effect was somewhat spoilt by a lingering stink of cat pee.

'Saint Galgano is supposed to have stuck his sword in here to symbolise his renunciation of his former life as a nobleman and soldier. It's claimed to have been here ever since the twelfth century.'

Mimi stared at it in fascination. They were alone in the little chapel, but she kept her voice down all the same.

'Maybe I should do something similar, the day I give up acting and settle down, assuming that ever happens.'

'You'd never give up acting, would you? Loads of actresses have children and keep on going.'

Mimi looked across at Bee. 'You're probably right. Besides, I don't have a sword to plant in the ground, anyway. And the way my agent keeps getting me to sign contracts, I'll probably still be acting on my deathbed.'

Outside, they surveyed the view over the fields to the hills beyond, most of which were capped by fortified villages, and to one side of the building they came upon the source of the cat pee: a group of feral-looking cats were stretched out on window ledges and flower beds, fast asleep, no doubt after a busy night dealing with the local rodent population. Bee clicked her tongue in an attempt to wake them, but didn't get so much as a twitch out of them. She glanced across at Mimi.

'All right for some.'

'I don't blame them. It's really, really hot today.' And it was.

From there, they drove up the very steep hill to Chiusdino and walked around the tortuous, narrow medieval streets, hugging the shade wherever possible. As anticipated, the view from up here was panoramic, all the way across to the peaks of the Apennines in the far distance. Although there was a restaurant aptly named *Caffè Panoramico*, they decided not to risk sitting down in close proximity to other guests for fear of recognition, so they settled for a bottle of water and a banana each from a local shop.

By the time they got back to the villa, it was late afternoon and both of them were feeling weary, but as they pulled up outside the villa, Bee was suddenly roused from her somnolent state. A familiar dusty pickup was parked there and, leaning against the bonnet, chatting to Umberto, was Luke. As he saw her, Bee for a moment thought his eyes lit up, but it was only a fleeting second and she couldn't be sure. What she was sure about, however, was that her own eyes definitely did.

'How does a glass of fresh lemonade in the garden with the man of your dreams sound?' Bee could tell from Mimi's tone that she was teasing, but she blushed all the same.

'It sounds wonderful, but I bet he says no.'

'We'll see.' Mimi was still grinning as they climbed out of the car.

'Good afternoon, gentlemen.' Mimi went over and shook hands with both men. 'Bee and I were wondering if you felt like joining us for a glass of cold lemonade, Luke.'

Bee came across to join her, feeling unexpectedly shy, almost like a teenager again. More for something to say than any other reason, she translated for Umberto's benefit, and saw him nod emphatically.

'An excellent idea. Ines has just made a new batch this afternoon.' The old man turned towards Luke. 'You will join us, won't you, Luca?'

To her surprise, Bee heard Luke reply immediately.

'I'd love a glass of lemonade. Thank you, ladies. Have you had an interesting day?'

Mimi nodded enthusiastically as they followed Umberto towards the front door, watched by the peacocks who had very sensibly taken up position in the shade of a big clump of oleanders. 'Very. I've had a fascinating tour of historical Tuscany with my very own guide.'

'And nobody recognised you?'

'No. It all went well, didn't it, Bee?'

By now, Bee had collected herself and she was able to respond in a normal voice.

'We went to San Galgano and Chiusdino and then stopped off to view a number of other tiny little places on the way back. And nobody so much as raised an eyebrow at us.'

They walked in through the lobby, along the corridor and out into the back garden, heading for the rattan armchairs set in the shade. As they did so, a black shadow emerged from the flower border and came trotting across to greet them.

Luke nodded towards him. 'The coolest place for Romeo is underneath the thickest bushes. Either there or in the river.'

Mimi crouched down to make a fuss of the dog and glanced towards Luke as she did so.

'You know, that's one thing that's missing in this lovely villa – a swimming pool.'

Luke nodded. 'That's in the plans for next year. You'll have to come back again.'

Mimi grinned at him as she straightened up and the dog transferred his affections to Bee. 'I'll definitely be back next year. You can be sure of that.'

'But in the meantime there's always the pool in the river. The water's clean and at this time of year it's not too cold.' Luke turned to Bee. 'Just go down to the river, turn right and keep going upstream until it gets really steep. There's a lovely little pool there. I often used to swim there.'

'I know exactly where you mean, Luke. That's where I went for my very first picnic shortly after getting here. Do you realise that's almost a month ago already? I was tempted to go for a swim, but it was just after the accident and I was told to avoid risks of infection, so I didn't go in.'

'Well, your cuts have all healed up really well now, haven't they? Presumably there would be no problem for you to go for a swim.'

She could feel his eyes on her and she struggled unsuccessfully to stop herself from blushing.

'You're really looking heaps better, Bee.' Mimi joined in, a mischievous smile on her face. 'Although your cheeks are a bit red at the moment.'

Bee saw her wink and felt her cheeks glow all the more. Fortunately, Umberto chose that moment to emerge from the kitchen with glasses of ice-cold lemonade. By the time he had distributed these, Bee had regained her composure.

'Thanks a lot. My cheek is definitely getting better. I'm sure there's no reason why I shouldn't go for a swim now. I'm seeing the doctor in a week or two and I hope he's going to tell me that I'm going to come out of it looking okay.'

'You already do, Bee.'

Luke's voice was low and it sounded sincere. No sooner had he spoken than he dropped his eyes and crouched down to scratch Romeo's tummy. Mimi's caught Bee's eye and grinned.

'We must give this natural pool a go, Bee.'

Bee nodded back at her.

'I'll take you up there one of these days, Mimi. It's a super place.'

Mimi, however, still hadn't finished matchmaking. 'And you should join us, Luke.'

Bee spluttered into her lemonade at the thought of Luke with his shirt off.

He looked up, but now, the sparkle had gone out of his eyes.

'I haven't been there for ages. I really should.'

His tone was sombre, in spite of his words, and Bee wondered if it had been a special place for him and his fiancée. Seeing his solemn expression at least served to shake her out of her state of teenage embarrassment and she found herself smiling encouragingly at him.

'Maybe we'll see you there one of these days.'

He didn't answer.

—

That evening, after a shower and a change of clothes, Bee walked down to Luke's father's house and found him sitting outside underneath the olive tree once more. To her surprise, she noticed that the garden was looking a lot tidier than the last time she had been there. The tallest weeds had for the most part been removed and somebody had clearly been busy with secateurs. She was quick to comment.

'Hello, Riccardo, have you been working in the garden?'

'Yes. And about time, too.' He waved her in. 'Come and have a drink, Bee. There's wine in the kitchen or I've got cold mineral water and a bucket of ice out here if you prefer.'

This was Bee's second surprise of the evening. She had been expecting to find her neighbour with his usual glass of wine in his hand. To see him with just plain water was remarkable, and commendable. She decided to add a bit of positive reinforcement.

'It's so hot, I'd love a drop of cold water. I'll go and get myself a glass.'

She went into the house, glancing into the studio as she walked past. There was yet another new canvas on the easel, clearly still in its embryonic early stages. This, too, was commendable progress, if what he had told her about having done virtually no painting for ages was true. Maybe Riccardo was getting his painting mojo back.

She grabbed a water glass and returned to the garden. This time she sat down on the bench alongside him and the two of them sipped their water and admired the view in silence for some minutes, but it wasn't an uncomfortable silence and it wasn't totally silent. Above them the swallows were circling noisily as usual and somewhere in the distance the peacocks were screaming at each other. For the first time she heard what had to be a goat. Maybe this meant that Berlusconi was out on the prowl once more and she was glad she didn't have any washing on the line. Other than that, it was calm and peaceful. She wondered wistfully if there was any way this peace might be made to extend into the relationship of the father and the son.

'So, what about sitting for me, Bee? I'm keen to get on with your portrait.'

'That's what I came to see you about, Riccardo. Whenever you like this week. Tomorrow or the day after maybe? You tell me what you prefer.'

Riccardo nodded gratefully. 'Thank you so much. I've got to go to the doctor's tomorrow. How about the day after tomorrow some time in the morning?'

'That sounds great. I'll see you, say around ten, and I won't forget to wear something that shows off a bit more skin than usual.' She grinned at him. 'But don't get your hopes up. Just like Mimi, I've got a no-nudity clause in my contract.'

She was delighted to see him smile back, a real, uncomplicated smile this time.

'In that case, I'd better review my plan to cast you in the role of Venus emerging from her shell in my next painting after all.'

'I haven't got the hair for it.' She ran her fingers through her hair and definitely it felt a bit softer. Rather than the kind of cut favoured by the US Marine Corps, it was now, just over six weeks since the accident, beginning to resemble a fairly radical urchin cut. Also, the stitches on the main head wound were feeling less and less prominent and no longer tender to the touch. Maybe, she told herself, it wouldn't be too long before she would be able to leave here and restart her life. If that was what she wanted to do.

'I noticed you've started a new canvas, Riccardo. It looked like a series of figures sitting round a table. Is that going to have a Renaissance flavour as well?'

He nodded. 'That's the plan. I was watching a discussion programme on TV last night and the idea came to me. There they were, talking endlessly about all the problems in the world, and it occurred to me that groups of people have no doubt been doing that very same thing throughout the whole of history, but to no effect. I thought I might call this one: *History Teaches us Nothing.*'

Bee nodded approvingly. 'You're dead right there.'

They sat for a few more minutes before Riccardo gave the conversation a startling new direction.

'So, what did your boyfriend think of Montegrifone?'

Bee looked up in surprise, wondering how news of Jamie's visit had percolated through to this hermit.

'He's not my boyfriend.' For some reason she definitely wanted to make that clear – to everybody on the estate. 'He used to be, but it all fizzled out a few months ago.'

'A-ha, so, don't tell me, he came here to try to woo you back? I spotted you talking to him by his car just before he left, and he looked a bit forlorn.' He added a word of explanation. 'I've started taking a few walks. I've been shut up in here for too long.'

Bee found herself smiling at him. 'I'm delighted you're getting out and about. That's great news. As far as Jamie's concerned, he wouldn't know the first thing about wooing, but I think you might be right. He did sound a bit nostalgic. But that episode of my life is closed now, so I sent him packing.'

Riccardo was still smiling. 'Ah… to be young and beautiful. You women don't realise the power you have over us men. You beguile us, use us, and then discard us at will.'

Bee found herself smiling back at him. 'I've never ever set out to beguile any man, least of all Jamie. No, it had to be done and I feel all the better for it.'

'So you're footloose and fancy free once more. Or do you have another poor unsuspecting victim in your sights?'

'Right now, I'm just fine as I am, Riccardo. This way, I can concentrate on my career without relationship complications.'

The look he gave her was highly sceptical. 'And your career is so important to you?'

'Yes, of course. I've been studying all my life to get to this stage. I'm at a crossroads at the moment and I need to concentrate all my efforts on sorting out which direction to go in.'

'Romance isn't high on your list of priorities, then?' The sceptical look was still on his face, but he moved on. 'And when does your work restart?'

'Not long now. Probably in September.' She went on to tell him about what had happened at work and how she was actively looking around for a different job. He shook his head ruefully.

'So, one way or another, you'll be leaving Montegrifone?'

'I'm afraid so.' She distinctly got the impression he was sorry she would be leaving. His next words confirmed it.

'I'll be sorry to see you go.'

'And I'll be sorry to leave this wonderful place and all of you.'

She meant it.

Chapter 15

The following afternoon, Mimi was tied up again on the phone to the US, so Bee decided to go for another good long walk, in spite of the heat.

When she went to the kitchen to collect the ever-willing dog, Ines had a suggestion for her. 'Have you been to the little church yet?' She called it the *chiesetta* and Bee dimly remembered seeing that name on the map Umberto had given her.

'No, I haven't. Hang on while I dig out Umberto's map and you can show me where it is.'

The little church was perched on the flank of the hill-side on the other side of the road down which they had driven to the villa just over a month earlier. She had got so used to living here at Montegrifone by now, it seemed even longer in the past than that. Certainly, her 'normal' life back in London felt much further away. She hadn't explored that side of the valley yet, so she readily agreed to Ines's suggestion.

She decided she could just wear her sunhat, rather than adding the scarf to help hide her face. At least from a distance, it really didn't look too bad at all now. From close up, of course, the damage to the skin was still visible, but even these marks were starting to fade and smooth themselves out a bit. An email that morning had confirmed the follow-up appointment with Doctor Bianchi at the hospital the following week and she was nervously awaiting his verdict on her progress and the long-term prognosis.

She and Romeo set off at half past two. The sky was cloudless, the late July sun scorching, and the temperature very high. She had spread sun cream all over her exposed skin and she was grateful for it. They both hugged the shade as they made their way down through the vines to the river and along towards the bridge. The river itself was now little more than a miserable trickle and they crossed it without even bothering to use the bridge, Bee stepping easily across without getting her trainers wet and Romeo deliberately looking for one of the few remaining little pools and flopping gratefully into the water to cool down. Bee looked on enviously. Yes, she thought to herself, the one thing missing from this gorgeous valley was a swimming pool. Maybe she would take Mimi up to the one she had discovered on her first walk. And, of course, if she were to find Luke there...

She was lost in her thoughts as she reached the road. These thoughts mainly involved Luke in tight-fitting swimming trunks, climbing out of the clear water towards her, dripping wet, a broad smile on his face and love in his eyes. As daydreams went, it was pretty damn good, but she was suddenly snapped back to the here and now by the sight of a wedge-shaped animal, roughly the size of a spaniel, scuttling across the road in front of her. She stopped dead and, beside her, the dog did the same. She stared blankly, blinked a few times, wiped her eyes and stared some more. There was no doubt about it. What she had just seen could only be one thing. She glanced down at the dog who had made no attempt to chase the animal.

'Did you see what I saw, Romeo? That was a porcupine. I didn't know they had porcupines here in Tuscany.'

From the expression on the bewildered dog's face, neither did he.

As they crossed the road without encountering any cars, Bee was presented with irrefutable proof that her animal recognition skills were faultless, at least on this occasion. There, lying at the side of the road was what could only be a porcupine quill, almost a foot long. She picked it up and studied it. It looked for all the world like the central shaft of a bird's feather, the top half black, the bottom half white, and the pointed black end was as sharp as a needle. Very carefully, she stuck it into the side of her straw sun hat, feeling rather proud of her trophy. She looked down at the Labrador.

'You're not silly, are you, dog? You wouldn't want to catch one of those on the end of your nose.'

They began the steep climb to the little church. It was higher up than it looked and by the time they got there, Bee was perspiring freely. The church really was little. In fact, it wasn't much bigger than an average house. She was fascinated to see that the windows and doorway were formed of rounded Roman arches, rather than the more recent Gothic 'broken' arches. It had to be early medieval, probably at least eight, maybe nine, hundred years old. It was a sobering thought. So much had happened in the world since this humble little church had been built and, no doubt, it would still be here long after Beatrice Kingdom, Romeo the dog, and all her current companions in the valley were dust.

The walls were made of local stone, and the roof of sun-scorched terracotta tiles. Bee and Romeo headed gratefully for the shade of the porch and stopped for a breather. The door in its arched stone frame was made of solid timbers, pinned together with huge dome-headed nails. The old planks were wide and weather-beaten, the sturdy iron latch worn smooth by the touch of a multitude of hands over the years. It all looked very, very ancient and Bee loved it.

She shrugged off her little backpack and felt the sweat cold against her back. She retrieved the big bottle of water and took a drink. It was already tepid. Leaning against the wall of the porch, she looked out at the view before her. They were now considerably higher even than the villa on its hill, and it seemed absurd that she had been unable to spot the church from there, but the stone was the same colour as the soil around it, and a few cypress trees on the slope in front of her served to add further camouflage to the little building. She took a few photos of the scene with her phone and sent one to her mother. Up here there was an excellent mobile signal, so she phoned home to tell her about Jamie's visit and the way things had ended up. Predictably, her mother was saddened.

'So it really is all over? You made such a lovely couple.'

Bee made no comment and fortunately the conversation turned to less contentious issues. After she had described her day out with Mimi the previous day, her mother must have heard something in her voice.

'You know something, Bee, you're sounding really happy. The Italian air must agree with you.'

'I think you're right, mum. It's such a wonderful place here and I've met some lovely people. And my furry friend at my feet is delightful.'

'And is there maybe a special someone there for you?'

Ever since her teenage years, Bee had always hated having conversations about boys with her mum. Now, almost twenty years on, it wasn't any easier. She did her best to nip it in the bud.

'There's nobody here, Mum. The place is virtually deserted apart from Umberto and his wife.'

Maybe Jamie had been right about her being a poor liar, as her mother carried straight on with her cross-examination.

'No nice boys looking after the vineyards?'

'There are the farm workers and the estate manager, but I'm just fine on my own, mum.'

'Anything you say, dear. Anyway, you'll find someone soon, I know. After all, it's about time you started thinking about settling down, you know.'

'Mum...!' Bee's voice tailed off in frustration. Doing her best to keep her voice level, she changed the subject. 'Anyway, you're right about my feeling better. Maybe it *is* the Tuscan air.'

After ringing off, she took a photo of Romeo as he lay sprawled on the worn flagstones of the porch and sent it to her mum as a peace offering. She added a few words of description: *the only male in my life over here.* It wasn't strictly true, but it was all her mother needed to know – at least for now.

Pocketing her phone, she reached for the heavy iron ring of the latch and twisted it. She pushed with her shoulder and the door opened with an eerie creak, but the blessedly cool air that came out from there more than calmed any nerves she might have had. She felt a movement at her feet as Romeo jumped up, nosing his way inside, and she followed him, closing the door behind her.

It was very dark in the church after the brilliant sunlight outside and pleasantly chilly. As her eyes began to get used to the gloom, she started to make out a few rows of pews, an altar at the far end and a handful of statues lining the walls. The narrow windows – only one of them boasting stained glass – shed enough light for her to be able to make her way around the building, marvelling at how tiny it was. At a push, probably no more than thirty or forty people could have squeezed inside. Everything was ancient and dusty, and the place smelt of mould. However, halfway along one wall, she came upon something more modern. A stone slab was set in the wall and it was clear that the inscription had been carved quite recently, as the outline of the letters was still crisp. She took a closer look. The heading was familiar:

Famiglia Negri di Montegrifone

Beneath this was a long list of names and dates, going back all the way to 1513. She scanned through them all until she crouched down to read the last name on the list and felt a twinge of sadness.

Cosimo Negri 1932-2017

This had to be Luke's grandfather. No doubt in years to come, the names Riccardo and Luca Negri would also be added. She was in awe of a family that could trace its roots so far back, but this only emphasised the fleeting nature of our time on this earth. She sat down on one of the pews, feeling remarkably contemplative. Seconds later, a warm furry head landed on her knee as Romeo came to offer comfort. She stroked his ears as she sat and reflected, not only on the history of this illustrious family, but on her own life. Maybe her mum was right after all. Maybe it was time to think about settling down.

She sat silently for a good few minutes, thinking about her life to date and her probable future, until the unmistakable high-pitched whine of a mosquito by her ear stirred her. She stood up, rousing the dog who had by now stretched out on the cool flagstones at her feet, and made her way back out into the sunlight. As she closed the door behind them, she resolved to come back up here again. There was an uncommon tranquillity to the place and she had felt comfortable here, even on the hard wooden bench.

She slipped her sunglasses back on, retrieved her backpack and stepped out of the shade of the porch and into the sun. The air was dry and hot enough for her to feel the heat in her throat as she breathed in. She made a decision and glanced down at the dog.

'You know what you need, Romeo? A swim.'

He wagged his tail hopefully and she set off with him down a track that curled across the hillside back to the road, heading in the direction of the little pool she had found on her first longer walk. With the aid of Umberto's map and Romeo's local knowledge, it took less than half an hour to get there, but she was bathed in sweat by the time she finally heard the waterfall and saw the pool. As she reached it, there was a loud splash as the dog plunged straight in, surfacing a few moments later with an expression of delight on his face. You didn't need to be able to speak Labrador to understand his message, 'Come on in. The water's fine.'

Bee took off her backpack and felt her T-shirt sticky against her skin. She sat down in the shade of the trees and watched as the happy dog splashed about in the cool, refreshing water. Once he had climbed out, shaken himself, and sprawled out on the rock at her feet, she listened hard for any other sounds of life, but could hear nothing. No voices, no footsteps, no tractors. Just birds singing, the ever-present bees, and a distant cow lowing. She hadn't thought to bring a costume, and for a naughty moment she even considered stripping off her damp clothes and plunging naked into the pool, but natural caution prevailed, so all she removed were her trainers and socks so she could dangle her feet into the remarkably cold water.

As it turned out, it was just as well she had resisted the temptation to go skinny dipping. She had only been sitting there for a few minutes when Romeo raised his head from the rock, pricked up his ears and then jumped to his feet, nose pointing downstream, tail wagging. By now, Bee could hear rustling in the bushes and the sound of cracking twigs as somebody approached. She took heart from the fact that Romeo was wagging his tail, but even so, it was a relief when she saw who it was. She sat up and beamed at him.

'Hi, Luke.'

'Hi, Bee. Hot enough for you?'

'It's boiling. In fact, I've just been toying with the idea of stripping off and diving into the pool. It's just as well I didn't.'

He grinned and she was delighted to see the lines around his eyes soften. 'Speak for yourself.' For a moment, she sensed his eyes on her body and there was no doubt in her mind, she rather liked the sensation. 'Anyway, to be honest, that's what I've come to do.'

He squatted down beside her, making no attempt for the moment to discard his shorts or his T-shirt. He was close enough to touch, and memory of her recent daydream almost made Bee's cheeks flush, but she controlled it this time. She wasn't a giddy teenager, after all.

'I thought you said you hadn't been here for a while.'

He nodded, the sombre expression back on his face.

'Not for almost a year. Not since… you know the story of Dawn, I imagine. Umberto told me he's given you the potted history of Montegrifone, so I assume you got the bit about the heartbroken farmer losing his Australian fiancée. She and I used to come here a lot. It was sort of our special place.'

She could hear him trying to sound upbeat, but his eyes betrayed him. She felt like reaching over and giving him a hug, but, of course, she didn't. Instead, she just nodded.

'He told me a bit, but I only discovered who you really were by reading your father's Wikipedia entry.'

His eyes narrowed.

'Umberto told me you've been speaking to my father.'

'You don't mind, do you?'

'Of course not. You're free to talk to whoever you like.' His eyes dropped. A long pause followed, but she made no attempt to break it. Finally he looked up again. 'How is he?'

'He's fine, I think. He said he had a doctor's appointment today, but that was probably just routine. He's a bit slow on his feet, but he looks and sounds fine.'

'Good.'

That was all he said. Bee deliberated whether to ask him about his relationship, or the lack of it, with his father but decided it wasn't her place to intrude. The fact that he was even talking about him was, she sensed, a major development, so she left it at that and turned to a safer topic.

'Umberto and Ines are lovely, Luke.'

'They certainly are. I don't know what I'd do without them.'

'There's a real family feeling when I see you with them. If I didn't know differently, I would have imagined they were your parents or your grandparents.'

'They're the closest thing to family I've got left. I was really close to my grandfather, and when he died I was really devastated.'

'And your mum died before that?'

She saw him nod his head. 'While I was still quite young. It was cancer. My grandparents brought me up, helped by Umberto and Ines. That's why I'm so close to them even now. I still think of Ines as sort of my surrogate mum.'

'And your father?'

Bee held her breath as she posed the question. All she got back from Luke were six words.

'My father's a waste of space.'

She didn't know how to respond to this and decided it would be better to let the subject of his father rest, so she lay back, pretending to snooze. After a while, he got to his feet and glanced down at her.

'Well, seeing as I'm here…'

Through the safety of her dark glasses she watched him remove his T-shirt to reveal his muscular shoulders and lovely V-shaped back. She averted her eyes rather primly as he slipped out of his shorts and by the time she looked back, he was only wearing his swimming trunks. For a moment she and Romeo exchanged glances and she felt sure the dog had read her mind. This was indeed a very handsome man. The dog distinctly winked, before turning and launching himself bodily into the water, splashing both of them as he hit the surface.

Luke climbed carefully down the rocks until he could slide into the water. Romeo doggy-paddled happily alongside him and Bee felt a definite twinge of envy, although, from Luke's grimaces, it was clear that the water in the pool was far from warm. He and the dog had a brief wrestling match for possession of a broken branch that the Labrador won, before Luke rolled onto his back and floated on the surface of the crystal-clear water, arms outstretched, with a blissful expression on his face. Bee's sense of envy increased and she resolved to bring her bikini one of these days and follow suit.

After ten minutes or so, he emerged from the pool, accompanied by the dog who showered her with cold water as he shook himself. After the initial impact, the cool sensation was very welcome, although the aroma of damp Labrador wasn't. Luke towelled himself off and sat down on an outcrop of rock just along from Bee. He smiled at her and she did her best to concentrate on his face, rather than his broad chest and his strong stomach muscles.

She glanced back at him, pleased to see him looking relaxed. Small talk seemed to be in order, so she tried farming.

'So, what's happening on the farm at the moment?'

'It's all pretty much concentrated on the vines now. We've been checking the new grapes to see they're developing well. In a few days' time it'll be August and we'll be spraying them to keep any mould or blight away and then, before long it'll be September and the *vendemmia* starts.'

'That must be a very busy time.'

'You can say that again. We tend to work pretty much all the daylight hours, so it's a tiring few weeks.' He smiled at her. 'Still, that's what we're all about. Without the grapes we can't make the wine.'

'And is it looking good for this year? Umberto said hail could be a problem.'

'So far so good. He's dead right about the hail, but the grapes are getting a lot of sunshine this year, with just enough rain from time to time. If it carries on like this until September and we don't get any hail, it should be a great year. Fingers crossed.' He caught her eye. 'Umberto may have also told you we're struggling for cash after my granddad's death. A good vintage will be a big help.'

'He told me. He also said you've had art experts looking at the paintings in case you had a forgotten old master hiding away here.'

'There actually is one, you know. Or at least, there was.'

Bee looked up with interest. 'What, a valuable old painting?'

'Yes, very. The family used to own an original painting by Simone Martini. You know the name I presume?'

'Wow. Of course I do.'

Simone Martini was one of the most famous Italian artists of the Middle Ages, responsible for the iconic *Annunciation*, now hanging in Florence's Uffizi gallery. A work by him would be worth many, many millions. Bee felt her skin tingle at the thought of such a treasure being anywhere near her.

'When you say "used to own", what does that mean?'

'It means it's lost.'

'Lost?'

'Lost, stolen, destroyed... who knows? During the Second World War, in the summer of 1944, the Germans were retreating from Montecassino, south of Rome, and the so-called Gustav Line, to prepared positions north of Florence.'

Bee nodded. This was not new to her. 'The Gothic Line.'

'Of course, I'd forgotten you're a historian. Anyway, my great-grandfather went to great lengths to hide or bury anything of value in the villa for fear of losing it to the Germans, or indeed the Allies as they came up through Tuscany.'

'Sounds like a sensible precaution.'

'It would have been, but for one thing. He didn't trust anybody else to do the hiding, so he did it himself. All well and good, except that only a few weeks later, he dropped dead.'

Bee gawped. 'Without revealing where he had put it all?'

Luke shrugged helplessly and gave her a tired smile. 'Exactly. A massive heart attack, apparently. Believe me, we've turned the whole place upside down, but with no success. We've even had divers in the well, but still nothing.' He corrected himself. 'No, that's not strictly true. Umberto and my grandfather did manage to locate some jewellery in the cellar, and I'll never forget finding a little cloth bag of gold coins underneath a loose floorboard in our house. That's the *Podere Nuovo* where my father lives. But we never found the big one.'

'If you did find that, it would solve your money worries, wouldn't it?'

'And some! We live in hope that maybe it'll turn up again some day, but I'm afraid it's a forlorn hope.' He stretched his arms up above his head and breathed deeply. 'Still, that's the way it is and there's no point in crying about it.' He glanced across at her. 'But if you feel like doing a bit of sleuthing, please go ahead. But I don't hold out too much hope. For all we know, it may even have been stolen years ago.'

'Or if it was hidden in a damp environment like a cellar, it may have rotted away.'

'Don't remind me.'

Luke lay back against the warm rock and closed his eyes, while Bee dreamt dreams of discovering a hidden masterpiece. From time to time, she glanced across at him and she knew she really liked this handsome man who lived in such a wonderful place, but who somehow had had such bad luck in his life, losing his mother, his fiancée, his beloved grandfather and, to an extent, his father. She knew she was developing feelings for him, but she knew that this, like the discovery of the Martini painting, was a forlorn hope. Even if he were to get over the loss of his fiancée – and it was clear he was still heartbroken – there was no way a relationship between them could develop beyond a brief holiday romance.

Enticing as that sounded, she knew she wanted more, and the insoluble problem was that her job, whatever that was going to be, would inevitably call her away from here. Tempting as it might be to give up on her career and settle down here and become a farmer's wife – although he had given little indication of having anything like that on his mind – she knew that she, like Luke's fiancée, would want more. As she had told his father, her career meant a lot to her and she couldn't imagine giving it up – even for Luke. And the more she got to know him, the more she was convinced that the last thing she would ever want to do was to hurt him by getting together with him and then leaving, just as his fiancée had done, particularly at this time when he was carrying such a burden of responsibility on his shoulders for the future of the estate and everybody who worked there. With considerable regret she knew nothing should ever happen between them, much as she might dream about it.

After a bit, seeing him so relaxed, she decided to risk broaching the subject of Riccardo again.

'Luke, your father invited me in to see his paintings the other day. He's a very talented artist.'

She saw his eyes open, but he didn't respond.

'But the two of you don't get on?'

'Is that what he told you?' He kept his voice low, but his expression had hardened.

'No, not at all. He just told me he rarely goes out and hardly ever sees anybody.'

There was a long pause before he spoke, his voice now little more than a whisper.

'I was only ten, Bee. I lost my mum and then, just when I needed him the most, I lost my dad. He sent me off to England to a very posh, but frighteningly Spartan, boarding school, and that was just about the last I saw of him.'

He looked and sounded bereft, and Bee could imagine the impression this experience must have made upon a little boy.

'Umberto said something about him having a break-down after your mum's death.'

'Who knows? All I know is that he deserted me in my hour of need. I used to come home for the holidays, but his door was always bolted and I stayed at the villa, not the *Podere Nuovo* which is where I was born and grew up. If it hadn't been for my granddad, along with Ines and Umberto, of course, I'd have been totally lost.' He caught her eye. 'So, yes, you could say we don't get on.'

'And you don't intend to try?'

He shook his head, but made no reply. After a minute or two, Bee decided she had better abandon the subject. She reached into her bag and produced the bottle of now lukewarm water, She offered it to Luke, but he shook his head.

'I'm fine, thanks.' There was a pause before he surprised her by picking up the subject of his father once more. 'What're his paintings like?'

'Your father's? Wonderful. Anybody can see what a talented artist he is.'

211

She wondered if she should mention the fact that he was painting her portrait, but decided against it for now. Instead, she threw it back to Luke.

'You must have seen his work, haven't you?'

'I saw some of his paintings when I was little, but I don't remember much about them. A few months back I checked him out on the internet and I saw some of his later stuff. You're right, he's a very good artist. Pity he wasn't a better father.'

The fact that he had taken the trouble to check his father out sounded promising but, for now, Bee decided to let the subject drop. She took a big swig of water, returned the bottle to the bag and pulled herself to her feet.

'I'd better get off home and take a shower. If the weather carries on like this, I think I'll come armed with a bikini next time.'

She was pleased to see a smile return to his face.

'You really should. The water's cold because it only emerges from the rock a few metres further up, but you soon get used to it and they say it has medicinal properties. You never know, it might help your wounds to heal.' He caught her eye. 'Although you're looking so much better already. When are you going back to London?'

'Some time later in August. It depends on Mimi. I've got an appointment at the hospital next Friday and I'll see what the doctors say.'

'The hospital in Siena?' Bee nodded. 'How are you getting there?'

'I'll drive up in our little Fiat. Umberto says parking can be a problem so I'll set off early.'

'What time's the appointment?'

'Around ten o'clock in the morning, I think. I thought I'd leave about nine, or even earlier.'

'I've got to be in Siena at ten-thirty on Friday. My meeting shouldn't last too long. I could give you a lift there and back if you like. That way, you'd have no trouble parking.'

'Are you sure? That would be lovely, thank you.'

'When you get back home, just text me the exact time of your appointment. Have you got my number?' Seeing her shake her head, he reeled off the number and she keyed it into her phone.

'Thanks, again, Luke. That's very kind. Now I think I'll head back to the villa.'

'I would accompany you, but as soon as I dry off, I've got to go on up the valley and check on something.' He caught her eye. 'Don't get too excited about this, but one of the boys said he found a deer carcass that looked as if it had been mauled by wolves. That's a bit too close for comfort, so I'm going to check.'

Bee's eyes opened wide. 'Just be careful, please. I'd hate anything to happen to you.'

He smiled at her. 'So would I, but it's very unlikely. They only operate at night and I've only ever seen one in the last four years, and it ran off as soon as it saw me. I'll be fine.'

'Like I say...'

'I'll be careful. Promise. Anyway, I'm glad I came for a swim. I'd been putting it off for too long. I enjoyed doing it and I enjoyed seeing you. It's stupid to put off doing things just because of a few bad memories. Life goes on, Bee. I've got to remember that.'

On an impulse she leant down and kissed him on the cheek.

'I'm glad you came.'

As she straightened up again she heard his voice, sounding quite emotional.

'Thanks, Bee. Thanks a lot.' He hesitated for a moment and she heard him clear his throat. However, when he continued, he sounded almost normal again. 'Do you want to take Romeo with you?'

Bee glanced down at the dog who was stretched out, comatose, on the rock.

'I'll be fine. You hang onto him. He is your dog after all...'

'He belongs to the whole place, really, so any time you want him, just whistle.'

Bee had never been very good at whistling, but she smiled at the two of them and headed back home.

Chapter 16

The following morning, Bee put on a tank top and went down to Riccardo's house to model for him. As she walked down there, she found she had a companion. A large black shape emerged from the vines as Romeo came back from his morning tour of the estate. After making a fuss of him, Bee carried on to Riccardo's house, the dog now trotting alongside her as if she were his mistress. She found Riccardo waiting at his front door.

'Hello, Riccardo. Look who's come with me. Have you two met?'

'I've seen him around, but we've never been formally introduced.'

Bee smiled. 'Riccardo, this is Romeo. Romeo, Riccardo. Say hello nicely.'

The dog wandered affably through the gate to where Riccardo was standing and paused at the step, tail wagging hopefully. After a moment's hesitation, Riccardo emerged and bent down to give the Labrador a stroke. He was leaning on his stick and Bee could see how uncomfortable it was for him to bend over. Still, she was pleased to see him make friends with the dog. When all was said and done, Romeo was Luke's dog, so this had to be a step in the right direction as far as a rapprochement was concerned.

Bee joined them on the front step. By now, Romeo had rolled over onto his back and Riccardo was crouching down to scratch his tummy. When the time came for him to straighten up again, Bee saw how heavily he was resting on his stick, so she grabbed him by the other arm and helped him to his feet.

'Your leg playing up again today, Riccardo?'

He nodded. 'To be honest, it's my hip. I saw the doctor yesterday and they're going to give me a hip replacement some time soon. The sooner the better as far as I'm concerned.' He shook her hand and nodded approvingly at her choice of top.

'Thank you for wearing this. It'll be perfect. Come in and we'll get started. What about your four-legged friend here? He belongs to Umberto, doesn't he?'

'He spends a lot of time at the villa, but he actually belongs to Luke and he has the run of the valley. I'm surprised he hasn't come calling before. He'll probably come in where it's cool and sleep, if you don't mind. Otherwise we can leave him outside and he'll wander off to see somebody else.'

At the mention of his son's name, Bee saw Riccardo flinch, but the moment quickly passed and he ushered them both into his studio. As Bee had predicted, the dog soon stretched out on the cool terracotta tiles as Bee took up position on a stool in front of the easel.

'Here, Bee, I wonder if you'd mind putting this on?'

She looked up and saw that Riccardo was holding a heavy gold necklace that she recognised from the painting. As she clipped it behind her neck, she queried its provenance.

'Is this real gold? It's heavy enough.'

She saw him nod and she was very impressed.

'Wow, it must be worth a packet.'

'It belonged to my wife.'

His tone was very sombre and she saw the same expression of sorrow on his face that she had observed from time to time on his son's, making the family resemblance even more evident, and she wondered why she hadn't noticed sooner.

'It's beautiful.'

'Thank you. I'm glad you like it. I bought it for her with the proceeds of the first of my paintings to be sold in the States. I bought it from a New York antique shop. Ironically we subsequently discovered it's Italian, maybe even Tuscan. It either dates back to the Renaissance or it's a very good nineteenth-century copy. Either way, it's old.' He picked up a paint brush. 'Now, if you're ready, let's get started. Try to keep fairly still, but don't worry too much. If you have to scratch your nose, just try to resume the original pose again afterwards.'

Bee was there for the best part of two hours altogether and the dog slept the whole time. She and Riccardo exchanged a few words, but he was obviously concentrating hard and she didn't want to disturb him. As it was, it gave her time to think and, once more, she found herself reviewing her life, wondering what sort of reception her scarred face would receive back in London and how she would feel to leave this wonderful place... and its inhabitants. Before coming here, she had feared being lost in a green wilderness, but instead, she had made some wonderful and lasting friends and she really felt at home here now. Yes, it was going to be tough.

Once he finally declared himself satisfied, Riccardo called her over to take a look at the result of his morning's work. Bee stood up, stretched, and walked across to see for herself, removing the heavy necklace as she did so. What she saw came as a considerable surprise. The face beneath the wonderful head of hair was without doubt hers, but he had painted it as it really was now, scars and all. It was a stunning piece of work and the expression he had managed to create was at the same time poignant and hopeful. Without taking her eyes off the picture, she asked him why.

'Riccardo, I thought you were going to give me... her my face as it used to be. How come you've left the scarring?'

Part of her was dismayed at the sight of the scarring while, deep down, she found herself seriously questioning whether that mattered. At least it was a true and honest representation of her, no holds barred. She heard his voice.

'I hope you don't mind too much, Bee. If you object, I can easily paint over the left cheek and make it the same as the right. That was my original idea but, somehow, the contrast between untouched and touched appeals to me greatly. I think it gives the painting so much more power, don't you?'

Bee had to agree. Somehow he had caught her very innermost thoughts, the internal conflict between her life back in London and how she was here in Tuscany. What struck her most forcefully, however, was how she looked. Yes, her left cheek was scarred, but it was no longer the frightening mess it had been. In fact, if anything, it brought extra humanity to the image on the canvas. With difficulty she dragged her eyes away from the portrait and looked up at him. His expression was uncertain, wondering what her decision would be.

'I absolutely love it, Riccardo. Of course you mustn't change it. I think it's a stroke of genius to paint me as I am. What are you going to call it?'

He looked greatly relieved. 'I'm still working on that. I was wondering about *Gioconda Nuova*, but that might be a bit cheesy.'

Bee smiled. *La Gioconda* was the Italian title of the painting known elsewhere as the *Mona Lisa*, whose enigmatic smile was one of the most famous images in the world. Was she herself similarly enigmatic, she wondered?

'Whatever name you give it, I love it. I absolutely love it.'

'And you don't mind airing your damaged face? After all, that's the reason you're here at Montegrifone, isn't it? To avoid exactly that.'

Bee nodded absently. 'No, I really don't mind.' Her head cleared and she felt a rush of emotion that threatened to choke her voice. She cleared her throat and did her best to put into words what she was feeling. 'I'll tell you this, Riccardo: you've done me a favour, a real, massive favour. You've shown me what I really look like and it's not the end of the world. Yes, I'm scarred, but I'm still me underneath. I've been scared stiff of the effect this accident might have on my life, but I see now this was just stupid vanity. I'm still me, in spite of what's happened...'

She suddenly felt an overwhelming urge to cry that she was powerless to resist, and the next moment she was sobbing like a little girl. She was dimly aware of a pair of comforting arms catching her by the shoulders before she buried her head against his chest and wept her heart out. But, even through her tears, she knew that she wasn't crying because she was unhappy. Very much the opposite. These were cathartic, purging tears, releasing so many of the fears that had been plaguing her for weeks now since the accident. When she finally recovered enough to lift her head from his chest and step back from his supporting arms, she was smiling.

'Thank you, Riccardo. You've helped me more than I can possibly say.'

–

Luke came to pick her up at nine o'clock on Friday. He was looking very smart in a grey suit, shirt and tie. Bee nodded approvingly.

'This makes a change from shorts and a T-shirt.'

He smiled. 'I'm afraid it's because I've got to go and talk to yet another lawyer and this one's always terribly formal.' He pointed downwards. 'You maybe haven't noticed, but I've even cleaned the front seat. Suits and dirty pickups don't really mix.'

They headed back up the valley. It was now almost six weeks since she had first arrived here and she was so familiar with everything, it felt almost as though she was leaving an old friend behind. Not for the first time, she reflected on how tough it was going to be when the time came for her to leave for good.

The drive to Siena took barely half an hour and Luke dropped her by the main entrance to the hospital. She walked in and up the stairs to her appointment with Doctor Bianchi. She was wearing her wig, and nobody recognised her until she reached his office. To her delight, she found Rosa waiting to greet her. She had no hesitation in giving the kindly nurse a big hug.

'*Ciao*, Rosa. How good to see you again. Thank you again for being so caring and so kind at a time when I was so scared.'

'Good morning, Beatrice, you're very welcome. You look wonderful now. I'm so happy for you.'

They chatted for a few minutes until Doctor Bianchi arrived. He also looked delighted to see her. They all went into his office and Bee removed the wig so he could give her a close examination. He took his time, checking her blood pressure, inspecting the cuts, and making sure that all the swelling had gone. He then quizzed her on her general health, particularly interested to know if she had been suffering from headaches, before giving her his verdict.

'I'm pleased to see that everything's healed up very well. The fresh air and exercise you've been getting have all contributed to returning you to full physical fitness once more. In fact, I wouldn't mind betting that you're fitter now than you were before the accident.'

'I've borrowed a dog and I've been doing lots of walking in the country. You're right, I do feel really fit. So, what about the scars?'

He took his time before answering. 'The scars on your head have all healed well and are already almost completely masked by your hair, so I really think we can forget about them now. As for the scarring to your face, you've got a choice. It's all healing well and I'm sure that in six months' time all you'll be left with will be a few pale patches and a certain amount of very faint tissue damage. From a few metres away, you'll look just like your old self.

From close-up there will always be a bit of damage visible, but nothing too unsightly and, of course, there's always make-up. However, if you like, we could see if we could improve things by some skin grafts and plastic surgery. This would probably involve a couple of operations, but in a few months you should be as good as new.' He caught her eye. 'It's up to you. You decide.'

Bee had already given a lot of thought as to how she would react to a variety of hypothetical scenarios she had imagined. What the doctor had just outlined had been one of many.

'So you're saying that with another couple of operations – presumably involving more time in hospital – I could look the same as I did before the accident?' She saw him nod. 'Alternatively, in six months' time, without any more medical intervention, I won't look perfect, but I won't look too bad?'

'Better than that, Beatrice. You'll look almost as good as new, and your face will have gained a lot of character in the process.' He smiled at her. 'You will always be a beautiful woman. You already are. It's just a question of how perfect you want to be.'

She flushed and smiled weakly at him, her mind busily engaged with weighing up the alternatives. The image of her face as painted by Riccardo came back to her and she began to realise she was almost certain what she was going to do. Still, just to be on the safe side, she decided to take her time.

'Could I get back to you in a day or two? I'd like to think this over a bit first.'

'Of course, all the time in the world.'

Luke picked her up just before twelve. She had been sitting in the coffee bar at the hospital waiting for his meeting to finish, and during that time she had been turning what the doctor had said over and over in her head. On the one hand, the idea of her face returning to its original state was enticing, although she didn't like the sound of two more operations. The thought that she could just do nothing and find herself looking almost normal in six months' time had great appeal, but there was always the big unknown; how would other people react?

Luke studiously avoided mentioning her visit to the doctor, but he did have a suggestion.

'Bee, how would you feel about letting me buy you lunch? I'd enjoy your company if you haven't got anything more interesting to do.'

Bee had to stop and think. On the one hand, she knew she would enjoy spending time with him, but she didn't want to let things take a more intimate turn between them. The idea, beguiling as it was, of getting involved, only for her then to go off and possibly break his heart again was out of the question. He must have sensed her reservations.

'And, in case you're worried about being recognised, I can promise you I'll take you to a restaurant where you'll almost certainly be the only foreigner. No fear of bumping into a horde of paparazzi.' He hesitated. 'What's the collective noun for paparazzi? "Horde" doesn't seem tacky enough somehow.'

'How about a "scum" or a "slick" of paparazzi?' This wasn't the problem and she knew it. Still, she told herself, it would be rude to refuse. 'Well, yes, Luke, I'd love to have lunch with you, but there's no need for you to pay. I've loved spending time at Montegrifone, and with Romeo for that matter. I should be paying for the meal.'

He glanced across at her and she saw the pleasure on his face. 'That's great. But, please, let this one be on me. My treat. OK?'

The restaurant was roughly halfway between Siena and Montegrifone and Luke hadn't been joking. It was most definitely off the tourist trail. They had to negotiate a bewildering muddle of narrow lanes to get there and when the road disintegrated into a steep, winding, rough *strada bianca*, leading up the hillside, it was so bumpy it was just as well they were in the pickup with four-wheel drive. Bee grinned across to him as they lurched through some massive potholes.

'No fear of meeting any Lamborghinis up here.'

'Most definitely not, at least not the sports car type. By the way, any time you want Marco or me to give you a ride in our Lamborghini, you've only got to say the word.' He smiled at her. 'Not as flashy as Joey's but far more practical. As for this place, I know Michelangelo, the owner, very well and he tells me the highway authorities keep asking him if he wants them to tarmac the road and he keeps saying no. He's not the most commercially minded restaurateur you'll ever meet. He values his privacy more than his bank balance.'

You could have walked past the restaurant without realising it was there. It was a scruffy-looking ancient stone building that looked more like a run-down farm than a place to eat. Luke drove round the back and, there, everything changed. The car park was already more than half full and this side of the building was immaculate. A series of arched openings linked the restaurant to a wide

224

terrace dotted with tables, many of them occupied. The terrace was sheltered from the sun by a wooden structure covered with vines from which bunches of green grapes were already hanging.

'Outside all right for you?' Luke climbed out of the car and came round to meet her.

'Absolutely. The view is stunning out here.'

The tree-capped hills were steeper here than down at Montegrifone, and an unbroken sea of vines disappeared into the depths of a valley before reappearing on the far side again, giving the whole area the appearance of a meticulously planned grid. Here and there were little clumps of pine trees and cypresses and the few uncultivated areas were a mass of poppies and other wild flowers.

As they walked across to the terrace, an immaculately dressed lady appeared to greet them. As she spotted Luke, her face split into a big smile.

'*Benvenuto, Luca.* We haven't seen you for quite a while.' The lady's attention turned to Bee. '*Signorina, buongiorno.*'

Bee gave her a smile and a nod as Luke replied.

'Good afternoon, Francesca. I hope you're all well.'

'Yes indeed, thank you. Would you like to follow me, please?'

Bee and Luke were shown to a table in the far corner of the terrace, sheltered from all but the most inquisitive eyes by two massive lemon trees in ornate terracotta pots. The trees themselves were laden with bright yellow fruit. After taking her seat, Bee looked across at him.

'I think the paparazzi would have a really hard time finding us here. It would take a machete just to get a look at the other customers.'

'I took a chance and booked a table this morning, hoping you'd say yes. I asked them to put us somewhere not too conspicuous and they took me at my word.'

'Well, thank you. This is perfectly—'

'*Ciao Barone, come stai, carissimo?*'

She was interrupted by the arrival of what was pretty obviously the owner. He was a big man with an even bigger smile on his face and he was wearing an immaculate chef's uniform, minus the hat. Bee saw Luke jump to his feet and the two men embrace warmly.

'*Ciao*, Michelangelo. It's so good to see you.'

Michelangelo kissed Luke nosily on the cheeks, but didn't release his grip on his shoulders.

'I haven't seen you for ages. Is everything all right?'

Bee saw Luke smile.

'Everything's fine now, Michelangelo.' For a second he glanced across at Bee. 'Really fine.'

Michelangelo released his hold on Luke and came round the table to shake her hand.

'Any friend of Luca's is a friend of mine.' He grinned. 'And so very beautiful.'

He stood and chatted for a few minutes and then, after he had gone back to the kitchen, Luke did a bit of explaining.

'Michelangelo and I go back a long way. We went to the same school until my father sent me off to that prison in England. Every summer holiday he and I would play together every day, and we've stayed close friends ever since.'

'So he knows your father?'

'And my grandfather, and Umberto and Ines. He's almost like my little brother.' He corrected himself. 'Well, quite big nowadays.'

'I notice he called you baron?'

Luke smiled again. 'He always does that just for laughs. The only baron was my grandfather. That's all over now.'

'Well, I think it sounds very grand. To be honest, seeing as Italy is a republic, I didn't think there were many aristocrats left.'

He smiled. 'You'd be surprised. Italy's not like France, you know. Nobody chopped any heads off, not even Mussolini. Poke about in the old castles and villas all over Italy and you'll run into more counts and princes than you can shake a stick at. And barons are two a penny. But that's all gone now. We're all just plain *Signore* and *Signora* these days, and that suits me just fine.'

The meal was predictably excellent. They started with a local speciality: slices of polenta, mixed with pieces of local ham and rosemary, fried in olive oil, and eaten with wild boar pâté. Luke chose lasagne with courgettes as his pasta course, while Bee had a fresh artichoke salad, and then they both had lamb chops grilled over charcoal as their main course. A bottle of red wine with no label appeared on the table and it was every bit as good as the Montegrifone wine.

As they ate, they chatted about everything from grapes to medieval history, but no mention was made of Luke's father, at least for now. After a while, Luke enquired gently what the doctor had said and Bee related the two choices she had been given.

'I told him I needed a bit of time to think about it and that I wanted to talk it through with friends first. Can I ask you what you think I should do?'

'Firstly, thanks for including me among your friends. Second, it's got to be your decision and yours alone. Don't let yourself be pressurised by family or colleagues into doing something you don't want to do.'

He took a mouthful of cold mineral water as he hunted for the right words.

'If you want my honest opinion, all I can tell you is that you are one of the most beautiful women I've ever met, and I mean as you are now. And I say that even though you're here alongside Mimi Robertson. Ask yourself whether you need to go through yet more surgery when you already look stunning.'

Bee felt herself flush with embarrassment.

'Thank you, Luke. That's so sweet. I'll tell you something: I've been doing a lot of thinking about my appearance over these past few weeks and I've finally realised that what counts is what's beneath the surface.' She took a deep breath and decided to take a chance. 'I was at your father's house yesterday and he really brought it home to me.'

She saw him look up in surprise, but she decided to carry on.

'He asked me to model for him – just my face – and to my amazement he painted me as I am, scars and all. It really got me thinking and the more I do, the more I'm coming round to deciding I'm not going to go through with any more surgery. This is the new me now. Take it or leave it.'

'It's your decision and yours alone but, for what it's worth, I'm with you on this. I'm sure you're doing the right thing.' There was a pause before he continued, a note of surprise in his voice. 'It's good to know my father's managed to be helpful to somebody at last.'

Chapter 17

As the long, sunny days continued and the stifling heat of August gripped Montegrifone, Bee's yoga continued to improve, her scars continued to fade, Mimi learnt her lines and they both managed to relax. She and the movie star were by now becoming ever closer friends and they talked about everything, including Luke. Bee repeated her rationale for not wanting to embark on a relationship with him, beguiling as this might appear, for fear of breaking his heart and hers in the process, and Mimi queried her decision.

'That's what you've decided, even though I'm sure he's crazy about you?'

Bee shook her head. 'I think he likes me a lot and I certainly like him, but from what Umberto has said, he's got too much on his plate at the moment and he's still bleeding from his fiancée's departure.'

'But he took you out to lunch and you say he turned up at the swimming pool. Surely that's a sign that he's moving on?'

Bee nodded slowly. 'I suppose so, but, to be completely honest, it's as much out of self-preservation as anything else. I feel convinced that if I let myself fall for him – and I know it wouldn't take much – I'll find it impossible to leave him when the time comes, so bang goes my career.

Would I be prepared to give that up? What worries me is the thought that I would almost certainly end up like his fiancée – isolated and bored – and it would all end in tears.' She took a deep breath. 'No, better to keep him at arms' length. For both of our sakes.'

Mimi nodded slowly. 'I get what you're saying, but I hope you know what you're doing. True love doesn't come round that often.'

Bee shook her head sadly and agreed, but her mind was made up. It was better this way – even though it was very, very frustrating.

She searched high and low for the long-lost painting or any residual treasure, but the only Martini she found was a dust-covered bottle of vermouth in a corner of the cellar, almost glued to the floor by a thick cloak of dusty cobwebs. The current owner of the cobwebs turned out to be a scary-looking, large, hairy spider who clearly took a dim view of being turned out of his home. Bee retreated in the face of his aggressive attitude and left it to Umberto to retrieve the old bottle. Alas, the contents turned out to have the consistency of swamp mud, with a smell to match. Otherwise, as far as treasure was concerned, she drew a blank.

As the end of their stay was fast approaching, Bee decided the time had come to risk going down to visit the farm shop in search of a few souvenirs. The shop had been one of Luke's innovations and it apparently sold all sorts, not just food and drink. Although she had been tempted to visit it earlier, natural prudence had stopped her, even though Umberto told her he had made sure nobody down there would give her away. Apparently he had told Loredana, the woman who ran it, that the guests at the villa were spies, or something equally sinister. Now, with just a few days to go, Bee reckoned she could take her chances.

The shop turned out to be a good bit bigger than she had expected and they had all manner of goods there, from whole legs of ham hanging from the ceiling to strawberries straight from the garden, still warm from the sun. There were two other customers in there when she arrived, but they had left by the time she had had a good look around and picked up a couple of lovely linen tea towels for her mum, and she was able to introduce herself to the matronly lady behind the cash desk. A badge on her ample bosom announced that this was Loredana.

'Hello, Loredana, my name's Beatrice. I'm staying up at the villa.' She wondered, with a little smile, if she had really believed Umberto's story about Mimi and herself being spies.

From Loredana's reaction, it appeared she had. No sooner had she heard where Bee was staying than she leapt out, remarkably nimbly, from behind the counter, caught Bee by the arm and almost dragged her through a multi-coloured plastic fly curtain out of the shop and into the storeroom. Once away from the non-existent prying eyes, Loredana greeted Bee in a hoarse whisper, her eyes darting apprehensively from side to side.

'Good morning, Signorina. Don't worry, your secret's safe with us.'

'Us?'

'Me and my daughter.' Loredana looked up and then almost deafened Bee as she hollered a few inches from her ear. 'Daniela, come in here. Quick.'

Bee was still trying to get the ringing out of her ear as a door at the end of the storeroom opened and a very pretty girl appeared.

'*Sì, mamma?*'

'Daniela, come and meet this young lady. Her name's Beatrice and...' Her voice dropped to a whisper once more. '...she's staying up at the villa.' She tapped the side of her nose in conspiratorial fashion.

Bee saw immediate comprehension in the girl's eyes.

'*Signorina, buongiorno.*'

'*Buongiorno, Daniela.* I'm pleased to meet you. Thank you both for keeping our presence here a secret.'

'That's quite all right.' Loredana answered for both of them, her tones still hushed. 'Now, is there anything we can do for you? Anything you need?'

'Not really. I just came down to pick up a couple of presents to take home with me.'

Loredana looked almost disappointed. Clearly, after what Umberto had told her, she had been expecting to be asked if she could procure some weapons-grade plutonium or a night sight for a sniper rifle. However, swallowing her disappointment, she smiled back.

'We look forward to seeing you any time, Signorina.'

Mimi and Bee both walked with the dog most days and swam regularly in the pool and they continued their historical excursions. Mimi's face was almost fully back to normal by now, but they both quite enjoyed the cloak and dagger element of these trips, Mimi evidently relishing being anonymous in the midst of the crowds of tourists when the two of them slipped incognito into wonderful old places like Pienza and Montepulciano. Hiding in plain sight was what she called it and she went out of her way to look as drab and uninteresting as possible. Even so, Bee soon lost count of the number of admiring looks they both received from Italian men of all ages. Clearly, the men around here had x-ray eyes. Still, nobody appeared to recognise Mimi for who she was and that was the object of the exercise.

One day, as they were sitting under a large parasol outside a little trattoria just up the hill from the beautiful abbey of Sant'Antimo, Bee's phone rang. It was Gayle, ringing from America with stimulating news.

'Hi, Bee. How's it going?'

Bee gave her an upbeat account of their progress and Gayle sounded genuinely pleased for both of them.

'That's terrific news. Is Mimi there? Have you ladies an idea how long you want to stay at the villa? It's booked until the end of August, but if you need it longer, just say the word.'

Bee and Mimi had been talking about this very subject that morning in the car and Mimi had indicated she would probably have to head back to LA towards the end of the month, and that was barely a couple of weeks away now. Bee relayed this to Gayle, after which Gayle came to the really interesting part of the conversation.

'The other reason I'm calling, Bee, is to let you know I might have found you a job.'

Bee sat up so abruptly, her knee hit the underside of the metal table and she spilled her mineral water. As it dripped through the mesh table top onto her thigh, she sat back and listened with rapt enthusiasm.

'Have you heard of *History of the World TV*? It's a new channel being set up as we speak. It goes live in October, I believe. The clue's in the name. You can guess what it's going to be all about. I was talking to one of the senior Vice Presidents last night at a thing here in Hollywood. When I mentioned your name and how great you'd been for us in Siena, he almost bit my hand off. He said they're actively looking for somebody with your background and qualifications to work alongside the commissioning editor, vetting programmes and pitches that are proposed to them. Might you be interested?'

Bee could hardly contain her excitement. 'It's lucky this is a phone call or I might just bite *your* hand off, Gayle. It sounds amazing.'

'Well, listen. The guy'll be in Rome at the end of this week and he's asked me to fix up an interview with him there if you're interested.'

'*If* I'm interested...?'

'That's what I thought. I'll get on it and email you the details. No promises, but like I said he sounded very keen.'

Bee's mind was racing. 'Thank you so very much, Gayle. Have you any idea where the job would be? Where's their centre of operations?'

'Just a few blocks away from our building in LA, but he was making noises about a European base as well. Get all your questions ready and see what he says.'

'That's amazing, Gayle. Thank you oh so very much.'

After ringing off, Bee passed the good news on to Mimi, who looked and sounded delighted for her.

'That's terrific, Bee. Being selfish, I hope the job's in LA. That way you and I could carry on hanging out together.'

Bee grinned at her. 'That would be really great, although part of me rather wishes it might be a bit closer.'

'Closer to where?' Mimi knew her too well by now. 'Closer to your mum and dad, closer to London or, maybe, just maybe, closer to a certain hunky farmer?'

Bee blushed. She saw Luke on average every other day and he always stopped and chatted. There was no doubt that the two of them got on very well together and her attraction to him was increasing, rather than decreasing, but she stuck by her resolve not to leap into a relationship, however tempted she might be, because she knew she was going to have to go off and leave him. She felt sure this would break his heart. And what was ever more certain was that it would break hers at the same time. It was quite clear he could never move away from Montegrifone. It had been in his family for so many generations and he belonged to it just as much as it belonged to him. Sadly, it was equally clear that there weren't any jobs for lecturers in Medieval History in the middle of the Tuscan countryside. It had been tough for her and maybe for him as well, although so far he'd kept his feelings well hidden. He was no fool, and if she could work out that there was no future for the two of them together, no doubt he had done exactly the same.

'I'm not going to count my chickens as far as this job's concerned. I'll go and talk to the man in Rome and see what he says.'

–

The email from Gayle arrived the next day, giving the details of the interview time and location. It would take place in a hotel bang in the centre of Rome, in Via Nazionale, at two o'clock on Friday. As a PS, Gayle had added, *Don't take less than a hundred grand, and if you're coming over here to work in LA, make sure you tell him you need dental and medical as well.*

Once Bee had got over the shock of realising that a hundred thousand dollars would be twice what she was currently earning as a lecturer, she hurried off to tell Mimi, who was very supportive and helped her a lot in her preparations over the next few days. As the new channel would presumably be dealing with all eras of world history, Mimi became question master. With her laptop open in front of her, she quizzed Bee on everything from the cave paintings of Lascaux to the D-Day landings. She also gave her some fascinating tips on body language and put Bee through her paces on how to walk into the room, stand and sit. A lot of this was completely new to Bee who, up to then, had just assumed that walking was walking and sitting, sitting. Clearly she was wrong.

By the time Friday morning came and Bee drove up to Siena to catch the train to Rome, she was as well-prepared as she could be. The train was comfortable and not too packed and she got to Rome with a couple of hours to spare. Keen to see as much of the Eternal City as possible, she took the bus down to the Colosseum and then walked slowly back from there. She had only been to Rome once before, very briefly for a conference, and she was soon in a sort of historical haze as she came across magnificent buildings, statues and landmarks dating back hundreds, if not thousands, of years. By the time she got to the very posh hotel where the interview would take place, she was still in a state of suspended animation.

When she spoke to Mimi about it afterwards, she found it hard to recall exactly what the Vice President, 'Call me Leonard', had said to her, or what questions he had asked. The upshot had been a promise to get back to her in a few days. He hadn't committed himself, but she definitely got the impression she had done all right in the interview. The one thing she did remember to ask was where this job might be situated. His reply, however, had been opaque. As Gayle had said, the new channel's centre of operations was indeed in LA, but they were 'evaluating the advisability' of setting up a European base. All would, apparently, come clear in the promised email.

As they sat out in the garden that evening watching the sun drop towards the horizon and sipping ice cold rosé, Mimi raised a potential problem.

'Say they offer you the job, Bee, what about your lecturing position? Can you get out of that at the last minute? It's probably only a month or so now before the new term starts, isn't it?'

'I've already thought of that. I contacted the HR department the other day as soon as I heard from Gayle, and they've basically said they'll leave it up to me.' She glanced across at her friend. 'They have definitely got a very guilty conscience about the way I've been treated, so they won't make a fuss. She also said they'd give me a glowing reference.'

'I should think so too. So you're good to go, then?'

'Well, let's see if he sends me the promised email first.'

After dinner that night, Mimi felt her appearance had improved sufficiently for her to have her first conference call with Hollywood, so Bee left her to it and went for a walk. The sky was clear and the sun had set by now. Instead of blue, the sky above her was now purple, and the swallows wheeling overhead had been replaced by bats. Although she was on her own, Bee felt quite safe and secure here at Montegrifone. By now she had learnt the names of all the different hills, copses and fields. She knew which vines were Merlot, which Cabernet Sauvignon and which were Malvasia. She even knew the names of some of Berlusconi's companions, and she could recognise Hercules, the big black and white bull who lived down by the river. They say familiarity breeds contempt, but that wasn't the way she saw it.

For a change, she walked down the track in the direction of Luke's house, the white surface of the *strada bianca* reflecting the moonlight and showing her the way. As she passed the olive groves, she suddenly spotted a dark shadow on the road ahead. She stopped and smiled in the darkness.

'*Ciao*, Romeo, how are you tonight?'

Strangely, the figure didn't move, so she raised her voice as she walked towards it.

'Romeo, is that you?'

She was within twenty or thirty paces when she realised this wasn't a familiar figure after all. At that same moment, so did the animal ahead of her. There was a rapid movement as it leapt to its feet, gave a guttural snort, and she clearly made out the unmistakable shape of a very large pig-like animal outlined against the white of the *strada bianca*. The beast stood there, motionless, for what was probably only a matter of a few seconds, but that to Bee felt like an eternity. Memories of what she had been told about how dangerous wild boar could be came flooding back and she was petrified. Then, mercifully, just as the tension was becoming unbearable, it turned and charged off into the olive grove.

She could feel cold sweat running down the back of her neck as she listened to the heavy animal's noisy progress across the field away from her. She was still standing stock still, waiting for her racing heart to slow down when she suddenly heard more noise and saw another dark shape in the road ahead. Two shapes. Her heart gave another somersault and she was about to turn and run when she heard his voice.

'Bee, is that you?'

Just in case she might be in any doubt, seconds later, a very bouncy Labrador arrived ahead of his master. Bee was so relieved to see them, she ran up to Luke and took refuge in his arms, burying her head in his chest. She felt him catch her protectively round the shoulders and heard his voice at her ear. He sounded very concerned.

'What's wrong, Bee? What's happened? Are you all right?'

She hung onto him for a few more seconds before pulling herself together again. At her side, she could feel the reassuring presence of the dog. Reluctantly, she relinquished her hold on Luke and stepped back, reaching down to stroke Romeo's head as she did so. She felt Luke's hands on her shoulders, steadying her, and she saw the moonlight reflect in his eyes right in front of her. Clearing her throat, she explained what she had just seen. He listened intently before answering.

'I've been afraid of that. The grapes are getting quite big now and this is when the wild boar start coming in. We did a tour of the perimeter fences a few days ago and we've identified a number of breaks. They should all be fixed in the next few days but, in the meantime, it might be better if you stay around the villa at night, or give me a call. I'd be happy to come for a walk with you. Romeo and I would make sure nothing happened to you.'

'I'm sure you would. Thanks for the help, Luke. Sorry for the maiden in distress act. It was just such a shock. I hadn't realised they were so big.'

'They're big all right, and they can be dangerous. You'll be fine during the day, but, like I say, give it a few days before you come out alone at night again.' Sensing that she was all right again, he released his grip on her shoulders and stepped back, leaving her with a sensation of regret. 'Anyway, Romeo and I are here now. If you'd like a bit of company, it's a beautiful night for a walk.'

'I'd love that, Luke. And here I was thinking how comfortable and safe I feel here.'

'And you are. It's a damn sight safer than some parts of London at this time of night, I'm sure. So, how was your trip to Rome?'

Bee recounted her experiences as they walked slowly back in the direction of the villa and he sounded pleased for her. Up to a point.

'So you might find yourself moving to the US? That's a long way away.'

The same thought had occurred to her.

'That's not definite. He did say they were thinking about setting up a European base somewhere.'

'It would be good if you were close by.'

She could hear something in his voice. Emotion, maybe?

'I'd like to stay close by, too, but it's out of my hands.'

'Romeo's going to miss you when you've gone, Bee.' She sensed a moment's hesitation. 'I'm going to miss you.'

Bee stopped and turned towards him. 'I'm going to miss you, too, Luke. A lot.'

There was silence between them, broken only by the croaking of frogs in the dried-up stream bed. They stood like that for some time, close enough to touch, but not touching. She wasn't sure what was going to happen, but if he were to sweep her into his arms and kiss her, she knew she wouldn't object – far from it. For a moment, she thought about making the first move, but the memory of his pained expression reminded her that it wouldn't be fair on either of them.

Finally, he found his voice.

'Having you here has been wonderful, Bee. You've brought me happiness and, from what you've told me, you've maybe done the same for my father. Thank you so much. I'll never forget you.'

Those final four words said it all. The message was clear. He was saying goodbye. Somehow, hearing him say it brought home to her just how much she was going to miss him and this magical place, and she felt a rush of emotion. She hastily dropped down on one knee and hugged the Labrador with both arms for quite some time. When she stood back up again, the moment had passed and she was in control once again. She reached up and kissed him briefly on the cheeks.

'And I'll never, ever, forget you, Luke.' For a moment, her resolve wavered. 'If things had been different...' She heard her voice waver and he can't have missed it. She felt his hands reach for the sides of her head and hold her tightly right in front of him. Then he dipped forward and let his lips rest on hers for a millisecond, before releasing her and stepping back.

'I'll walk you to the door.'

As they climbed back up the hill to the villa, Bee had a thought. She glanced across at him, seeing his eyes flash in the moonlight.

'Could I ask you something, Luke?'

'Of course. Anything.'

'You know you said I've brought happiness to the valley? Well, you know what would make *me* very, very happy would be if you felt like sitting down and talking to your father.' Sensing his reserve, she carried on quickly. 'I've started getting to know him a bit now and I get the impression he's not really a bad man.' She smiled at him in the dark. Even if he couldn't see it on her face, he would hear it in her voice. 'Would you do that? As a favour to me if for no other reason.'

By this time they had reached the lawn and the security lights came on, revealing him clearly. He blinked a couple of times and looked down at her.

'I'd do anything for you, Bee. Believe me. But there's so much history, so much mistrust, so much hurt between us, I think you're asking the impossible. Not of me. I promise you I'm prepared to sit down with him and talk, but from what I know of the man, he'll say no.'

'So, you're saying that if I can get him to come and talk, you'll do the same?'

'That's right but, Bee, don't hold your breath. I've been fighting this particular battle for the last twenty-five years.'

'Thank you, Luke. That makes me very happy.'

To prove it, she kissed him again, chastely, on the cheeks before heading for the door.

'Goodnight, Luke.'

'Goodnight, Bee.'

Chapter 18

The next day, she and Romeo went down to see Riccardo. She found him with a brush in one hand, no doubt hard at work. He invited her in, but she hesitated.

'Only if I won't disturb you. If you're busy, Romeo and I can go for a walk.'

He shook his head. 'Come in, come in. It'll be nice to have some company. And it's good to see the dog again. We always used to have one in the house. My wife was crazy about dogs... well, all animals really.'

'But you've not thought about having one since?'

He caught her eye and she saw the same expression of sadness she had noted on his son's face. 'Memories, Bee, memories.'

They went through to his studio, where he was working on another new canvas, this time a complex, almost geometrical composition of rows of vines crisscrossing. It was delightful. Bee sat down on a stool to one side and watched him work in silence while the dog stretched out with a heartfelt sigh on the cool terracotta floor. After a bit, she told him about her lunch with Luke the previous week. At first, Riccardo made no comment, but some time later he brought up the subject again by himself.

'Where did Luke take you for lunch? To Michelangelo's I bet.'

'That's right. He told me they're old friends and he said you know him too.'

'I've known Michelangelo since he was tiny.' He gave a little smile. 'I believe he's filled out a bit since then.'

Bee nodded. 'Indeed. When's the last time you saw him?'

Riccardo paused for a moment. 'It must be twenty-five years ago… longer. He was just a boy.'

'So you haven't been to his restaurant?'

'Oh, I've been there all right, but it was long time ago. My wife and I often went there in the days when his father was running the place. I haven't been back since her death.'

Bee gave him an encouraging smile and he rallied, glancing at his watch. It was eleven o'clock. He rested his brush on the edge of the palette and looked up at her.

'Do you have any objection to drinking in the morning?'

'It depends what I'm being given to drink.'

'Champagne.'

She grinned and nodded her head. 'There's no wrong time for drinking champagne.'

'Excellent. There's a bottle in the fridge and you know your way round the glasses in the kitchen by now. Would you mind going and fetching them.'

Bee needed no further encouragement. As she hunted for suitable glasses, she wondered if there might be a special reason for this.

When she got back to his studio, she soon found out that there was.

He made short work of opening the bottle and filling two glasses. As he handed one across to her, she saw his eyes twinkle.

'The reason we're drinking champagne is because I've got some news to celebrate.'

Bee clutched her glass and listened attentively.

'I took a photo of the portrait you so kindly sat for and sent it to my agent. We've barely been in contact for God knows how long and it turns out he now has offices in London, Zurich *and* New York. Business must be good. Anyway, it's certainly the first painting I've sent him for a couple of years, maybe longer. He replied immediately. He loves it and wants me to take it over to him. He says he's got people queuing up for my work.'

Bee smiled broadly and reached across to clink her glass against his. This was excellent news on many levels. He was painting again. His work was still in demand. And, in particular, he was telling her about it. Seeing as he had been living more or less as a hermit, virtually without communicating with anybody, she felt honoured and delighted for him. Hopefully he was coming out from underneath his pall of gloom. After swallowing a mouthful, she decided to go for it. Nothing ventured, nothing gained.

'I was speaking to Luke last night, Riccardo. He told me he'd like to sit down and talk to you.' She kept the fingers of her free hand crossed behind her back. This wasn't exactly what Luke had said, but it would do. It was a while before he replied.

'You're wrong, you know, Bee. He'd never do that. He hates me.'

It was all so Shakespearian somehow, a family torn apart by death and desertion. And pig-headed stubbornness. To say she felt mixed loyalties was an understatement. Still, she did her best to act as mediator.

'He doesn't hate you, Riccardo. He told me that. What he said was that he lost his mother and then his father as well, just when he needed him most, and he had a very tough time growing up as a result. I'm sure you must have had your reasons for doing what you did, but surely you can imagine the impact it must have had on a young boy. He needed a father...' She held her breath, fearing an outburst. She was, after all, meddling in something that was no business of hers. She took a big mouthful of wine and let the bubbles fizz over her tongue before swallowing.

He picked up the bottle and topped up their two glasses in silence. She could see that this was a displacement activity to give himself time to think and she made no sound, not even to say thank you. Finally, after setting the bottle back on the ground at his feet, he started to talk.

'I loved Elizabeth, Luke's mother, more than anything in the world. Standing by helplessly as I watched her fade away and die was the hardest thing I've ever done and I wouldn't wish it on anybody. After her death, I was drained, empty, lost. Everything I saw around here, including my son, reminded me of her and it was driving me crazy.'

Bee reached across and caught hold of his hand, but he didn't seem to notice.

'I knew I needed time to get over her death. I sent Luca off to school in England as it was what his mother would have wanted.' He stopped, his eyes staring blankly across the room into the distance. 'She always said she wanted him to be educated in England. Then, as soon as I knew he was settled, I barricaded myself in here. I couldn't face the idea of meeting anybody, anybody at all.'

'I heard that you'd had some kind of breakdown. Is that right? You must have been traumatised.'

His head turned slowly towards her and she saw his eyes focus once more.

'I must have gone a bit crazy, I suppose. You know something, Bee? I have absolutely no memory of the first few years after Elizabeth's death. It's all gone. Wiped. Looking back on it now, I know I should have sought medical help, but, way back then, that never occurred to me. By the time I came out of whatever I'd been going through, as far as my relationship with Luke was concerned it was too late. He was away at school or staying up at the villa with my father and I never saw him. Things weren't much better with my father. We rarely saw each other and we argued when we did. He told me to speak to Luke, but I didn't have the nerve. I said I'd wait for Luke to come to me and, of course, he didn't. And I don't blame him.'

He shook his head ruefully.

'The thing is, Bee, I always was a pretty awful father. All that counted for me was my beloved Elizabeth and my art. I never did the sort of stuff normal fathers do with their kids. No games of football or fishing trips, and I never had any interest in farming, winemaking or the estate. Luke was always closer to his grandfather than he was to me. I don't blame him for not wanting to have anything to do with somebody like me.'

Bee could hardly believe her ears. How stubborn could people be? Surely, after everything he had gone through,

Riccardo should have been able to speak to his son, and his son to him? Not for the first time, Bee thanked her lucky stars for having had the good fortune to be born into a relatively *normal* family, however frustrated she might become with her mother from time to time.

'You're still his father and you really should speak to him, you know. If you just tell him what you've told me, I'm sure he'll understand.' She took another mouthful of champagne. 'Anyway, that's up to you and it's no business of mine, but why don't you meet him one evening for a glass of something? I told Luke I was coming to see you and he said he'd meet you if you agreed.'

Riccardo looked up sharply. 'You sure he said that?'

'Yes. But I won't say anything to him until I hear from you.' She finished her drink and stood up, conscious that he had a lot to think about. 'Anyway, I mustn't stop you working.'

She leant over and kissed him on the cheek.

'Just think about it, all right?'

He caught hold of her hand and squeezed it, but he didn't reply.

–

A couple of days later, Bee and Mimi went for an early morning walk accompanied, as usual, by the Labrador. It was mid-August now and the temperature was so high during the middle part of the day that both of them preferred to stay indoors. Dark clouds ringed the horizon and Bee had enough experience of the valley now to recognise that rain was on the way almost inevitably accompanied by thunder. She kept her fingers crossed that there wouldn't be any damaging hail to ruin the grape harvest.

They set off down the track in the direction of the *Grifoncella*. As they walked, they chatted. Mimi was now in regular video contact with Hollywood and she relayed the news that the film she had been making that winter in Yorkshire would be having its premiere in London in the autumn.

'I'll make sure you get an invitation. I don't know how long I'll be in London for, but at least, it'll give us a chance to catch up.'

'Thanks a lot. That sounds like fun. Mind you, for all I know, I might be living in LA by then.'

'Still no email?'

Bee shook her head. It was almost a week now and the waiting was starting to get on her nerves. The end of August was approaching fast and she still didn't know what she would be doing next month. It was frustrating, to say the least.

Mimi smiled and Bee could see she was trying to cheer her up. 'Well, if you're in LA, you can fly over to London for the premiere with me in my plane. There'll be bags of room.'

That also sounded like fun. Bee found herself smiling back, in spite of the uncertainty about her future.

'Anybody else likely to be flying with you?' She gave Mimi a knowing look.

'Joey, you mean? Well, to be honest, I just spoke to him this morning and he said he's coming over again to see us.'

'Us or you?' Bee grinned.

'He said us.'

'He meant you.'

Mimi had the grace to look slightly embarrassed. 'Whatever. Anyway, seeing as we're almost at the end of our stay, I thought I might take him out for dinner just before we leave, if I can squeeze him into the 500. Even if we're recognised, by the time the paparazzi get wind of it, I should be on my way back to the States again. That place you went to with Luke sounded gorgeous. Maybe you'd give me the details.'

'I don't really know, but you never know, Luke might still be home. It *is* early, after all. We'll be at the *Grifoncella* in a few minutes and we can ask him for the contact details.'

When they got to Luke's house, she was in for a surprise. As they turned the corner, they were just in time to see pretty, dark-haired Daniela from the farm shop emerge from Luke's door and climb onto an old bike. As the girl cycled off down the track, Bee and Mimi stopped and exchanged glances. It was barely eight o'clock in the morning and Daniela was leaving. Could it be she had spent the night there? A sensation swept through Bee that wasn't hard to identify. She was actually jealous, even though she knew there could never be anything between her and Luke.

'Maybe she does the cleaning for him.' Mimi was once more doing her best to be supportive.

Shaking her head in a vain attempt to rid it of such thoughts, Bee went in through the gate and walked up to the front door, followed by Mimi. She couldn't see a bell, so she rapped on it with her knuckles as the dog stood poised, tail wagging hopefully, his nose at the crack of the door. They had to wait almost a minute and they were about to turn and leave when there were noises inside and the door opened.

Luke was looking flushed.

'Bee, Mimi, hi. Sorry to keep you waiting. For a moment there, I thought Romeo had discovered how to knock on the door.'

He was wearing a T-shirt that stuck to his damp chest and his hair was still running with water. He looked particularly cheerful this morning and Bee's antennae bristled.

'Hi, Luke. Did we catch you at a bad time?'

'I'm sorry to keep you waiting outside the door, but I'd just leapt into the shower. Would you like to come in?'

By this time Romeo had pushed past him into the house, so they followed him inside, hearing the door close behind them.

'Just go straight through to the kitchen if that's all right with you. Just follow the dog.'

Bee glanced around as they walked along the corridor as directed. It was remarkably cool in here, presumably due to the shade provided by the big trees in the garden behind the house. The floors were old terracotta, the beams supporting the ceilings were tree trunks, and the kitchen was a delight. Like his father's at the *Podere Nuovo*, Luke's was still very traditional-looking, except for a battery of modern units and no fewer than three ovens along one wall. Clearly somebody liked cooking. Or somebody had liked cooking.

'Coffee? I was just about to make myself an espresso. Or would you prefer a cappuccino? Will you join me? This machine makes pretty good coffee.' Luke came in after them and indicated they should take a seat at the huge old table.

'A cappuccino would be lovely, thanks.' Mimi, realising Bee was struggling, stepped in. 'Same for you, Bee?'

Bee nodded and sat down as Mimi went on to explain about Joey's impending arrival and Luke supplied her with details of the website and directions as to how to get to Michelangelo's restaurant.

As he passed on the information and busied himself with the coffee machine, Bee looked around and stroked the dog who had come over to sit by her, leaning against her knees, his nose on her lap. She gazed down at him as she ruffled his ears, still trying to come to terms with the fact that Luke would appear to have found somebody after all. Mind you, she told herself firmly, it made a lot of sense for him to find himself a partner here in the valley, seeing as he would never want to leave. Nevertheless, however logical that argument might sound, it didn't make it easier for her to accept.

Luke's voice was gradually drowned out by the sound of the milk heating up. He worked quickly, his back towards them, before completing his task and turning towards them with two big frothy cups of coffee and a plate of what looked like homemade biscuits.

'These are fresh this morning. Loredana makes them. You've been to the farm shop, haven't you? You must have met her. Her daughter, Daniela, dropped them in just before you arrived and they're still warm.' He looked a bit bashful. 'It's my birthday, you see.'

'Congratulations. Many happy returns, Luke.' Mimi jumped up and kissed him on the cheeks, shooting a jubilant look across at Bee as she did so. They really did know each other very well by now.

A flood of relief swept over Bee as she heard that the pretty girl from the farm shop hadn't spent the night with him after all and she too stood up and hurried round the table towards him. Taking him by the shoulders, she pulled his head down towards her so she could kiss him on the cheeks.

'A very happy birthday, Luke.'

For a moment their eyes met and then, by mutual agreement, they both looked away again. He mumbled his thanks and turned back to get his own cup, while Bee and Mimi returned to their seats. As he sat down opposite them, Bee gave him a smile.

'Dare I ask? Twenty-one again, or is it twenty-two now?'

He smiled back. 'Thirty-six, but who's counting? I imagine that makes me about ten years older than either of you.'

Mimi declined to comment, but Bee's smile broadened. 'I wish. I'll be thirty-two next April.'

He was tactful enough to look surprised. 'You're looking good, Bee.'

Beside her Mimi agreed. 'Isn't she?' She glanced at Bee. 'The scars are disappearing by the day.'

'Mimi's right, Bee. And your hair's growing really fast. If you end up in Hollywood, you'll take the place by storm.' Ignoring her blushes, he continued. 'Any word about the job yet?'

She shook her head. 'It's only a matter of days now before we leave. It would be nice to know where I'm going.'

Chapter 19

That afternoon, as distant clouds began to bubble up all around and the humidity reached unbearable levels, Bee decided to go for a swim. Mimi was locked away in her room doing yoga and skyping, quite possibly with Joey, so Bee went by herself. As she left the house, she made a spur of the moment decision to go via the little church. She had enjoyed the sense of peace she had felt in there last time and she knew she wanted to go back before their time in the valley ended.

She bumped into Romeo down at the river. He was lying in one of the last remaining pools in the dried-up river bed, with just his nose above the water, looking more like a seal than a dog. He was only too pleased to join her as she climbed the hill. In spite of the approaching clouds, the sun still beat down unmercifully and by the time they got up to the little church, she could feel sweat running down her back. She pushed the door open and followed Romeo inside.

The sun was shining in through the stained-glass window at the far end of the church at such an angle that it spread a multi-coloured stain across the altar and onto the floor. She sat down in the front row, her feet coloured blue and purple by the sunlight, and the dog thudded down at her feet, stretching out luxuriously on the cool floor tiles, grunting happily to himself. She wasn't a religious person, but it felt very peaceful in here and a sense of serenity gradually enveloped her. She closed her eyes and let her mind whirl.

Returning to London and her old job would be so very different. And if, by any chance, she were to get the TV job, it would be even more of a change. A move across to the other side of the world would be a massive undertaking.

She stretched out a foot and rubbed the dog's tummy, eliciting a sigh of satisfaction from him. She glanced down and, once again, she distinctly got the feeling he winked at her.

'I'm going to miss you, dog.'

And not just him. Of course, there was Luke. She knew she had fallen for this kind, handsome and troubled man, but they were irrevocably divided by her career and his attachment to Montegrifone. The strength of her jealousy this morning when she had wrongly imagined he had hooked up with Daniela was the proof of just how deeply he had got under her skin. Leaving him, even though nothing had happened between them, would be tougher by far than her separation from Jamie.

She was still turning this all over in her head when she heard the sound of a powerful engine approaching. This roused her and the dog and they went out to see who it was. As she closed the church door behind her, she looked round and saw Luke driving a massive silver tractor and trailer, accompanied by the usual cloud of dust. Romeo, recognising his master, went running out to greet him, tail-wagging. Bee followed suit, although she kept any tail-wagging to a minimum. Luke switched off the engine and opened the side door of the cab, jumping easily to the ground. As he scratched the dog's ears, he looked across at Bee.

'I spotted you and Romeo a few minutes ago when you were climbing the hillside and I remembered I'd promised you a ride in my Lamborghini.' He gave her a broad grin and she found herself smiling back at him. 'Mine's maybe not quite as fast as Joey's, but it's a lot more practical.'

She went across to him and kissed him on the cheeks. It was really good to see him.

'*Ciao*, Luke. Thank you for the thought.'

'A promise is a promise. Where are you off to now?'

'I was just thinking about taking Romeo for a swim in the pool. It's really hot today and I might well join him. I don't know how you can bear being inside that glass bubble on top of the tractor.'

He grinned again. 'Aircon. Here, I'll give you a lift down the hill and you can see for yourself.'

He turned towards the tractor and gave a whistle. The dog immediately leapt to his feet and followed him to the trailer. Luke undid the back of it and Romeo jumped up, standing there, tongue out, wagging his tail excitedly. Luke returned to the tractor and beckoned to Bee.

'Here, I'll help you up.' He held out his hand towards her.

Bee came over, took his hand willingly and let him guide her up and into the cab. To her surprise, it was remarkably cool inside. He showed her how to perch on a sort of shelf alongside him while he climbed up after her and slid into the driver's seat, pulling the door closed behind him.

'You going to be comfortable enough up there?'

'I can always hang onto you if it gets bumpy.' Secretly, she found herself rather hoping it would get bumpy.

He started the engine and she immediately noticed two things. First, it was far less noisy in there than she had expected and second, the air conditioning really did work well. She felt a cool breeze sweep over her, bringing welcome relief from the heat. With a practised action, he swung the huge vehicle and its trailer round in a wide circle and set off back down the track again. The cab swayed a bit, but Bee hung on to the edge of the seat, rather than his broad shoulders, although she was sorely tempted. She had resisted temptation so far. It would be a pity to spoil her record in the last few days.

In a matter of minutes, they were back down onto the road and shortly after that he turned off onto another dusty track that Bee recognised as leading to the pool. She glanced back over her shoulder and saw the happy Labrador, firmly planted on his four feet, nose sniffing the air and his tail wagging, no doubt fully aware where they were headed. Finally, as they reached the edge of the trees, Luke slowed and stopped, reaching forward to switch off the engine. In the sudden silence he turned towards her.

'This is as far as I can take the tractor, but you know where you are, don't you?' Bee nodded. 'I'd love to come and join you in the pool, but they're waiting for me back at the farm.'

Bee felt a little stab of disappointment. Seeing him without his shirt on for one last time would have been good, but maybe it was for the best. There was a limit to just how much willpower a girl could muster, after all.

'Well, thank you for the ride. I'm very impressed with your Lamborghini. That's something I can tick off my bucket list.'

She followed him out of the cab and jumped the last few feet to the ground. He caught her in his arms and steadied her. Her self-control faced another challenge as she bounced up against his chest. Seemingly unaware of her internal turmoil, he stepped back, released his hold and went over to the trailer to let the dog jump out. She found herself laughing as Romeo did exactly what she had done and launched himself bodily into his master's arms. Luke caught him easily and lowered him to the ground before returning to the tractor. As he swung himself back up into the cab, he gave her a lazy wave of the hand.

'Enjoy your swim, Bee.'

'Thanks, Luke.'

Yes, she really was going to miss him.

–

When she got back to the villa, she was in for two surprises. The first came from Mimi, who was sitting out in the garden, engrossed in her reading. As the dog ran over to nuzzle her, she looked up and saw Bee.

'Have you read this, Bee?'

There was no doubt about it. What Mimi was holding in her hands was Jamie's screenplay, *A Big Mistake*.

'I don't think so. I don't recognise the title. He said it was a new one, so probably not. Why do you ask? Is it okay?'

Mimi's face split into a grin. 'It's more than okay. I love it. I really do. But I think you should read it.'

'Jamie'll be really pleased to hear that. Pass it on to me when you finish it. I'll take a look at it.' It occurred to her that Jamie was going to freak out when he heard that Mimi Robertson, no less, liked his work.

'I've already read it once. I'm almost through reading it a second time.' Mimi was still grinning. 'I'll give it to you this evening. Somehow, I think you'll find it interesting. Very interesting indeed.'

The second surprise was the arrival of the email from Call-me-Leonard at HOWTV. Bee clicked on it and read it eagerly. Two things immediately became clear. They were offering her the job of Associate Commissioning Editor and this was at a salary that was even more than Gayle had said. Bee was flabbergasted and found herself doing a mad little dance around her room, squeaking to herself in delight. Finally, she settled back down again and read it through to the end. The last paragraph was of considerable interest.

> After a lot of deliberation – thanks, again, for your patience, Beatrice – we have decided to establish a European hub. If you accept this offer, in the first instance we would like you to come here to our head office in LA as soon as possible for four weeks so as to familiarize yourself fully with our aims and ethos, after which we would anticipate your being based back in Europe. We are currently in negotiations about a number of possible locations. The shortlist currently includes Zurich, Brussels and London, although this list is not exhaustive. A decision will be taken

very soon and we will, of course, inform you
as soon as it is decided.

Bee picked up her laptop and dashed back down the stairs. As she reached the kitchen, she found Ines and Umberto by the sink. She rushed over to the bemused pair and hugged them warmly, kissing them on the cheeks. She carried on towards the back door, stopping briefly on the doorstep to call back over her shoulder.

'Umberto, if you can find a bottle of fizz, now would be the perfect moment to open it.'

She ran down the steps and out to where Mimi and Romeo were curled up side by side on the rattan sofa. She opened the laptop and brandished it under Mimi's nose.

'It's arrived, Mimi! They've offered me the job.'

Mimi took the laptop from her and read it through carefully before looking up, a beaming smile on her face.

'That's fabulous, Bee. Really well done. I bet you're pleased.'

'Over the moon.'

At that moment Umberto came out with an ice bucket and a bottle of champagne. He had only brought two glasses, but Bee hurried back into the kitchen and brought out two more, along with a bewildered Ines. As she poured the champagne for the four of them, Bee outlined what she had just been told and she saw genuine pleasure on the faces of the old couple. Even Romeo came over and stood up on his hind legs to add his congratulations. Behind him, Mimi had a practical suggestion.

'When you go back to them, get them to email you the contract. If you like, I can get my legal team to give it the once over.'

Bee was still grinning stupidly. 'That would be great. Thanks so much, Mimi. Are you going to be in LA next month? Hopefully we can meet up.'

'I can do better than that, Bee. You can come and stay with me.'

Bee's eyes opened wide. 'I couldn't possibly.'

Mimi patted her on the arm. 'Bee, I live in a house with twelve bedrooms. At the moment, there's only me, Mary Jane the housekeeper, Howard my butler, driver and security guard, and a guy who comes in to skim the pool and cut the grass. I've enjoyed your company here. I'll enjoy it there. That's if you want to.'

'Of course I want to. That's amazing. Thank you so very, very much.' Bee could hardly get her head around the realisation that this wasn't just any old friend offering her a bed for a few nights, but an invitation to sample the kind of lifestyle ninety-nine point nine per cent of the world's population could only imagine and envy. It still felt incredible that she and Mimi had become such good friends.

That evening, after a bit too much champagne and rosé, Bee found herself back in her room lying in bed with Jamie's manuscript. She took a bottle of mineral water out of the fridge and settled down to read his screenplay.

It was well past midnight by the time she finished it and there had been an expression of disbelief on her face since the second page. It was remarkably well written, but that wasn't it. It was the story of a thirty-something man, Johnnie, whose obsession with his career had made him neglect and finally split up with his stunningly beautiful – Bee rather liked the sound of that – girlfriend. Her name was Dee and she was a famous fashion model. It was only after the break-up that he came to realise just what he had done and what he was missing, so he set about trying to get her back and followed her to a host of exotic locations, including a vineyard in Italy.

The story concluded with an emotionally charged scene on a beach on a Greek island that almost had Bee in tears. By this time Johnnie had become quite desperate and when he saw Dee with a handsome male model named Gérard, he feared the worst. He climbed to the top of a cliff, high above the Aegean, maybe even ready to fling himself over the edge. Luckily for him, however, this was a romantic comedy and the Dee character climbed up after him and resolved everything with a passionate kiss and a happy ending.

Bee finally set the manuscript down and lay back against the pillow, totally astounded. In all the years she had known Jamie, she had genuinely never believed he had a single romantic bone in his body. And this film, if it ever got made, would be absolutely dripping with romance. Apart from anything else, this confirmed without a doubt that Jamie's visit to Montegrifone had not just been to bring over his screenplay for Mimi. He really had been trying to get Bee back.

What, she wondered to herself as her eyes grew heavy and she drifted off to sleep, was she supposed to do about him now?

Chapter 20

At the end of their stay, to thank everybody at Monte-grifone before leaving and to celebrate their return to health, Mimi and Bee decided to throw a party for all the people they had met here and to thank them for keeping their presence a secret all this time. Mimi prepared the invitations while Bee went to the farm shop and bought all the food and drink they would need. They made all the preparations themselves, barring Ines and Umberto from their kitchen on the day and insisting that they come along with everybody else as honoured guests. The elderly couple protested, but Bee and Mimi were adamant. They wanted to do this themselves, to say a big thank you all round.

Bee went down to Riccardo's house in person a few days earlier to deliver his invitation. She had heard nothing more from either Luke or him about a possible meeting between father and son and decided to leave well alone. This was a long-running tragedy, and, in fairness, it would have been expecting a lot of an outsider to come in and fix it just like that. Still, she and Mimi had discussed it and both of them felt that Riccardo should be invited to the party. Whether he chose to attend or not was up to him.

When she got to the *Podere Nuovo*, the front door was closed so she went round to the back. The kitchen door was open and there was a strong smell of wine in the air. She found Riccardo in there with a massive glass container almost the size of a dustbin on the table, with rows of bottles around it. The container itself was a huge ball of green glass set in a straw cover, for all the world like a huge version of an old-fashioned Chianti wine bottle. She stopped at the doorway and called inside.

'Riccardo, it's me, Bee. Can I come in? Can I help?'

'Come in my dear and yes, you most certainly can.' Riccardo gave her a smile and beckoned her in. 'The boys have just delivered a fresh *damigiana* and I'm bottling it up.'

'It's absolutely massive, Riccardo. How much does it hold?'

'The label on the neck says fifty-three litres.'

'Wow. How long's that going to last you?'

'The way I used to drink twenty years ago, probably no more than a month. Nowadays, more like half a year.'

Bee did a rapid bit of mental arithmetic and worked out that Riccardo must have gone through a seriously alcoholic phase at the height of his depression. Thankfully his consumption had returned to a much more acceptable level nowadays.

'So, how can I help?'

'I'm running out of room on the table. I wonder if you'd feel like stacking the bottles I've already filled down there in the larder, please.'

She glanced across the room and saw that he had cleared the bottom shelves of the narrow cupboard in the corner. She went across to the table and picked up one of the full two-litre bottles, capped with its metal cage apparatus, and took it over to the larder. It was remarkably heavy and cumbersome. She started on the bottom shelf, which was made of a single piece of lovely old wood. It looked as though it had been there for centuries and, from the thickness of it, it was clear it would be well able to take the weight of a dozen or more of these hefty bottles. She started stacking it with bottles as Riccardo carried on siphoning the red wine from the massive flask through a clear plastic pipe.

It was a very simple process. As each bottle on the table was filled, he would block the end of the tube with his thumb to stop the air getting in while he transferred it to the next bottle. He had been doing this for some time now and his thumb and most of his right hand were unexpectedly stained blue, rather than dark red. Working together, Bee and he were able to drain the *damigiana* into about twenty-five of the big bottles. By this time the bottom shelf and the one above it were jam-packed and Bee's back ached from all the bending. When the big flask was finally empty, they were left with a quarter of a bottle. Riccardo allowed the wine left in the tube to drain back into that bottle and then hobbled over to the dresser and picked up two glasses. He filled them both and pushed one across to Bee.

'Bee, thank you yet again for your help. With my bad hip, I was dreading all the bending and getting up again. Here, sit down and let me drink to your health.'

Bee sat down willingly on an old wooden chair and he took a seat across the table from her. Raising his glass, he reached forward and clinked it against hers.

'Cheers, Bee and thanks again.'

She took a big mouthful of the wine and murmured approvingly. This was something else she was going to miss when she left Montegrifone. Somehow, knowing the place, the vines and the men in the cantina made it all the more special. They chatted for a few minutes, mainly about her new job, his impending hip operation, and the continuing uncertainty about where she would end up, before she invited him to the party.

'Mimi and I are leaving this Saturday, so we thought we'd organise a little party at the villa on Friday night to say goodbye to all the friends we've made here. Please will you come?' She crossed her fingers under the table. 'There's just one thing. Luca will be there.'

There was a long silence, during which Bee let her eyes range around the kitchen It was a lovely old room, with a high ceiling supported by hefty tree trunks. For the first time she spotted an old photograph in a silver frame on top of the dresser. She hadn't seen it there before. It was a family group of three figures, clearly taken in the garden of the *Podere Nuovo*. Alongside a youthful Riccardo was a very pretty fair-haired woman and, in her arms, a cheeky-looking little boy. Riccardo with his long hair and tie-dyed shirt looked every inch a hippy, his wife, Elizabeth looked blissfully happy, and little Luke had the sort of broad smile on his face Bee had only glimpsed once or twice since meeting him.

Finally, Riccardo looked up.

'Can I think about it, Bee?'

'Of course. There's no need to make your mind up right here and now. Please come, but if you decide not to, don't worry. I'll come and say goodbye to you on Saturday morning.'

—

The party was a great success – well, almost.

As there were likely to be twenty people or more by the time they all brought their partners and children, Bee and Mimi decided to make it a stand-up affair with lots of canapés and nibbles. Bee was somewhat surprised to find that Mimi turned out to be an excellent pastry cook. The film star spent all day at the oven, making two huge quiches and sausage rolls from her mother's special recipe, alongside little vol-au-vents filled with mushrooms. Bee prepared fried polenta topped with pâté and Gorgonzola, smoked salmon and slices of goats' cheese on toast, as well as a couple of pizzas bought from the farm shop and sliced into segments.

Bee managed to get the barbecue going without setting fire to the tinder-dry garden and started grilling a load of chubby little sausages to be served on cocktail sticks, dipped into a huge dollop of French mustard in the middle of the plate. She was delighted and relieved when, of all people, Joey came out and took over the cooking partway through. This was the third time this month he had flown all the way from California to be with Mimi and to give her a lift back to LA. There was no denying his commitment and Bee could see that Mimi was impressed, maybe more. He also turned out to be very competent at the barbecue and revealed to a surprised Bee that he had worked as a chef at a burger bar in Beverly Hills for a year before he got his big break. He was surveyed closely by the Labrador, nose firmly trained on the sausages the entire time, as well as by Daniela from the farm shop with a faraway expression on her face. Unlike the dog, her attention wasn't trained on the food. It wasn't every day she met a Hollywood idol after all.

Bee had a little smile to herself as she watched the expressions on the faces of the guests as they were ushered, shyly, into the presence of not one, but two internationally acclaimed film stars, bizarrely here in the wilds of the Tuscan countryside. Just like Bee's reaction two months earlier, it must have appeared incredible to them to be moving in such rarefied circles. In fact, it took a few drinks and a few minutes before natural Tuscan ebullience allowed them to adjust to the presence of their illustrious hosts and normal noise levels resumed.

Communication between the different nationalities was surprisingly good. Bee was delighted to hear Mimi taking a stab at some basic Italian and Umberto's son, Marco, producing some unexpectedly good English learnt at school. And Bee still hadn't got over the discovery that Joey spoke Italian. Admittedly, it was second or third generation Sicilian, learned from his grandparents while growing up in the Bronx, but he made himself understood pretty well, and Bee could see that, not just Daniela, but most of the women and girls at the party soon fell under his spell. Not that this presented a problem to the men among the guests. Most of them had their eyes out on stalks as they followed Mimi's every move.

There was no shortage of liquid refreshment either. Everybody seemed to arrive with something different, including Umberto with a bottle of grappa. Bee and Mimi had already crammed the fridge full of rosé, champagne and cold beer and felt sure it would be more than enough. For the drivers and children there were soft drinks and lots of mineral water.

Bee went around, topping up glasses, but soon found herself out of a job as Ines and Loredana gently but firmly took over. Freed from her duties, Bee circulated chatting to everybody, being introduced to partners she hadn't met before, and keeping a watchful eye on the gaggle of little children belonging to the farm hands. Marco and the others were a bundle of laughs and Bee was soon giggling along with their girlfriends and wives as they were regaled with hilarious anecdotes. Unsurprisingly, many of them involved Berlusconi the goat and his voracious appetite. The noise was almost deafening. Tuscans definitely didn't do sotto voce. Bee was delighted to see that Luke, although their employer, was accepted into the group as an equal and he was looking remarkably relaxed for once.

There was just one problem. There was somebody missing. Luke's father didn't come after all.

Bee kept checking for any sign of him, but without success. From his house, she had no doubt he would have been able to hear the noise, so he couldn't have forgotten. As dusk fell, she almost ran down the road to knock on his door but then decided against it. It was his choice and, she told herself, no business of hers. Yes, it would have been wonderful to engineer a meeting between the father and the son, but it wasn't her place to push it. She was saddened by his no-show but deep down, not really surprised. The idea of meeting his son again after so long would have been scary enough, but for this to take place under the prying eyes of so many astonished onlookers would have been truly daunting.

By the time they had all helped themselves to slices of Mimi's homemade apricot and strawberry tarts accompanied by lovely creamy ice cream from the farm shop, eaten quickly before it melted, it was quite dark outside. They lit candles and sat under the stars. By now Romeo was happily sprawled in the midst of them, surrounded by the little kids who looked as tired as he did. Finally, Bee and Mimi began a coffee marathon, serving powerful little shots of espresso coffee to the adults while Umberto came around dispensing liver-crippling quantities of grappa to the unwary.

Bee sat down on the rattan sofa with Ines and Loredana, her hand over her glass as she spotted Umberto and the grappa bottle circulating, and thanked them for all they had done for her. Ines brushed away her thanks.

'It's been a pleasure. So, time to leave Montegrifone? Any regrets?'

'Lots.' Bee looked around the group, doing her best not to focus on Luke. 'Everything's been so wonderful. Living in such a marvellous historic setting – to a historian like me it's been a dream come true – and discovering just how lovely the countryside can be. Above all, the people have been great. Ines, you and Umberto have looked after us so wonderfully I feel like part of the family now. I'm going to cry my eyes out when I leave tomorrow, I'm afraid.'

'But you will come back and see us, Bee, won't you?'

'I'll definitely come back. Tuscany's in my blood now. I'll be dreaming of Tuscany forever.'

Later on, she found herself sitting beside Mimi, a couple of candles on the table illuminating the scene. Mimi caught hold of her arm and gave it a squeeze.

'I was just thinking – I haven't had a haircut, a manicure or a facial for two months and, you know something? I don't think I've ever felt so good.' She smiled at Bee. 'And you look gorgeous. It must be the Tuscan air.'

Bee blushed. '*I* look gorgeous? You look stunning. I've still got a way to go, but I think I'm reasonably presentable again.'

'Much more than that. My friends in Hollywood are going to love you.' Mimi grinned. 'Although I'd better tell them your heart already belongs to another.'

Bee genuinely didn't know how to respond to that. Luckily Mimi didn't dwell on the subject.

'It's going to be hard to leave all this, isn't it, Bee?'

'Terribly hard. But I'm definitely coming back.'

'That's good to hear because I thought you might be interested to know that I've just booked the villa again for a month next summer. Promise me you'll come.'

Bee glanced across at her, her eyes shining.

'Just try and stop me, Mimi. Thank you so much. And thank you so much for being such a warm and wonderful friend.' She reached over and gave Mimi a hug. As she did so, a thought occurred to her. 'But as I'll be working for an American company, I probably won't have much in the way of holidays.'

'You just come for as long as you can. And as for friendship, I can't begin to tell you how much I've enjoyed your company. I don't know how I'd have coped all alone here without you. The very least I can do is make it possible for you to come back here. Besides, it'll give you a chance to see you-know-who again.'

Bee nodded, but didn't reply. She really wasn't looking forward to saying goodbye to him the following day.

Mimi gave her arm a supportive squeeze. 'I'm so sorry it didn't come to anything.'

'Me too, but sometimes it's better to face facts and accept that some things just aren't meant to be. Not all dreams come true.'

'Says who?'

'Says six thousand miles between LA and here for a start.'

'*Amor vincit omnia.*' Mimi winked at her. 'Besides, you might end up working in Switzerland and that's just over the border.'

'Yes, I know they say love conquers all, but it's not as easy as that. Besides, who's said anything about love? For Romeo the dog definitely. For anybody else here, affection, definitely affection, but surely that's as far as it goes.'

'If you say so, Bee.' Mimi didn't sound convinced.

But then, neither was Bee.

The guests gradually melted away in dribs and drabs until the only people left were Joey and Luke, sitting on the rattan sofa, the dog at their feet. By this time Bee was feeling very emotional and she was almost in tears as Mimi came out and whispered in Joey's ear. As the two of them disappeared into the house, Bee was left alone with Luke, doing her best to keep the tears at bay.

'Sorry to be leaving?' From the expression on his face in the candle light, it was clear he was fully aware that it was a rhetorical question. 'Still, you'll come back and see us, won't you?'

She turned towards him and wiped her eyes with the back of her hand.

'Definitely. I'm going to take every opportunity I can to include a visit to Tuscany in any future trips to Italy.' She sniffed, picked up a paper napkin and blew her nose. 'I'm sorry to be so emotional, but I've really enjoyed my time here and I've met so many lovely people.' She caught his eye. 'Particularly you, Luke.'

There was a second or two before he broke the silence.

'You're leaving tomorrow? From Florence? Pisa?'

She had to clear her throat before replying as firmly as possible.

'Pisa.'

'How are you planning on getting there? Could I offer you a lift to the airport? I'd like to do that.'

Bee nodded. 'If you really don't mind, that would be very kind. Joey's driving down to Rome airport with Mimi so, seeing as we gave the 500 back a few days ago, I was going to get a lift with them into Siena and then take the train, but I think it might mean a change.

'Then that's decided. I'll drive you to Pisa.' He reached down and picked up an empty tray, apparently keen to get away. 'It's probably best if we clear the plates into the kitchen before Berlusconi and his friends come calling.'

She reached out and caught his arm, turning him towards her once more.

'Wait, Luke. There's something I have to say.'

She saw his eyes sparkle in the moonlight.

'I've loved being here, Luke, and I've loved meeting you. I just want you to know that if things had been different...' Her voice began to peter out, but she collected herself. '...if things had been different, I would have liked to get to know you so much better.'

She saw him nod his head and when he spoke she couldn't miss the emotion in his voice.

'And me, Bee. You're a lovely person and I'll never, ever forget you. I hope you have a wonderful life.'

And he turned hastily away.

Chapter 21

Saturday was a draining day, physically and emotionally. Bee got up very early so she could wash the dishes from the night before, but she found Ines already hard at it. Bee gave her a hand before going up to finish packing her things and then it was time to bid farewell to the two Hollywood idols.

Mimi had tears in her eyes as they hugged on the doorstep and she repeated her invitation to Bee to stay with her when she went over to LA to begin her new job in less than two weeks' time. The fact that they were going to see each other so soon made the parting easier, but Bee was feeling very emotional as Joey's car disappeared down the drive. What had started out as a babysitting exercise for a potentially difficult and spoilt diva had produced a real friendship that Bee felt sure would go the distance, in spite of the abyss that existed between her and the glamorous world of the movies. Living with Mimi had been a wonderful experience, and Bee was really glad she had been able to play her part in helping the megastar learn to relax and enjoy life so much more. In return, Mimi had proved to be a supportive, encouraging and generous friend – to the point of offering her hospitality in her own home in LA. Bee knew that profound trust now existed between the two of them and she felt privileged to have been allowed into the private life of a living legend. They had definitely done each other good.

After they left, she hurried down the track to say goodbye to Riccardo. However, try as she might, although she knocked numerous times, she was bitterly disappointed to receive no answer. She went round to the back door but found it locked and his little car missing. In the end, all she could do was slip a note under his door with her phone number and email address, adding the words, *So sorry not to have been able to say goodbye. Please stay in touch. x Bee.*

She went back to the kitchen to say goodbye to Ines and Umberto and she was touched to see both of them with tears in their eyes. The Labrador no doubt picked up on the mood of the humans around him and his big brown eyes looked even more mournful than usual as he rested his nose on her knee. She made a huge fuss of him before leaving him in the company of these two charming old people. As she had expected, she cried her eyes out as she left.

During the drive to the airport she and Luke didn't talk much. Partly this was because she was tired, partly because she was feeling very emotional and didn't want to start crying all over again, and partly because she knew that leaving him and his home was one of the most difficult things she had ever had to do in her life. When they reached Pisa airport, she refused his offer to come in with her and told him he should drive straight off again. After piling her bags onto a trolley, he came over and stood in front of her.

'Thank you, Bee, for everything you've done for us, and I mean all of us.' She heard him clear his throat before continuing. 'Your stay at Montegrifone has brought some much-needed joy to a place where joy's been in short supply for a good while now. I really hope you'll come back to see us again. As often as you can.'

She nodded. 'I'll be back, Luke, I promise.' She could hear the emotion in her voice and she had no doubt he would be able to hear it too. 'I've loved meeting you all and I know my time here's done me good, not just physically, but as a person. I'm the one who should be saying thank you.' Her voice broke. 'I'm really going to miss you, Luke.'

He took a step towards her and wrapped his arms around her, crushing her to his chest. She felt his lips on her damaged cheek and then his voice in her ear.

'And I'm going to miss you, too, Bee.'

And then, before she could respond, he released her and turned away. He climbed back into the truck and drove off with just a little wave of the hand, without looking back, leaving her feeling more alone than she had felt for ages. She felt so drained by now, she could barely control the tears that were stinging the corners of her eyes.

–

It was five o'clock by the time she got back to her flat in south London feeling totally deflated and still close to tears.

To her amazement, as she opened the door, she saw a pile of mail neatly stacked on the hall table. Dropping her bags, she walked through to the living room and got another surprise. There was a vase of fresh flowers on the table. The window was open and the place felt airy and clean, not nearly as stuffy as she had been expecting.

The scent of the flowers as she walked in suddenly took her back to the villa and she stopped, lost in thought, the familiar stinging at the corners of her eyes welling up again. She knew she would never forget her time at Montegrifone and that one special man. With an effort, she wiped her eyes and took a few deep, calming breaths. She had no doubt that she would be dreaming of Tuscany for a long time to come.

Returning her attention to the room, she saw that there was a note with a key on the table alongside the flowers. Both were from Jamie. He and she had corresponded quite a bit recently, after she had broken the amazing news to him that Mimi loved his screenplay and had sent it straight to her agent in LA. Jamie had been understandably delighted and almost pathetically grateful. In spite of everything, Bee had found herself beginning to think fondly of him once more. Not fondly enough to consider getting back together with him, in spite of the unexpectedly romantic nature of his screenplay, but she had forgiven him for taking advantage of her mother's naiveté and then turning up at Montegrifone uninvited. The note, written on the back of an envelope that had once contained a bank statement, was brief. His handwriting was his usual scrawl but, by now, she knew how to decipher it.

> *Welcome home, Bee.*
> *Thanks again for what you've done for me. I owe you. Hope to see you some time. Good luck with your life.*
> *With love*
> *Jamie*

PS I found I still had a spare key. Here it is back again.

PPS There's bread and milk in the fridge.

Bee went through to the little kitchen, made herself a cup of tea, and settled down to phone round and let people know she was back. She started with her mum and moved on to friends she hadn't spoken to for months. The result of her phone calls was an invitation to come along and meet up with a bunch of people from the university who wanted to wish her well in her new job. Although she was feeling weary, she agreed to see them at their local pub near the university at eight that evening.

Finally, she phoned Jamie. He sounded genuinely pleased to hear from her.

'Hey, Bee. Glad to hear you're home safe. How was Tuscany?'

'Tuscany was great. Just great. I already wish I was back there. Thanks for the flowers and the milk and stuff.'

'You're very welcome. Tell me about your new job.'

So she told him. He sounded very impressed, in particular that she would be staying with Mimi for a month. 'That all sounds amazing, Bee. Maybe we'll meet up in Hollywood some time.'

'You're moving over there?'

'If Dolores manages to sell my screenplay, you bet.'

'Dolores?'

'My new agent. That's right, I've finally got one after all this time. And she's based in Hollywood herself.' He sounded ecstatic. 'She was put onto me by Mimi Robertson's agent. She says she loves my work.' Bee heard him hesitate. 'To be quite honest, I met her for the first time when she was in London a week ago and I think there's a real spark there.'

'Spark?'

'You know, a romantic spark. I liked her a lot and I think she feels the same way about me.'

Somehow, Bee wasn't surprised. The combination of his finding somebody who lived in Hollywood, 'loved' his work, and might be able to turn his dreams into reality, had been pretty well guaranteed to result in infatuation on his part. Whether it was reciprocated or not was another matter altogether. The good news was that, in spite of the evidence to the contrary provided by his screenplay, it appeared he had got over any disappointment he might have felt at her refusal to take him back.

'Well, good for you, Jamie. I wish you all the best for the future.'

And she meant it.

A couple of hours later she travelled into Waterloo on the train. As usual it was crowded, stuffy and dirty. If she had needed any confirmation that her decision to leave her old job was the right one, this certainly helped. As she watched the anonymous buildings flash by on either side of the train, she found herself comparing them to the scenery at Montegrifone. No cypress trees, no rows of vines, no yellow butterflies, no medieval or Renaissance architecture. The difference was staggering and she was feeling terribly nostalgic by the time she got out at the other end.

It was about twenty degrees colder here in London than it had been in Tuscany, and she rather wished she had brought a thicker jumper as she walked along to the pub. Once she got inside, however, it was almost as stiflingly hot as it had been in the train. She immediately had to face a barrage of questions about the accident, her health and her new job. As she told them all about it, she could see envy on a number of the faces. In return, they passed on the latest news from the university, including the bombshell that the gropey professor was being pursued through the courts by no fewer than three other women for sexual harassment. Bee was delighted to hear it.

As she sat there, however, listening to all the gossip and sipping a pint of lager, she suddenly realised she felt out of place, even though she and her friends had been coming here for years now. The funny thing was that, whereas she had always felt comfortable in such surroundings before, she now felt like a fish out of water. Clearly, she had been away too long or maybe her months in Tuscany had somehow changed her.

As the evening progressed, she was unable to shake this sense of discomfort. She only drank half of her pint of beer and refused any more as all it did was to make her feel even more tired. She was pleased and relieved that her appearance didn't seem to be putting anybody off too much and, in fact, she had a lot of very positive comments about how she looked. She was even approached by an unknown man with the offer of a drink, dinner or more, and presumably if she had looked too frightening, that wouldn't have happened. She gave him a smile and thanked him, but said no. There was only one man in her head for now and she knew it was going to take months, maybe years, to get over what might have been.

In consequence, when she finally made her excuses and left the pub early, it was with mixed feelings. On the one hand, she was pleased and relieved that she appeared to have been accepted back as her old self, not some kind of freak. On the other hand, there was the realisation that, as far as she was concerned, it was now London that felt alien to her. Had she got so used to lizards, goats and Labradors that pints of lager, university gossip and being chatted-up by random men were now every bit as strange to her as the Tuscan countryside had once been?

Back at the flat she felt a definite sense of relief to be in her own space once again. Maybe that was all it was. She had got used to being away from the crowds and it would take her a while to get accustomed to being among people again. Yes, she told herself, maybe that was it.

Her resolve lasted for all of five minutes while she made herself a mug of camomile tea before sitting down and opening her laptop to check her emails. When her eyes alighted on one from luca@montegrifone.com, her heart gave a distinct flutter and she knew it wasn't just the solitude of Tuscany she was missing. She clicked on the message and read it eagerly.

> Ciao Bee. I thought you might like to have
> this as a souvenir of your time here at Monte-
> grifone. Very best wishes. Luke.

Along with the email was a photo, taken in the garden behind the villa, of Luke, Umberto and Ines, with a comatose Labrador lying stretched out at their feet. As Bee stared down at the photograph, she felt her eyes well up and tears begin to run down her cheeks.

Chapter 22

Although the photo from Montegrifone had reduced her to tears, the fact that Luke had omitted to add even one little *x* before his signature reinforced her conviction that she had been right in ensuring that no relationship could spring up between the two of them, enticing as it would have been. This thought helped to calm her still raw emotions as she took the train to Newbury to see her parents the following day. The last thing she wanted was to have a full-on emotional breakdown in the presence of her mum as she knew she would never hear the last of it.

Her mother and father were both waiting for her at the station and she hugged them warmly, really pleased to see them again. As they drove home, she began to give them a detailed description of Montegrifone and most of its inhabitants, and this continued over lunch. She deliberately downplayed the part Luke had occupied in her life and concentrated mainly on Umberto and Ines and, of course, Romeo the dog. Her mother apologised profusely for revealing the address to Jamie, and Bee was able to reassure her that no harm had been done and, in fact, that she and Jamie were back on speaking terms again. However, something in her mother's eye made her add a hasty qualification.

'Before you say anything, mum, I'm not about to get back together with him. That's all over.'

'I'm so sorry, dear.'

'There's no need to be. Both he and I are fine as we are.'

She went on to tell them all about the new job and she was delighted to see her father's eyebrows shoot up when she told him how much they were going to be paying her. Predictably, her mother was more concerned by the possibility of her only daughter ending up on the other side of the world. Bee did her best to reassure her.

'I don't think I'll be based in California. I'm only going there for a month to learn the ropes. They're planning to open a branch somewhere in Europe and they're still trying to decide what's best. They told me they might even set up offices here in London.'

'I do hope it'll be London, dear.'

Bee, on the other hand, was ever more convinced that she wanted to get away from London and make a complete break, but for now she didn't mention that to her mum. There would be time for that as and when the decision was made.

As they tucked into the summer pudding with ice cream, her mother turned the conversation to more personal matters and Bee groaned inwardly.

'When you spoke to me about the people where you were staying in Tuscany, you mentioned the estate manager. Did you like him?'

'Yes, mum, I liked him. I liked all the people there.'

'But you liked him most of all…?'

Her mother's radar was uncanny. Ever since her schooldays, Bee had been unable to work out how on earth her mother managed to home in on the boys she really liked, rather than the regular procession of hopefuls who appeared at their door from time to time. She took a mouthful of Tesco Valpolicella and sat back, recognising that she had been rumbled.

'Yes, mum, if you really want to know, I liked... like him a lot.'

'But nothing happened?'

'Nothing *could* happen, mum. It wouldn't have been fair on him.' Now that she had started, she found herself giving them a brief summary of Luke's often tragic background, ending with the words that had been going round and round in her head for so long. 'He lost his mother, his grandfather and then his fiancée. I couldn't be responsible for breaking his heart one more time.'

'That's a very grown-up attitude.'

Bee managed to grin at this. 'In case you hadn't noticed, mum, I *am* grown-up. I'm a woman of thirty-one, soon to be thirty-two.'

'I know you are, dear. I just meant that not many girls would have behaved the same way, I'm sure. And what about him? Do you think he felt the same way about you?'

'Yes... maybe. I don't know, mum. Anyway, it was good to meet him and I know I'll never forget him.' She caught her mother's eye. 'He said the same thing to me.'

-

Over the next few days, Bee threw herself into making all the practical arrangements before commencing her new job. There was still no word as to where the European headquarters might be and she wondered if she should hang onto the flat for another month, just in case she ended up back here in London again. However, with the huge amount they would be paying her, she knew she would easily be able to afford somewhere better and she might even be able to start thinking about putting down a deposit and buying her first place. Also, a change of apartment would definitely underline the fresh start she was making in her life. In consequence, she gave notice to her landlord and set about packing up her things.

She managed to speak to almost all her friends and met up with a number of them before setting off to LA. Among these was Annabelle. She was an art historian and she had helped Bee a lot with her doctoral thesis. They spent a pleasant afternoon together in a café near Victoria station and it was while they were talking shop that Bee had a moment of enlightenment. Annabelle, as always, was talking about medieval art and she suddenly said something that set bells ringing in Bee's head.

'Of course, back then nobody painted on canvas. Most of the paintings were either frescoes, painted direct onto walls, or panel painting.' In case Bee might be unsure what she meant, she elaborated. 'I'm sure you know that artists painted on wooden panels throughout the whole of the medieval period, and it wasn't until the Renaissance that canvas appeared.'

'Wooden panels… of course.' Bee's mind was racing. Of course she had known this already, but had forgotten. Suddenly things began to fall into place.

Unaware of the turmoil going on inside Bee's head, Annabelle carried on.

'Poplar or plane were the favourite materials and they didn't cut the tree lengthways, but obliquely, so as to end up with pieces that were as large as possible. Then they used animal glues to stick on a sheet of linen, and built up the surface with layer upon layer of gesso. The results—'

Bee cut her off before she could go on. 'Sorry, Annabelle, but these panels, what sort of size were they?'

'It all depended on the size of the tree. The bigger the tree, the bigger the panel. I've seen some as big as a tea tray.'

'You know Martini's *Annunciation*?' She didn't wait for an answer. 'He painted that on wood, right?'

'Absolutely. All his religious works of the time were either painted straight onto the walls of churches or on wooden panels. The *Annunciation*'s a big painting, so it's made up of a series of bits of wood fixed together. Smaller paintings might just occupy a single panel. Why do you ask?'

Bee stared wild-eyed across the table at her, barely able to contain her excitement.

'I may just have discovered a painting by Simone Martini, that's why.'

'You've what?' Now it was Annabelle's turn to look astounded. 'You mean, an unknown painting?'

'One that's been lost for the last seventy or eighty years. At least, I think I might know where it is.'

Bee hugged her flabbergasted friend and wasted no time in racing back to her flat. She had no contact details for Riccardo, but she did have Luke's mobile number. She took a deep breath and called him. He answered almost immediately and she felt a thrill at the sound of his voice.

'*Pronto.*'

'Hi, Luke, it's me, Bee. Listen, something's just occurred to me.'

'Bee, hi. Are you all right?' He sounded surprised and concerned.

'I'm fine. Look, don't get your hopes up too much, but I've got a feeling I might have found your Simone Martini painting.'

'You've what?' His reaction was the same as Annabelle's had been. 'Where…?'

'I think I know. In your dad's house, your old house, there's a cupboard in the corner of the kitchen. You know the one I mean?'

'Where he used to keep the wine bottles.'

'Right, and he still does. The thing is, a week or two ago, I was helping him bottling up a *damigiana* of wine. As he filled the bottles, I stacked them on the shelves in that cupboard and, Luke, I noticed that the bottom shelf is made out of a single piece of very old timber.'

'And you think…?' He sounded bemused.

'Martini painted on wooden boards, and his smaller stuff could have been on just a single plank. The painting you've been looking for wasn't painted on canvas, but wood. I should have remembered that, but I wasn't thinking.' She took another deep breath. 'I have a feeling that if you take that shelf out and turn it over, you'll find it's what you've been looking for: the answer to all your problems.'

'You think my grandfather hid the painting in the kitchen?' Luke sounded breathless. 'In such an obvious place, for all to see?'

'Hiding in plain sight, Luke. It really could be.' As she spoke, she remembered Mimi using those same words to describe their visits to Tuscany's historic places over the past few weeks. Then something else occurred to her.

'Somehow, I think this might be the moment you and your father start talking again.'

'If the Martini's really there, he's going to *have* to talk to me. Listen, Bee, I don't know how to thank you…'

'Like I say, don't get your hopes up yet. I may be quite wrong. I'm just so sorry I didn't think of it at the time. I'm supposed to be an expert on the Middle Ages, after all.' She slumped down on the sofa, suddenly feeling weary. 'I'll keep my fingers crossed for you both. And, Luke, it's been good talking to you.'

'It's always good to talk to you, Bee.' His voice suddenly became huskier. 'I've been thinking of you a lot.'

'And I've been thinking of you, Luke. You want to know something? I've been dreaming of Tuscany every night since I got back here.'

She had in fact been dreaming not only of Tuscany with its hilltop villages and outstanding architecture, but of a certain farmer in his swimming trunks. She decided it was best not to tell him this.

-

Bee's phone rang at eight thirty the next morning, just as the kettle boiled. She saw that it was Luke and sat down at the kitchen table to answer, holding her breath in anticipation.

'Bee, you were right!' He sounded excited and her heart leapt.

'It's the Martini?'

'It has to be. I went round to my father's house first thing this morning and, together, we cleared the bottles and prised the shelf away. It was only tacked into the timber supports with short nails and it came out quite easily. And yes, turning it over, we've found the painting.'

Bee's heart sang. 'That's fantastic news, Luke, really fantastic. Please, will you do me a favour? Take a photo and send it over to me, would you? One of my close friends is a world authority on medieval art. She'll probably be able to tell straightaway if it's by Martini.'

'That's terrific. I'll do that now.'

'And you and your father? You're speaking?'

'I'm up at the villa with the painting now. I had to show it to Umberto. But yes, my father and I did talk this morning. Not a lot, as you can imagine, but we're talking. It's all been such a shock.'

'Then, will you do me another favour, please, Luke? If Annabelle agrees about the painting, will you go back and see him again? And when you do, will you take a bottle of champagne with you and promise me you'll drink it together? All of it. And while you're drinking, please start talking.'

'It's a promise, Bee.' There was a moment's hesitation from him. 'Bee, I can't tell you how much this means to all of us. You may just have saved Montegrifone.'

'You'd have managed, Luke, I have no doubt. Now, send me that photo.'

The photo duly arrived and Bee gazed at it in awe. In her eyes, there was no doubt that it was the genuine article. The *Annunciation* hanging in the Uffizi Gallery was unique for a number of reasons, one of which was the strange posture of the Madonna, curled back, as if unwilling to accept the news brought to her by the Angel Gabriel. Luke's much smaller painting looked like an early study for that part of the more famous picture, and the bent position of the Virgin was unmistakable. It had to be authentic. However, as promised to Luke, Bee sent it straight on to Annabelle, who called back less than five minutes later sounding absolutely delighted.

'I'd need to see it in person to be absolutely certain, but the photo you've sent me looks like an authentic Martini. I think you've found it, Bee. In fact, I'm sure you have. That's amazing!'

And it was.

'Thank you so much, Annabelle. Have you any idea what it might be worth, if it *is* authentic?'

'I thought you might ask me that. I've just had a quick check. Another painting by Simone Martini, *The Virgin Annunciate*, was sold by Sotheby's a few years back for just over four million dollars. It was a very small painting, so it's a fair bet your one could fetch a good bit more than that. The market for medieval art has never been stronger.'

'Wow! Thanks a lot, Annabelle. I'll pass on the good news.'

Bee got straight back on the phone to Luke and was delighted to hear the awe in his tone. Somehow she felt sure that this discovery would not just save Montegrifone, but would save, or at least help, both Luke and his father. She crossed her fingers in the hope that this would bring the two men back together again after all this time.

She and Luke talked for some minutes, but the sense of frustration she got from knowing he was a thousand miles away and that she was about to travel even further away tinged her pleasure at the sound of his voice with melancholy.

The following days were a whirl of activity. She packed up all her stuff and hired two of her former students to collect it all with a rented van, and deliver it to her parents' house in Newbury. After they had left, she tidied up the flat and spent a final few moments thinking back to the years she had been there, her relationship with Jamie, and how she was now making a fresh start. But there was no getting away from it, however exciting the next weeks and months of her new job promised to be, there was something, or someone, missing from her life. As she gazed out of the window over the overgrown back garden towards the identical row of drab houses beyond, she sighed for the beauty of her Tuscan paradise and the people who lived there.

One in particular.

While she had been at Montegrifone, she had managed to convince herself that there was no way he and she could ever be together because of their different jobs. She had told him, and everybody else, that her career was the most important thing in her life but now, back here and all alone, she wasn't so sure. Yes, the new job promised to be really stimulating but, however alluring this new direction in her life might prove to be, she had a horrible feeling it might feel hollow without Luke. She found herself facing the same dilemma that had plagued women since the dawn of time – family or career? She knew she wanted both, but she also knew this was an impossible wish.

Just as she was drifting towards melancholy, her phone bleeped. It was an email and she was delighted to find it was from Riccardo.

Dear Bee.

I hope this finds you well. I'm sorry I didn't have a chance to say goodbye properly before you left. I intended to, but lost my nerve at the last moment.

Thank you so very much for your exciting discovery. You can probably imagine what a difference this will make to the fortunes of Montegrifone and our whole family. I don't know how we can possibly repay you.

I was very pleased to meet you and I feel honoured to have been able to get to know you. Do, please, stay in touch and let me know as soon as you have any plans to come back to visit Montegrifone.

Kind regards

Riccardo (Negri)

The formal tone of the email made her smile, particularly his surname in brackets in case she didn't remember him. His comment about losing his nerve didn't surprise her. Although hopefully beginning to emerge from his long years of depression, she knew he was still very vulnerable. He hadn't mentioned his son and she hoped desperately that this discovery would turn out to be the catalyst necessary to rekindle the relationship between the two men.

She could only hope.

Chapter 23

September was an amazing, surreal month for Bee.

The headquarters of HOWTV couldn't have been more different from Montegrifone if they had been on a desert island. Everywhere she looked was tarmac, glass and concrete and, from the top floor, the views out of the windows were of block after block of buildings, with the iconic Hollywood sign just visible on the hills beyond. The good news was that inside the company people were friendly and helpful, and her immediate boss, Virginia, the Commissioning Editor, was delightful. Bee was greatly relieved. She had seen too many movies about hard-nosed American corporate bullies and had been fearing the worst.

She spent long days with Virginia going through the new channel's plans for the future and soon began to develop the knack of sifting the chaff from the wheat as submissions from production companies around the world came pouring in. Some were fascinating, some questionable, and some just plain rubbish. As the weeks went by, she and Virginia produced a solid schedule for the next few months and she definitely got the impression her efforts were appreciated. From her perspective, it was a fascinating job and every bit as interesting as she could have hoped, and should have been interesting enough to make her forget the Tuscan winemaker.

But she couldn't get him out of her thoughts.

As far as work was concerned, the one thing she still didn't know was where she would be based. The more she thought about it, however, the more she found herself hoping it wouldn't be London. Somehow she knew she wanted to make a complete break with the past and move on. Every day new rumours circulated, ranging from Prague and even Reykjavik, to there not being a European base at all. She did her best to curb her impatience.

She was greatly helped in this by the variety and excitement of her life outside the office.

From the moment she extricated herself from US Border Control at LAX airport, she found herself in a world of riches, privilege and excess. She was picked up from the airport in a limo and transferred smoothly and silently to Mimi's mansion in Beverly Hills. The house of the richest actress in Hollywood was ultra-modern and equipped with everything from a thirty-seat cinema to a massive swimming pool, tennis court and delightful subtropical gardens. Bee was touched to see that it now also boasted a snow globe of San Gimignano in the main living room. Most evenings, when Bee and Mimi got back from work, they went swimming or sat outside under swaying palm trees, sipping Prosecco specially imported from a little producer north of Venice as a reminder of Italy. Tuscany was still very much in their thoughts and Mimi was fascinated to hear about Bee's discovery of the Martini painting.

'So the love of your life's now solvent again.' She caught Bee's eye. 'You realise he could easily afford to employ an estate manager now, so he could come and live with you wherever you end up.'

Bee smiled ruefully. 'He's already told me he'd never leave Montegrifone. And I would never want to be the one to make him do something so drastic. His family's been living there for centuries and I can understand the depth of feeling that keeps him tied to the valley. No, it still wouldn't work.'

'Of course, you could still go over there and settle in Montegrifone with him.'

Bee shook her head. 'And give up my exciting new job?'

'Not even in the name of love?'

'No, not even for love.'

She almost believed it herself.

On a number of memorable occasions, Mimi took Bee along with her to parties at the homes of the rich and famous. Bee lost track of the number of household names in the movie business she recognised, and with whom she quite literally rubbed shoulders at some of the more crowded events. Also present at these events was Joey, now a permanent fixture in Mimi's life. Bee was delighted to see both of them looking happy and she got the feeling Mimi's wish of settling down might just be coming true.

Towards the end of the month, a week before Bee was scheduled to finish her initial four-week introductory period at HOWTV, Mimi's Yorkshire film had its premiere in London. As promised, she invited Bee to travel across with her and Joey by chartered jet. The plan was to fly over, attend the premiere on the Saturday evening, and then fly straight back again – a round trip of over ten thousand miles. Bee had never done anything like this before and had never been on a private aircraft either.

The chartered jet was luxurious and offered full length beds to sleep on. The co-pilot explained to her that these aircraft flew higher than normal airliners and, in consequence, there was very little turbulence and Bee managed to get a good few hours' sleep on the way there and on the way back. If she had wanted, she could have drowned herself in champagne and stuffed herself with caviar, but she exercised restraint and settled for some fresh fruit and a sandwich, knowing that a gala dinner awaited them in London. It was an amazing weekend but, when she got to London, she discovered she was in for an even greater surprise.

The film was great and Mimi's acting as flawless as usual. Bee felt sure the critics would give it and her really good reviews. After the premiere in Leicester Square, there was the gala dinner. Rather apologetically, Mimi explained that she and Joey would have to be at the top table with the great and the good, or not so good, while Bee had been allocated a place at one of the other tables. When she made her way to the assigned seat, feeling nervous at the thought of dining with nine complete strangers, she discovered that not all the other people at the round table were strangers after all. As she leant down to check her name on the name card, the man sitting in the next seat turned his head towards her and jumped to his feet.

'Hi, Bee. I can't tell you how great it is to see you again.'

He was wearing a stylish dinner jacket, and his short fair hair was freshly cut. With his tanned face, broad shoulders and even broader smile, he was looking really good.

Bee squeaked with delight and literally threw herself into his outstretched arms.

'Luke... you're here.'

It wasn't the most inspired observation, but she was secretly pleased to be able to say anything at all. The sudden upsurge of emotion she had felt at the sight of him had threatened to reduce her to tears. She buried her face in his chest and did her best to regain control of her faculties as he spoke into her ear.

'Didn't Mimi tell you she'd invited me?'

Bee stepped back so she could look up into his face, but still kept hold of his hands.

'Nope. When it comes to surprises, this has got to be one of the biggest.' She grinned at him. 'Wait till I get her home...'

'You're looking wonderful. Really stunning.' He sounded impressed.

Bee was wearing a very expensive designer dress that Mimi had insisted on buying for her to replace the silk blouse devoured by Berlusconi the goat, but Luke's eyes weren't on her clothes. He was beaming at her face.

'Your cheek has almost completely cleared up now and I love what you've done to your hair. You look like one of those sexy French film stars.'

Bee had insisted upon paying for the visit to Mimi's hairstylist herself and was still recovering from the amount it had cost. But she had to admit that José the stylist had done a wonderful job and she definitely liked Luke's choice of adjective. She beamed back at him.

'Well, you look like a film star yourself. The tuxedo really suits you.'

They both sat down and he kept her hand in his. As she devoted all her attention to Luke, she barely noticed that she was sitting opposite a couple of people she had met at one of the recent Hollywood parties.

'Tell me about the painting. Have you had it looked at?'

'Sotheby's sent an expert up from Rome and she's confirmed what your friend said: it's genuine all right. It's a study of the Madonna, very similar in style to the *Annunciation*. It's going into their autumn fine art sale with a guide price of between five and six million euros.' Bee could hear the awe in his voice. 'She told me she reckons it might well go for a lot more than that.'

'Wow! So that means your financial worries are over.'

'All thanks to you, Bee.'

Bee hesitated for a moment. 'And your father? Have you and he finally managed to talk?'

Luke nodded, a little smile on his lips. 'He's been doing most of the talking. I've been doing a lot of listening.' The smile broadened. 'But it's all good. I now understand what made him behave like he did. Did you know? He sent me to that boarding school because my mother wanted me to be educated in the UK, not because he was just trying to get shot of me.' He met Bee's eyes for a moment. 'If only he'd told me… Anyway, I've even persuaded him to see a psychiatrist. He should have done that years ago, decades ago, but better late than never.' He leant towards her and kissed her gently on her good cheek. 'That's from him. He sends his love.' Then he kissed her softly on her damaged cheek. 'And that's from me.'

Bee caught hold of his head as he was straightening up again and pulled him back down until she could kiss both his cheeks in return.

'That's for him from me.' She didn't let Luke go. 'And this is for you from me.' She kissed him, this time on the lips, and she felt her head spin, but all too soon she was interrupted.

'Hey Beatrice, it's great to see you again. And you're looking really good. Back to normal.'

Bee's eyes opened as she registered that the voice had come from none other than Amos Franklin, the director of *The Dark Prince*, who was now sitting a few places along from them. At his side was Gayle, looking far more glamorous that Bee had ever seen her in a dark red satin dress with a plunging neckline. Reluctantly, she pulled back from Luke's arms and felt herself blushing as she hastened to explain.

'Hello, Mr Franklin, hi Gayle. I didn't see you there. I'm sorry. It's just that we haven't seen each other for a while.' At the same time she waved vaguely towards the other people around the table. 'I wasn't concentrating.'

'I could tell.' Gayle was grinning back at her. 'So, are you going to introduce us?'

As Bee made the introductions, she caught a twinkle in Gayle's eye.

'So you've found yourself a souvenir of Tuscany.'

Bee was still blushing, but she did her best to answer in kind.

'Romeo the dog wasn't invited, so I've had to settle for the next best thing.'

Luke caught hold of her hand again and gave it a squeeze as he answered on the dog's behalf.

'We couldn't find him a tuxedo.' He was smiling and sounding relaxed. 'Besides, he's never been too interested in the movies, unless it's *A Hundred and One Dalmatians*. Whereas I'm a great fan of your movies, Mr Franklin.'

As Luke and Amos Franklin chatted about films, Bee settled back, delighted to see Luke looking and sounding so bright and cheerful. Clearly, the discovery of the painting had removed all his financial worries and had been the catalyst for the reunion of father and son. Had he maybe also managed to get over the loss of his fiancée and, if he had, what did that mean as far as he and Bee were concerned? Suddenly the perfectly balanced scales of career versus love showed signs of tipping, in spite of her best intentions. She knew she wanted and needed to spend time with him but, like Cinderella, she also knew she was going to have to disappear at midnight.

When Bee described the food to her mum on the phone the next day, she told her it was pretty good, but not as good as Michelangelo's restaurant. In fairness, the caterers were serving several hundred people, but it didn't matter. She barely tasted any of the meal and just basked in the company of the man she had missed so badly ever since leaving Montegrifone.

As the evening drew on, they chatted easily, pausing only to eat or when the speeches started. He told her that the grape harvest had been even better than expected and this boded well for the new wine. He was looking and sounding so much more cheerful, and the stress lines around his eyes had melted away, leaving a happy, handsome and very desirable man. Bee tried not to drink too much of the wine, which wasn't a patch on Montegrifone wine, because she knew that all her instincts were screaming at her to ravish him right here, right now, across the table. She felt pretty sure Gayle wouldn't bat an eyelid if she did, but the other diners might take a different view.

Finally, just before midnight, a waiter appeared at her shoulder with the message that the car to take her back to the airport with Mimi and Joey was waiting. Bee stood up regretfully and took her leave of the others around the table, before turning to Luke who was standing before her.

'I'm really, really sorry I have to go. I wish I could stay.' There was a break in her voice and the familiar stinging in her eyes once more.

'I wish you could stay, too, but I know you've got your job to do. I'll keep my fingers crossed that you come back to Europe before long. Maybe if you do, we'll be able to meet up.'

'I can't think of anything better. I really want to see you again, Luke.' In spite of her resolve, she knew she couldn't hide her attraction to this kind, gentle but strong man any longer. Why, oh why, did she have to disappear off to America?

He leant forward and kissed her briefly, softly, on the lips. As he did so, she felt herself go weak at the knees, and it was fortunate that Joey arrived at that moment to take her arm and guide her away as they made their way out to the car. As they left Luke at the table, through the wave of emotion that threatened to submerge her, Bee heard Mimi's voice calling back over her shoulder to Luke.

'You'll see her again soon, Luke. Don't worry.'

–

When Bee got in to work on Monday morning, she was feeling remarkably fresh for somebody who had flown halfway across the globe and back in the space of twenty-four hours. This was just as well, as she and Virginia were called into a top-level meeting at nine o'clock. Bee was impressed, and a bit intimidated, to see everybody there, right up to the CEO himself. Once everybody was settled, he announced the importance of this meeting to the assembled executives.

'Today is September twenty-nine. HOWTV goes live the day after tomorrow and I want to wish you all well.' He looked around the room shrewdly. 'I also want to hear from you that everything's in place and we're good to go.'

There then began a series of reports from the heads of the different divisions, but it was only when they got to Legal and Property that Bee suddenly sat up to attention. The short, chubby, lawyer in charge of that department broke the news to the room that a final decision had been made on the European headquarters.

'We've decided to go ahead with setting up a European branch office. Initially, this will be a fairly small affair, headed up by...' He checked his iPad. '... Ms Kingdom, Beatrice Kingdom.'

The CEO cut in. 'Stand up and give us all a wave, Beatrice. I want everybody to get to know you before you leave us and head off to Rome.'

Bee pushed her chair back and got to her feet, smiling nervously around the room. All the while, her brain was trying to process what she had just heard. Had he really said 'Rome'?

Unaware of her bemusement, the lawyer carried on in his deadpan voice.

'We've taken premises in the centre of Rome and we plan to begin with just a skeleton staff headed up by

Ms Kingdom. She will be responsible for ensuring that everything's up and running by the end of November at the latest.'

Bee suddenly realised she was still on her feet, grinning stupidly around the room, so she hastily sat down again.

That evening she couldn't wait to give Mimi the good news, but she soon discovered that Mimi had some fascinating news of her own. After Bee had revealed that she would be living and working in Italy, and Mimi had given her congratulations, Mimi went on to tell her something just as amazing.

'It's official, Bee. I'm going to be you.'

Bee took a mouthful of Prosecco and gave her a puzzled look over the rim of her glass. 'You're going to have to explain.'

'I signed the contract this afternoon. Pan World have bought the rights to your boyfriend's… your ex-boyfriend's screenplay. And I'm playing the part of Dee.' She held up her glass and clinked it against Bee's. 'Cheers, Bee, or should I say Dee? I'm going to be you.'

'Wow!' Bee really didn't know what to say. 'Does Jamie know?'

Mimi nodded. 'My agent and his agent set the whole thing up, so he's been kept in the loop. Apparently when she called him today with the confirmation, the line went silent for so long she thought he'd had a coronary.' She grinned. 'But he's fine, just amazed and very, very happy.'

'I bet he is. Well, good for him.' Bee was genuinely pleased for him.

'But, coming back to you, Bee, have you called Luke yet to give him the good news that you're going to be living and working only a couple of hours down the road from Montegrifone?'

Bee shook her head. 'It's the middle of the night over there right now. I'll send him an email after dinner.'

'You're sounding very calm and relaxed. If I were you, I'd be jumping up and down with delight. You'll be able to see him every weekend, maybe even work from Montegrifone some days. This has to be the best news you could have possibly hoped for.'

Bee took another sip of wine. 'It is, of course... It's just that this changes everything.'

'In what way?'

'Up till now, I've known, and he's known, that there could never be anything serious between us because of the sheer impossibility of the distances between us. Now, suddenly, I *can* be with him. What if he doesn't want me?'

Mimi reached across and caught hold of Bee's hand and squeezed it.

'Beatrice Kingdom, the Americans have an expression for what you are, you know. You realise you're bat-crap crazy, don't you?'

Bee smiled in spite of herself at the expression as Mimi expanded.

'I've told you before and I'll tell you again. Take it from me, he's crazy about you – in a good way, not in a bat-crap way. You tell him you're coming to live in Italy and he'll be down on one knee with a ring in his hand before you're out of the airport. Trust me, Bee. I know what I'm talking about.'

Bee found herself blushing. She wasn't so sure. But Mimi hadn't finished yet.

'So when are they sending you back across to Europe?'

'At the end of this week.'

'A hundred dollars, no, a thousand dollars, says Luke invites you to Montegrifone.'

'I won't take your bet, but I hope you're right. I'm just afraid he'll be scared off, now that the impediment has been removed.'

'Don't you believe it.'

Chapter 24

Bee was right not to take Mimi's bet. Luke was waiting for Bee at Rome Fiumicino airport and as she spotted him amid the crowds of the busy terminal, her whole being lit up as she felt a wave of joy spread throughout her. Whatever his feelings towards her might be, there was no doubt in her mind that she loved him dearly and it was useless to try to hide this from herself any longer. As he saw her, he ran towards her and caught her in his arms, lifting her bodily off the ground. He drew her to his chest and hugged her tight for several seconds before sweeping up her bags and carrying them out to the car park. They chatted in the car, but not about anything really personal. She heard about the latest exploits of Berlusconi the goat, who had managed to get into the kitchen and, to Ines's annoyance, eaten a freshly baked apple tart. She also heard about the results of a concerted attempt by local hunters to cull the marauding wild boar population. In consequence, everybody in the area had been eating wild boar pâté, wild boar sausage as well as roast, and boiled and grilled wild boar for days now. She asked about Ines and Umberto and received his assurance that they were both well and waiting to welcome her to the villa.

It took a couple of hours to get back to Montegrifone and the sun had just set as they drove in through the gates.

As the car tyres crunched up the hill on the *strada bianca*, the cypress trees alongside the drive looked for all the world like an honour guard of soldiers on parade and Bee felt a rising sense of homecoming. Somehow she knew she belonged here.

They emerged from underneath the massive umbrella pines and drew up on the gravel outside the villa. As Luke switched off the engine, Bee unclipped her seat belt and leant across towards him.

'It's really good to be back, Luke.'

'It's really good to have you back.' And he kissed her.

She had no idea how long she was in his arms, but they were finally interrupted by a heavy thud against the side door and a scrabbling of paws at the window. Bee relinquished her hold on Luke and turned to find herself looking straight into the eyes of the Labrador. She was already smiling, but her smile broadened as she saw him. She pushed the door open and did her best to fend off his friendly assault. Finally, she stepped out of the car and stood silent for a few moments, scratching the dog's tummy with her toe as he lay on his back at her feet, grunting happily to himself.

The impressive bulk of the villa stood out against the purple of the evening sky before her. Bats wheeled in and out of the trees above her head and somewhere in the distance she heard an owl hoot but, apart from that, it was as peaceful as she remembered. She heard footsteps behind her and then felt Luke's arm grip her shoulders and pull her to him. She let her head rest back against his chest as she savoured the moment. Then, as she looked up, the front door opened wide, spilling a shaft of light along the path towards them. Three figures appeared on the steps to greet them. To Bee's delight, she saw that these were Ines, Umberto and, along with them, Riccardo. Importantly, there were smiles on all three faces.

She swivelled round and raised her eyes towards Luke, smiling at him in the twilight. He was looking down at her with an expression of adoration on his face. He lowered his lips towards hers and, just before they touched, he whispered softly.

'Welcome home, Bee.'

She savoured his kiss and then they headed for the front door hand in hand. As they walked up the path, she looked up at him and whispered in her turn, 'I never want to leave.'

'You never need to.'

Epilogue

'The baby's crying.'

Umberto's voice resulted in both Mimi and Bee jumping to their feet. Here inside the villa it was cool, while outside in the mid-August sunshine, little moved as the temperature climbed once more.

'I'll go.'

Bee headed for the door, but Mimi beat her to it.

'You stay with Joey. I'll go.' She shot Bee a happy smile. 'She is my daughter after all – although she gets her powerful lungs from her father.'

'I've heard you scream even louder than that.' Joey looked up from the lounge floor where he was on his third set of one-arm press-ups. 'What about that time I spilt ice down your back?'

Bee grinned at the two of them. Mimi and Joey had arrived with four-weeks-old Siena at the beginning of August, and Montegrifone had already worked its magic upon them. The stress of work, of their celebrity wedding and of the birth of their child had swiftly slipped away and they both looked much more relaxed, even though Mimi had insisted she intended to do without the services of their newly engaged Scottish nanny for this month. Fiona, the nanny, had gone to visit relatives in Scotland while Mimi and Joey had come here to Montegrifone to look after their child all by themselves. As Mimi had told Bee with a smile, 'Just like real parents'. Little Siena certainly had good lungs, and the ability to employ them to the full most nights, but the new parents were managing fine with the willing help of Bee and Ines.

As Mimi disappeared, Bee glanced out of the window and spotted a silver tractor coming down the track through the vines. She recognised Marco at the wheel and wondered idly where Luke might be. He had promised to join them for afternoon tea any time now and later on, they were having a barbecue in the garden to celebrate his thirty-seventh birthday. Later still, Bee had planned a very personal birthday treat for him, but only he would get to experience this particular present. A sensation of erotic excitement had been building in her all day and she could hardly wait.

She returned her attention to the inside and once more surveyed the painting occupying pride of place over the mantelpiece. It was uncanny. She wondered whether Simone Martini himself would have been able to tell the difference. Riccardo really was a very talented painter. He had made this perfectly faithful reproduction in secret and had presented it to Luke on the night of the sale as they celebrated here in this room with champagne. Bee had taken a day off from work in Rome and had come up to join them, and the atmosphere had been euphoric.

The other cause for celebration that November evening had been, in Bee's eyes, far more important than the Martini selling for an amazing eleven million euros at auction. That evening, Luke had gone down on one knee, as Mimi had predicted, and proposed to her. She hadn't hesitated for a moment. The wedding had taken place in

Newbury in June, and Bee's parents had welcomed Luke and his father into the family with open arms. Her mother had even taken her to one side after first meeting Luke and whispered in her ear.

'I like this one even more than the last one.'

'This one is going to be the last one, mum.'

As for her previous boyfriend, Bee received regular bulletins via Mimi and her agent. He had also married, to Bee's amazement, and his wife was apparently steering his writing career with considerable success. The movie of his original screenplay, starring Mimi, was due to start filming this autumn and Bee had been helping Mimi learn her lines this month. It had been bizarre to hear Mimi saying things that she recognised as having originally been said by her to Jamie.

Suddenly a happy Labrador nosed the door open and came over to greet Bee before turning his attention to Joey, who was still stretched out on the floor and this soon developed into a cheerful wrestling match. Behind the dog came Bee's husband.

'Hello, gorgeous.' He came across and kissed her. 'The decorators have finished for the day. By the end of the week the *Grifoncella* should be finished and we can move back in.'

Bee had managed to reach a highly satisfactory agreement with her employers where she worked in Rome from Tuesday to Thursday and from home in the *Grifoncella* on the other two days. Not far from the office in Rome, she had found a sweet little *pensione*, run by an elderly couple not dissimilar to Umberto and Ines, where she stayed during the week. It was all working out really well, and she was able to spend four full days each week by Luke's side. And there was nowhere she would rather be.

'I can't wait.' She kissed him back. 'Have you heard from your father?'

'I got an email half an hour ago. It sounds as if he's having a whale of a time in New York. The exhibition's going well and his agent's been taking him to a load of galleries and art events, and he's even met a few familiar faces from years ago.' He smiled at her. 'That psychiatrist really knew his stuff. What an amazing improvement in less than a year.'

Bee, too, had seen and applauded the change in her father-in-law. Apart from the almost immediate physical improvement brought about by his hip operation, over the months since his rapprochement with his son, he had blossomed mentally, coming out of his shell and his house, and beginning to live a normal life again after a quarter of a century of miserable solitude.

The door concealed in the bookcase opened and Ines came in with the tea tray. Behind her, Umberto was carrying another tray, this one with an ice bucket and champagne.

'Happy birthday, Luke.' Ines set the tray down and went over to give him a hug and a kiss.

Bee saw how warmly he hugged her in return. As he had said, she was the closest thing to a mother he could remember.

'*Grazie*, Ines.'

'It's a pity your father isn't here. It would have been the first of your birthdays he's celebrated with you for twenty-seven years.'

'He'll be back soon. Once his exhibition's finished.'

The other major change in Riccardo had been the increase in his artistic output. After his painting of Bee's face had achieved remarkable critical acclaim, demand for his work had increased and his agent had convinced him to stage a one-man show in Manhattan this summer.

Umberto opened the champagne bottle while Ines disappeared back to the kitchen. Moments later, Mimi reappeared, this time cradling little Siena in her arms. At the same time, Ines returned with a wonderful iced cake decorated with thirty-seven candles. She set it down on the coffee table and gave Romeo a stern stare.

'No, Romeo, this is not for dogs.'

The Labrador made no attempt to approach the table but never took his eyes off the cake for a second, even while Joey squatted on the floor alongside it and set about lighting every single little candle. When they were all lit, Umberto distributed the glasses of champagne and proposed a toast.

'As the oldest person here, it falls upon me to wish you, Luke, a very happy birthday. I can't tell you how happy it's made Ines and me to see you once again with a smile on your face and a spring in your step.' He turned towards Bee and held out his glass. 'And we all know who we have to thank for that. And I'm not talking about your wonderful discovery, Bee. I'm talking about the joy you've brought to all of us.' He clinked his glass against hers as she blushed red. 'Here's to you, Bee and to your husband. Wishing you both every happiness.'

Everybody joined in the good wishes.

'Happy birthday, Luke. What present did you get?' Mimi kept her voice low so as not to wake the baby.

Luke stretched his free arm around Bee's shoulders.

'This lady here is my present. I can't imagine anything better.'

And he kissed her.

Acknowledgements

With warmest thanks to Michael Bhaskar, Kit Nevile, and all the team at my wonderful publishers, Canelo. Thanks also to all my friends in Tuscany for their input, advice and help. Thanks, as ever, to my wife for putting me straight on matters of Tuscan art and architecture, not to mention cuisine.